# honey don't

# *honey* don't

## tim sandlin

A MARIAN WOOD BOOK

Published by G. P. Putnam's Sons

*a member of Penguin Group (USA) Inc.*

*New York*

This is a work of fiction. Names, characters, places, and incidents either
are the product of the author's imagination or are used fictitiously,
and any resemblance to actual persons, living or dead, business
establishments, events, or locales is entirely coincidental.

A Marian Wood Book
Published by G. P. Putnam's Sons
*Publishers Since 1838*
a member of
Penguin Group (USA) Inc.
375 Hudson Street
New York, NY 10014

Library of Congress Cataloging-in-Publication Data

Sandlin, Tim.
Honey don't / Tim Sandlin.
p. cm.
"A Marian Wood book."
ISBN 0-399-14998-8
1. Presidents—Death—Fiction.
2. Washington (D.C.)—Fiction.   I. Title.
PS3569.A517H6      2003                    2002031712
813'.54—dc21

Printed in the United States of America
1   3   5   7   9   10   8   6   4   2

This book is printed on acid-free paper. ∞

BOOK DESIGN BY MEIGHAN CAVANAUGH

for carol, kyle, and leila

# acknowledgments

It would not be possible for me to live and work in Wyoming if others were not willing to support my efforts from the coastal cities. From the East Coast, I would like to thank Flip Brophy, Marian Wood, Anna Jardine, and Teresa Kraegel; from the West Coast, Charles Ferraro, Scottie "the Godfather" Schwimer, Tamra Davis, and Tab Murphy. Sarah Bird gave assistance from Texas. Karen Joy Fowler put the vehicle in gear.

Locally, Jaime Hall, Kyle Hong, and Carol Chesney researched odd facts so I didn't have to. Cranford died before this book was finished; I would like to remember his intensity and thank him for the use of his name.

Much of this book was written in Pearl Street Bagels here in Jackson. I thank the owners, Les and Maggie Gibson, for their tolerance, and to the employees who think they are the model for Honey, I lied.

The stream interrupted by rocks is the one that sings most nobly.

*Awed Afifi, nineteenth-century Tunisian Sufi dervish*


Being a writer means everything is relevant all the time.

*John Nichols*


We said the Serenity Prayer, and then we fucked.

*Cranford Nix*

# notice

I made this story up. None of the people in it are based in any way on real people. None of the events are based on real events. Even the Washington, D.C., in my story isn't based on the real place with that name. Travelers who use my Dulles Airport as a guide will find themselves lost.

The book is set sometime in the near future, or perhaps on a planet parallel to our own, so while a character may speak of a place-kicker for the Dallas Cowboys, he is not speaking about an actual placekicker, past, present, or future. If there is a real Damien's Donuts somewhere in the world, I apologize for saying your coffee is bad.

In closing, I will quote from Mark Twain's author's note to *Huckleberry Finn*:

> *Persons attempting to find a motive in this narrative will be prosecuted; persons attempting to find a moral in it will be banished; persons attempting to find a plot in it will be shot.*

# saturday

RC Nash's sense of destiny was reignited by a flight attendant feeling bumps on his forehead. It happened six hours into the redeye between Paris and Washington. RC was sitting in the very last row because that's where he always sat so he could be closest to the bathrooms. Either last row or first, and it had been years since he'd sat in first class.

As the flight attendant with the name tag "Melissa" leaned over to pick up his empty mini-bottle, she said, "Do you mind if I feel your head?"

After only one drink RC might have shown surprise at a stranger wanting to feel his head, but this was just the sort of thing he expected after three.

He said, "Why not?"

Melissa slid into the empty aisle seat beside RC and turned to run her fingers across his forehead, starting with the eyebrows and working her way up to a hairline that had been receding at an alarming rate ever since he passed forty. Her fingers were cool and distant, like air-conditioning over a bed, and they smelled faintly of airplane soap. RC hoped Melissa would find whatever she was searching for on his forehead. He couldn't stand the thought of letting down a female with expectations.

"I spotted your philoprogenic node all the way from the galley," she said. "You have a unique skull structure."

RC said, "Are you certain? No one ever noticed before."

"I mean everyone has a unique skull structure. Skulls are like snowflakes but most snowflakes look the same until you examine them up close. If you were a snowflake you would stand out like blood."

"Pardon me?"

"Blood stands out when you see it on snow."

"Okay."

"Okay what?"

"I understand you."

"Most people don't. Feel this."

She took his hand and ran it from the bridge of his nose through the area that mystics and New Agers refer to as the third eye. For RC it was the triangle of skin his grandma back in Wyoming had warned him about, where, if you pinch a pimple, the poison squeezes into your brain and you die instantly.

Melissa said, "You are a man of great destiny."

RC's heart gave a small lurch. He had once considered himself a man of great destiny, had even been so certain of fate's design that he saved all his high school homework for posterity. Then came the O.J. trial and his demotion from hard-news reporter to celebrity profiler, and RC had lost his vision. He no longer believed in future glory.

"Martin Luther King had an elongated philoprogenic node. So did Jesse James and John Lennon. I've been practicing phrenology for ten years and I've never seen an elongated philoprogenic. I've only read about them."

RC rubbed his node up and down. "Have you ever read about anyone who had one and didn't die from bullets to the brain?"

Melissa thought. "Joan of Arc, maybe. But she also had a ninth skull plate."

"So I'm a man of destiny doomed to a violent and painful death."

When Melissa spoke, it was in the tone normally used by angels of God, as if she expected her words to be repeated in a pageant someday. "You are destined to affect the future of the planet. Isn't that remarkable?"

"I think I'll pass."

"You can't pass on destiny. It's written there in your head."

"Listen, I bumped my head on a men's room door in Paris yesterday. That's what caused the philo-whatever node. It wasn't there last week, and it won't be there tomorrow."

RC could tell Melissa didn't believe him. It must be such a thrill to discover something colossal that she didn't want to face the reality of a knot on the head. "What were you doing in Paris?"

"I'm a journalist."

Melissa's face fell. It was as if RC had said, "I'm a real estate developer who sells crack on the side." All the zeal she had exuded moments earlier flew out the window and landed *plunk* in the Atlantic Ocean.

"Maybe you can change," Melissa said.

"I hope so, but right now what I want out of destiny is another drink."

RC could remember a time when the word *journalist* didn't make faces go blank and drain of all sympathy; a time when a world-class journalist returning from an assignment in Europe got laid on status alone. Men who weren't journalists claimed they were.

But that was before the carefully nourished holier-than-thou reputation won by centuries spent in the objective search for truth had gone belly up, replaced by a public image of journalists as no better than blowflies feeding off the corpses of lives sacrificed to fuel the public's insatiable demand for titillation. At least that's how RC viewed the demise of his calling. It didn't help that his own original sense of nobility had been laid to waste by O.J. Before the trial, RC had been a human being, blessed with dignity, comfortable with his position in the pecking order of right and wrong. He had reported hard news, which in RC's take meant any event affecting the freedom or food supply of any segment of society, and the only segment of society the O.J. trial affected was the media, so when his boss shipped RC to California with orders to find the meat of the story, RC reported on the media in a way both honest and offensive to practically everyone he knew or might possibly come in contact with.

As Melissa brought him drink number four—which RC did not think was so out-of-line on an eight-and-a-half-hour flight—she said, "People do change, you know. There's this book called *Chicken Soup for the Soul.* Have you read it?"

RC poured liquid from the mini-bottle into a plastic cup filled with ice. He said, "No, but I saw the movie and the woman I saw it with told me it was better than the book."

"I didn't know *Chicken Soup* had been made into a movie."

"Those brothers who did *Fargo* wrote and directed it. Harrison Ford and Winona Ryder play the lovers."

Melissa was disappointed in RC. "You're lying. I hate it when men think I'll believe any ridiculous line, just because I'm a flight attendant."

"It wasn't a lie, it was a joke. There's a difference."

"Journalists aren't supposed to tell jokes."

As the red-eye from Paris floated like a bloated pelican cross-ing the Potomac, another plane approached Washington from the south. That flight carried Jimmy Sebastiano, errand boy for the mob. Jimmy had the self-image of a man on his way up into the tangled web of organized crime, an intern, of a sort, paying his dues before taking his rightful place as Godfather of Philadelphia and eastern Pennsylvania. Like most of the new wave of mafiosi, Jimmy had learned his basic mob skills from movies. He knew older, more settled wise guys could afford to fake civility, They were allowed to pet cats and pass out shiny quarters to street urchins. The old farts didn't flaunt their ruthlessness, because everyone knew, one word from their lips and you were dead meat on a slab. But for the errand boy with ambition, a smile would be seen as weakness. Decency was a trait Jimmy Sebastiano could not afford.

When the college boy going home for the weekend had arrived to take his place by the window, Jimmy, in the aisle seat, did not give an inch. Make the bastard climb over, he thought. Make him realize in his bones how inconvenienced I am by his very existence.

The boy said, "Excuse me."

Jimmy put on his sunglasses.

Later, when the stewardess asked if he cared for a beverage, Jimmy said nothing. He simply took his sunglasses off and stared at her with a look he'd refined slowly, over hours, in front of a mirror. Eyelids low, chin up, pupils performing laser surgery on her skin. The look should have sent chills down the stewardess's spine, but instead Jimmy came off a bit like Lauren Bacall telling Humphrey Bogart to pucker his lips and blow. She shrugged and gave the college boy a Coke.

When the plane landed, Jimmy drew his carry-on attaché from under the seat in front of his and stood, looking around for someone to be rude to, but this was two a.m. in Washington, D.C. Nobody cared. Jimmy was the invisible punk.

He left the plane and beelined for the nearest pay phone. Using a counterfeit prepaid card, he punched numbers.

The voice on the other end said, "Talk."

Jimmy spoke without moving his lips. The effect was lost over the phone, but he needed the practice. "Tell Rat's Ass I'm in."

"That's Mr. Olivetti to you, Jimmy."

"Yeah, tell Mr. Olivetti I caught an early flight."

"How much did you bring?"

"Six hundred fifty, more or less."

"More or less?"

"Six fifty-six, plus change."

"We'll want it by eight this morning."

"Shit, when am I supposed to sleep?"

The voice didn't reply. Jimmy waited. The voice waited. So much of intimidation is based on menacing silence that Jimmy's conversations nearly always ended in thirty seconds of dead air.

Finally Jimmy said, "I'll be there."

"You do that."

Jimmy hung up and checked the coin return for change, then he sauntered through the almost empty terminal, disappointed there was no one around to watch.

RC gathered up the brown suitcase he'd used since college and a canvas carry-on with "Daily News" stenciled on the side, then made it past a Customs agent who appeared to be suffering through the down cycle of bipolar depression, and out into the moist Washington night. No stars shone. No moon. He could see the span on the airport Hilton, and a glow came from Virginia—what would have been Northern Lights if he was still in Wyoming but here were only halogens along Highway 267.

A short walk would clear his head. RC needed a clear head before he got home, because Kirsteen had been in a state of high pique when he left, and Kirsteen's piques only gained strength through absence. There'd been a misunderstanding over something he wrote in a profile of Heather Graham, something along the lines of, "Any man in his right mind would be thrilled to" blah-blah. His job was to create harmless fantasies and he created them, for Chrissake, but Kirsteen found nothing harmless in publicly admitting lust for the stars. A head fogged by four bourbons and jet lag wouldn't stand a prayer against her wrath, no matter how long he'd been gone or how late he came home.

So RC walked from international arrivals down to the main terminal exit. He didn't trust the taxis at international arrivals anyway. There were too many stories—some even written by him—about

Russian tourists starting out for the Lincoln Memorial and ending up in Atlanta. At the main terminal he found a driver, who, from his looks, wasn't a conspiracy freak. RC could smell cabdrivers with conspiracy theories. RC gave the driver a nod of "Let's go" and the driver nodded back "You got it"—two guys communicating. But then, as RC set his bags on the curb and reached for the back door handle, Jimmy Sebastiano rushed from the darkness.

Jimmy said, "Out of my way, old man."

RC knew right away what he was up against. The black leather jacket over the black outfit. Sunglasses in the middle of the night. Neck chain thick enough to control a pit bull. This was an East Coast urban male.

RC fell back on western politeness. "I beg your pardon, but I believe I was here first."

"No, you weren't."

RC bent down to appeal to the driver, who was studiously minding his own business. "I was here first, wasn't I?"

The driver said, "Looked that way to me, but what do I know?"

Jimmy said, "You don't know nothing."

RC looked back up the entry loop. No doubt another cab would be along soon. Even at this ungodly hour there were usually three or four drivers leaning on their hoods, smoking and bitching about the government and their kids who had it so easy. But RC was sick of being the only reasonable person in his own life.

"Where you headed?" he said. "Maybe we could share the ride."

Jimmy blinked three times, quickly, and swallowed. He grunted. "Foggy Bottom."

RC smiled. "Isn't it a small world?" He held the door open for Jimmy, but Jimmy didn't get in.

He said, "Maybe I don't want to share."

RC said, "It's fifty-five dollars plus tip."

"I don't tip." As Jimmy slipped past RC and ducked into the taxi, he told the driver, "Twenty-two ten F Street."

RC threw his bags in so they formed a low wall between him and the jerk. He said, "Not two blocks from my place. You can drop me off."

Jimmy leaned back and lit a cigarette, one of those extralong, skinny brown jobs preferred by your ostentatious element.

The driver said, "Sorry, bud, you can't smoke in here."

Jimmy said, "I'm not smoking." He turned his head and blew smoke in RC's face. "Do I look like I'm smoking?"

RC decided to hate Jimmy. "You are definitely smoking."

Jimmy inhaled deeply on the brown cigarette and blew smoke again. "This isn't smoking. It's exercising my freedom as an American."

RC rolled his window down, turned, snatched the cigarette from Jimmy's mouth, and threw it out the window.

"Hey!" Jimmy couldn't believe what had happened.

"What?" RC rolled his window up. He felt good. His hand had been quick as a flash. My God, he was fast. RC felt real good, and he hoped Jimmy would try something else. The kid had just come off a plane, which meant he probably wasn't armed. RC knew he could take the punk as long as weapons were not involved.

"I'm exercising my freedom too," RC said.

"You can't do that. I'm connected."

"It was either the cigarette or you and I chose the cigarette. You want to follow it?"

The driver said, "How about them Skins."

RC glared hard at Jimmy, who looked out his window at the passing strip mall. RC wanted to hit the kid but couldn't without more provocation. It was the Cowboy Code, taught to RC as a child. It's okay to hit another male, but only if he pushes first. Since RC had thrown the cigarette out the window, the last act of aggression was his; therefore the next move had to be Jimmy's or RC couldn't smack him in the jaw. Those were the rules, and although Jimmy didn't know squat about the Code, he instinctively knew better than to provide RC with any excuses.

RC held the tension a couple beats, then he said, "Yeah, how about those Skins?"

The driver visibly exhaled. "They got their butts whipped Sunday, didn't they?"

RC leaned forward to check the laminated card on the passenger visor—Mickey Winship. In his photo Mickey had long sideburns and a widow's peak. "I was out of the country, so all I heard was the score. What the hell happened?"

Mickey said, "Tampa Bay flat shredded our secondary, and they was holes in the line you could drive a golf cart through."

RC wanted to convey sympathy, so he said, "Shit."

Encouraged by the sincerity of this word, Mickey went on. "Tell me about it. I had fifty riding on that pitiful excuse for a team."

Jimmy smirked and glanced at his attaché case. RC spotted the smirk right off but decided not to pursue it. They'd already established who in the backseat had the hardest dick; there was no call to rub it in.

RC nodded and said, "What's wrong with the bums?"

Jimmy blurted, "They're all fags."

"You know this firsthand?" Mickey asked.

"Shut the fuck up."

RC said, "No, really, pard. We'd like to hear what you're basing your information on."

Jimmy's face had the expression of an eleven-year-old taking on a double dare. "For a fact, the special teams are a pack of queers."

"Name one."

"Farlow Stubbs."

RC tried to remember a Farlow Stubbs on the Redskins' roster. He followed the team fairly closely, even went to a game or two each season when he could get free tickets, but he'd never heard of Farlow Stubbs.

Jimmy plowed on. "My old lady used to know him in high school, real well. They were like best buddies, even though she's not a fag hag if that's what you're thinking. She's normal now, but she says he's queer as a male ballerina."

RC started to point out the raging heterosexuality of Baryshnikov, but decided it would be wisdom wasted on a jackass. "Okay. Name two."

"I don't have to name squat. All them football players are queer. They eat steroids and their balls shrivel up like peanuts."

The lights of Washington proper were rapidly approaching. It was basically too late to throw Jimmy out the window without the risk of witnesses.

RC said, "Buddy, you are what makes living in this town so wonderful."

Jimmy said, "Don't mess with me. I'm connected."

"You said that before, and I didn't know what it meant then either."

Greg Gamble played a handheld-computer game that buzzed and whirred and occasionally announced, *You're a dead dog now!* while Stonewall Jackson sat with his wrists draped over the steering wheel. Stonewall was cold; he was bored out of his mind; his one desire in life was to eat a meal in a room instead of a car. He had a college degree in criminal justice and had endured thousands of hours of training, and now, at the age of fifty-five, he was a professional having second thoughts.

The game made a *bleep* sound and died. Gamble cursed softly. "You ever know anybody to get past level three on Metroid?"

Stonewall stared at a window on the fourth floor of the building across the street. A red light was on up there, and he thought maybe he saw someone cross between the light and the window. "Parker Swindell's got a kid can do level eight."

"That's a kid. I mean real people." Gamble pressed the restart button, and fancy graphics appeared to show that he was entering a new world. Stonewall wished his life had a restart button.

He said, "Sometimes I sit in the dark and cold and I imagine what he's doing in there. Is he standing or lying down? Does she scream and beg for mercy?"

Gamble said, "Keep that up and you'll drive yourself nuts."

"I am nuts."

The phone *buzz*ed and Stonewall answered. He listened a few moments, then said, "No need. He doesn't know we're here." He listened longer. "Ducked out the employee entrance of a Starbucks on Connecticut. He thinks he's lost us." More listening. So much more that Gamble rolled his eyes and made "yak yak" signs with his fingers.

Stonewall said, "Right," and hung up. His gaze wandered from the fourth-floor window, across the stale red bricks, and on to the moths futilely swarming around a streetlight. Mist was creeping in from the bay. The city smelled like dry wells in a steam table.

"What'd I do to deserve the nooky patrol?" he said.

"Just lucky, I guess." Gamble smiled; he'd made it to level four.


Three blocks away and closing fast, RC was engulfed in his own second thoughts. When he left for Paris, Kirsteen had been in more than her usual fit of fury. She had broken glass. He had said things that couldn't be made better by a dozen roses and an orgasm. There was more than a possibility that the moment he came through the door the discussion would resume where it left off.

RC tapped Mickey on the shoulder. "I changed my mind. Let me out at Damien's, there on the corner."

Mickey slowed and veered toward the curb in front of Damien's Donuts, an all-night cubbyhole with the best doughnuts and worst coffee in the metro area.

Mickey said, "You leaving me alone with him?"

RC said, "You'll be safe. This boy's all bark."

As if to prove RC's point, Jimmy made a noise in the back of his throat that did indeed sound like a growl.

RC said, "Besides, he's only going another couple of blocks."

RC passed up money. "Keep the change." He opened the door and looked back at Jimmy. "I paid half, plus enough tip for both of us."

Jimmy said nothing. He was deep into a vengeance fantasy and he didn't want to spoil the moment.

RC got out, said, "Stay in touch," and shut the door.

Jimmy spotted the car right away. It was a black Ford Crown Victoria with U.S. government plates and two men in the front seat. They weren't even pretending to be undercover, just sitting there like narcs expecting curb service.

"Don't stop," Jimmy said. "It's down the end of the block."

"But this is Twenty-two ten."

"I meant Twenty-one ten."

Mickey grumbled something along the lines of a man ought to know where he lives, then drove on. As they passed the government car, Jimmy turned his face away and held a hand up beside his ear. He said, "Jesus," and Mickey said, "What's that?"

Jimmy paid in exact change. He'd meant to claim the extra money from RC went against the total bill since he hadn't agreed to any tip, but the stakeout rattled him. Now wasn't the time to start an argument with a taxi driver.

Jimmy walked back a block, crossed the street, turned left and cut into the alley behind his building. It was dark back there, but he knew of a fire escape low enough that if you stood on the dumpster and hooked it with a broken umbrella you could pull it down. He'd stashed the umbrella behind the dumpster in case of an emergency exactly like this one. Nobody could say Jimmy Sebastiano didn't plan ahead.

With the attaché case in his left hand, Jimmy scrambled up the iron ladder and across the roof between various vents and electrical boxes. Some of the tenants had small herb gardens up here, as if oregano grown in the D.C. air wouldn't poison the pasta. The yuppie scum. He let himself in a door that should have been locked but wasn't, because Jimmy had broken the bolt weeks ago.

The fourth-floor hallway was lit by a thirty-watt bulb in an iron fitting, like a catcher's mask. The lock stuck a moment before it turned with a whisper, and Jimmy crossed the dark living room to the window. The black Ford Crown Victoria was still there. Shit. What had he done to bring heat into his life? Rat's Ass would throw a fit. He'd probably fire Jimmy, or stick him on the street running numbers in the ghetto. Black people scared Jimmy. They didn't have enough to lose.

Gradually, almost subconsciously at first, Jimmy became aware of a noise. There was a rhythm to it, and a low moan. Then a distinct gasp and a *slurp* like a sneaker being pulled out of mud. Jimmy turned to cross the living room and whacked his shin on the beak of a cast-iron flamingo.

*"Christ."*

He froze, waiting. The sound was still there, a wet sound, like water flowing through bad pipes. Jimmy actually tiptoed to his bedroom door. He leaned his forehead against it, listening. The sounds were louder now, and clear on two levels. The high one he had heard before.

Jimmy eased the door open. The bedroom—his bedroom—was softly lit by candles on the nightstands on each side of the bed. At the head of the bed, he saw Honey's face, eyes closed, her mouth in a faint curve, as if she were eating a Hershey bar. It was her chocolate smile. Honey's breasts were small as bathroom Dixie cups and pale, with tiny perfect nipples. A trickle of sweat ran from her ribs into her outie navel, which, as Jimmy watched, quivered. The view of her crotch was blocked by the back of a man's head.

Jimmy roared like a pissed-off mountain lion. He flew across the room, grabbed the man by the neck, and threw him onto the floor. Honey screamed. The man screamed. Jimmy ripped open his bedside table drawer and came out with a knife. *Swick.* Candlelight glittered off the blade.

The man yelled, "Wait. I can explain."

Jimmy yelled, "I'll bet."

Honey yelled, "Dickhead."

Jimmy lunged and the man scrambled for the door, but no sooner had he gained his feet than he fell, tangled in the bikini thong wrapped around his ankles. The sight of the thong stopped Jimmy for an instant. He thought it was Honey's, and his mind was momentarily boggled by the mechanics.

Honey screamed, "Idiot," and grabbed Jimmy's arm, and he backhanded her across the face. The man on the floor jumped up and charged out of the bedroom. Jimmy took off after him.

From the bed, Honey shouted, "Look at him, you jerk." Who was she calling a jerk? Jimmy was the righteous party here. Honey should be begging for forgiveness instead of calling him names. The living room, with no candles, was darker than the bedroom. Jimmy heard the man running and he threw the knife. There was an *"Ouch!"* and a fall. The man's head hit Honey's flamingo with a sound like a shovel coming down on a day-old wedding cake.

Then silence.

Honey ran in and pulled the chain on the tall lamp next to Jimmy's beanbag chair. She said, "Look what you did."

"What I did? I oughta cut your heart out."

Naked, Honey knelt at the unconscious man's side. "I hope you're happy, big shot. You killed him."

Jimmy's face dropped three shades of pale. His mouth filled with acid reflux. It took a massive effort of self-will, but slowly, while Honey watched, Jimmy righted his sense of coolness.

"Good. I told you I'd whack any man you screw other than me. Jimmy Sebastiano don't make promises he can't keep."

Honey held her fingers in front of the dead man's nostrils in case she'd been wrong, but there wasn't much doubt. He was dead. She said, "Look at him."

Jimmy came forward one step, no more. He'd never been this close to a cadaver before. He knew how he was supposed to feel after his first kill and he knew how he felt, and so far, they weren't matching up.

He said, "What an old fart. You been turning tricks while I was out of town?"

Honey's voice was incredibly calm. "Jimmy, sugar pot, look who you just killed."

Jimmy studied the face. It was long and thin, deeply planed, with a large chin and dimples. "He's kind of familiar."

"It's Franklin, you pencil dick."

Jimmy walked to the feet end of the body to view the face right side up. He still didn't get it.

Honey said, "President Franklin."

"President of what?"

"President of the *Fucking United States* Franklin."

His nausea came back like a cold front crossing his chest. Water seemed to rush over his eardrums. "The President?"

"Yes, pinhead. You just killed the President of the United States. You feel like the hot-stuff Mafia bagman? Mr. I'm-gonna-be-somebody. You are sure as heck going to be somebody now."

Jimmy sat down hard. "Why was the President giving you tongue?"

Honey cooed. "I did it for you, sugar pie."

Jimmy was struck by a deep sense of unfairness. Life was a cheat. He'd been so secure in his place in the world, hauling gambling money up and down the East Coast, hanging out with tough guys who made their own rules. All Jimmy had asked for was enough cash to get by and a presentable girl to bang now and then. What had gone wrong?

Honey sashayed over and sat in his lap. She put her arms around him; her fingers twirled a lock of his Italian-heritage hair. She said, "I was hoping we might get invited to parties at the White House. That would be fun, don't you think?"

"I never thought about parties at the White House."

"And let's be practical here. You might get arrested someday, what with your career in organized crime and all. Me screwing the President could come in handy when you wind up in jail."

"Yeah, right. You two could hump like rabbits while I'm up the river."

She mock-slapped him. "No, silly, we could blackmail the President into getting you free. He'd have to do what we say from now on."

Honey leaned into Jimmy and kissed the top of his head. Her skin up against his face smelled faintly of baby powder and Starbucks Breakfast Blend. She said, "If he didn't do what we wanted I could go on *Montel* and expose the bastard. Or that hippie disc jockey you like so much, the one who talks to whores."

"Howard Stern."

"Yeah." She did her best imitation of a DJ. *"Women Who Blow the Executive Branch."*

Jimmy's voice was muffled by her breasts in his face. "Jesus, you gave him a blow job too?"

Honey nodded. "I did it for you, sugar booger."

"This entire neighborhood was built on a swamp," RC said. "That's why it smells like snake puke."

Leonard Levinson wiped the already clean counter with his rag. "I thought Foggy Bottom was named after Dolley Madison's ass."

It was a conversation Leonard had on the average once a night. In fact, it was a conversation he had had with RC not two months ago. The lonely customers wandered into Damien's Donuts between three and six in the morning, looking for a conversation starter, and if it wasn't the Redskins or the weather, it was the history of Foggy Bottom. Something about a government founded on a swamp real estate deal seemed to comfort those who ate doughnuts while the rest of the city slept.

"How about more coffee?" RC said.

"How about."

Damien's had been around since Roosevelt, although you could get an argument as to which Roosevelt. It consisted of four tables, a counter, and a dirty window facing E Street. Out back, through a door behind Leonard, five men who couldn't speak English were making raised glazed doughnuts, cake doughnuts, crullers, bear claws, éclairs—the works. RC sat at the counter. Two aged men in shabby suits shared a table by the window. Next to the wall, under a photograph of Lyndon Johnson shoveling a chocolate long-john into his wide-open gullet, a black man in clothing from the Salvation Army free bin sat scribbling in a three-inch-by-five-inch notebook. The black man punctuated his writing with an occasional grunt or *"Yes!"*

RC waited while Leonard poured the coffee. Conversation this hour of day had to be timed properly. There was a form to follow. RC wasn't supposed to speak before his first sip of the refill, and Leonard had to answer as he wiped the counter. They both knew and respected tradition.

RC sipped his coffee and grimaced, although he tried to hide the grimace. "You're a poet, aren't you, Leonard?"

Leonard wiped the counter. "Yes, I am."

"Poets are the only ones cut out to work the graveyard shift at doughnut shops. What do you write about?"

"Despair, as a rule. I have a couple of love sonnets I can pull out if a pretty woman starts hanging around."

"What would a kid like you know about despair?"

"Work here from midnight to seven and you'll learn more than you'll ever want to know about miserable people. See those two over by the window?"

RC turned to look at the two old men, who were what he could become if he stopped paying attention to personal hygiene. Neither one moved a muscle. Their blink reflex appeared dead, and RC wondered how they avoided dry eyes.

Leonard said, "Mr. Gelfino won't go home because his wife is waiting for him, and Mr. Sawtelle won't go home because no wife is waiting for him. They're trying to outlast each other here."

"Which one is Gelfino?"

"What difference does it make?"

"What about the black fella in the corner?"

"That's Cranford Nix. He doesn't have a home to go to." Cranford sucked the point of his Bic, then moaned and continued writing. Leonard said, "Cranford fills up one of those notebooks a night. I have no idea where he keeps them, but he'll stay here till mid-morning, then go over to Rawlins Park and sleep."

"Sounds better than my life."

"He says he's schizophrenic and happy."

Later, as RC walked up F through the smelly mist, he considered the advantages of homelessness. The only truly free humans he had ever known had been either outrageously rich or outrageously poor. Anything between the two came with baggage. At twenty, he figured it didn't much matter which end of the curve you were on, so long as you were on the end, but at forty-two, he preferred the extreme with insurance. Either way, he didn't think he could handle that much freedom. He would only manage to botch it up somehow.

Up ahead, RC spotted the black Ford Crown Victoria with government plates. He walked to the passenger window and tapped on the glass. Greg Gamble rolled the window down two inches.

He said, "Go away, RC."

RC said, "Have you questioned the quality of your life recently?"

Stonewall Jackson leaned into the steering wheel to look past Gamble at RC hovering in the window. "You know you can't report this. We'll pull your paper's credentials. The *Daily News* will never get government access again. The IRS will audit your taxes going back thirty years."

RC interrupted the flow of threats. "I mean, if I had to sit in a car at"—he pretended to check his watch—"four-thirty in the morning, waiting for my boss to finish sloppy seconds in a nice warm bed, indoors, I would question my career choice."

Jackson had been doing exactly that—questioning his career choice—all night, so having a broken-down reporter say it out loud was something of a shock, like having someone tell you what you'd been dreaming.

"This isn't your business anymore, anyway," Gamble said. "How many years has it been since you got booted off real news and put on the fluff beat?"

"What could be fluffier than a famous person committing adultery? If I was a true professional, I'd stick photographers on every exit."

"Lucky for us you don't give a shit," Gamble said.

"Don't try to hurt my feelings. Is the girl over eighteen?"

Gamble rolled the window up.

RC raised his voice. "Give me the scoop or I'll call *Dateline*."

Behind glass, Gamble flipped RC the bird. RC laughed out loud, which felt nice. It had been a long time since he'd laughed. He held his hands up in an air headline. "'President Gets Lucky with Bimbo,' by RC Nash, ace reporter."

Gamble rolled the window back down. "Don't even think about it. Nobody would believe you. With your record, even the *Enquirer* wouldn't touch the story."

RC's laughter plummeted straight into depression. The government geek was right. Since the O.J. debacle, RC had the credibility of a car salesman. It was a bitter lesson from history: No one believes the man who tells the truth.

Jimmy walked in a circle around the President's body. Dead and naked, he didn't look like such a big deal. His belly pooched out; he had flaps under his arms, and liver spots in places where real men don't have spots; his dick was Elmer's-glue white and no bigger than a .45 caliber slug.

Jimmy said, "I thought he'd be bigger."

Honey came from the bedroom wearing a man's white dress shirt with none of the buttons buttoned and a pair of tight shorts. She tied the shirttails across her abs so her breasts were more or less held in position.

She said, "The stud was wearing makeup. He rubbed rouge all over my tits. You look like you could use a drink."

"Have you seen my switchblade?"

"It's in him, isn't it?"

"I don't see it."

"Maybe it went in his back. Turn him over."

"You turn him over."

After several minutes of searching, Honey found Jimmy's knife stuck in a Kurt Cobain poster on the wall. She said, "You missed him by a mile."

"I missed him on purpose."

"Like I'm supposed to believe that."

"I only meant to scare the crap out of the jerk. Screwing somebody else's girl is completely wrong. I can't believe the President would do such a thing."

Honey pulled the knife out of the wall. It'd gone through Kurt's throat. "If you missed him on purpose, why is he so dead?"

"I've been trying to figure that out." Jimmy squatted on his toes at the President's head. There was a splat mark on his temple, and a spot of blood on the beak of Honey's flamingo. "I think he tripped on your underwear and hit his head."

"That's not my underwear." Honey stripped the thong from the President's feet. "It's his. I'll bet you anything I could sell it on eBay."

Jimmy's eyes traveled from the crushed skull down the President's body. "There's come on his belly."

Honey knelt by Jimmy. She touched the come with her index finger, just to be sure that's what it was. "He must have gotten off again when he died. I'm amazed—the first time took forever."

Jimmy groaned. "Honey, I appreciate it that you sucked him off for me and you didn't enjoy it, but I don't need the details."

"Who said I didn't enjoy it? You want a drink or not?"

Honey fixed Jimmy a Kahlúa and skim milk while he stood beside the window, staring down at the Crown Victoria. The Feds weren't staking him out after all. That was the only blessing in the night from hell, and even then, Jimmy felt a bit deflated. Federal heat had made him legitimate. They wouldn't send a black Crown Victoria to spy on a small-time bagman. Turned out they hadn't.

Honey smiled as she handed Jimmy his drink. "We should save some presidential sperm."

"God, Honey, don't be sick."

"I was going to ask for an autograph if you hadn't killed him."

"You want a souvenir, cut off a lock of hair."

Honey went back into the kitchen to rummage through drawers for scissors. She was humming a Cyndi Lauper song but Jimmy couldn't remember the title. Honey's humming irked Jimmy. She didn't seem to realize the seriousness of the situation.

He said, "What are we going to do with him?"

"What do you mean, *we*? You killed him."

"Yeah, but you screwed him."

Honey came back into the living room with a pair of scissors normally used for cutting up chicken. "Are you going to throw that in my face from now on, because if you are we should redefine our relationship right now." She waved the scissors in a way his mama had always said might put out an eye. "And another thing, budd-o, I didn't screw him, we gave each other head. There's a big difference. What I did wasn't even against the law, but killing him is."

Jimmy said, "Technically, I didn't kill him. It was an accident."

"Tell that to those two men sitting outside."

Jimmy parted the curtain and looked out at the black car again. "I thought they were watching me."

"Fat chance." Honey knelt at the dead body to consider where to clip the lock of hair. She decided on below the waist. Any groupie could save hair off his head. She said, "Those two stuck with us all night. That's how I knew for sure he was who he is, only I don't think he saw them." She checked out the President's eyes. They had milked over since his death—looked more like Ping-Pong balls than eyes.

Honey said, "He's kind of oblivious."

Jimmy chugged his drink. What he liked was Kahlúa and cream, but Honey had been ragging him about cholesterol. Next drink, he would make her fix him the real stuff. He had nothing to lose anymore.

"They'll electrocute me, for sure. I can't stand electrocutions. They fry you from the inside out."

"Maybe you could ask for a lethal injection."

Jimmy shuddered. As Honey snipped, she caught the little curls in her left hand. She glanced up at Jimmy and went into her coy voice. "Or we could escape."

"Jesus, Honey, you can't kill the President of the United States and escape."

"Somebody did with Kennedy."

A light of hope flickered across Jimmy's face. Someone had killed Kennedy and gotten away with it. "Kennedy's killers planned ahead. They didn't come home and find John drilling the old lady."

Honey pouted. "How do you know that?"

"I saw the movie."

"The movie was make-believe. It could have happened exactly the way it did here. Kennedy was a known pussy hound. All presidents are. It's a wonder every single one of them doesn't get syphilis."

Jimmy lit a cigarette and paced from the window to the flamingo, around the beanbag chair and back to the window. "We can't escape. It takes money to escape a worldwide manhunt."

Honey cut her eyes toward the attaché case on the floor, where Jimmy had dropped it in the excitement. "Don't you have money in that bag?"

Jimmy was aghast. "Gino'll tear my heart out if I steal from him."

"Is Rat's Ass Olivetti more powerful than the United States government?"

Jimmy considered the question. "I don't know. Maybe."

"Jimmy. Sugar booger. Be a man." Honey talked as she carried the handful of hair into the kitchen and found a Baggie. "You've assassinated the leader of the Free World. Ripping off Gino is diddly compared to what's going to hit the fan over that body on my rug."

Jimmy really did not want to go to prison. There were men in prison with no respect for personal sexual preferences.

"Where could we run to?"

Honey sealed the Baggie. The hair looked more like a dust bunny from under the bed than anything that had come off the President.

"Farlow will help us."

Deep in his gut, Jimmy had known that sooner or later Honey would fall back on "Farlow will help us." She always did.

He looked at the dead body and said, more to himself than Honey, "I hate Farlow."

The moment RC walked through the door he knew the townhouse had changed. It was atmospheric, as if the warmth had been sucked up the gas-fireplace flue and replaced by a cold fog. He turned on the light—nothing was visibly different. Same Danish modern couch and chair he couldn't sit in. Same globular paintings he didn't understand. Same anorexic lamps. The home entertainment center hadn't moved. Kirsteen was Danish modern, but he'd never seen that as an excuse for surrounding herself with black and silver. He was western, and he didn't insist on horseshoe doorknobs or elk antler chandeliers.

He checked the thermostat and solved the mystery. Kirsteen had turned the heat off, which meant she'd left in a huff. Which meant she would not be back. For a Danish native, Kirsteen had the lowest tolerance for cold RC had ever seen. And she hated snow. One flake and she was ready for Cancún.

Snow wasn't unique on her hate list. Kirsteen hated practically everything, starting with the United States and all the people in it. RC could never fathom why she had chosen him from among the options in a city chock-full of filthy-rich foreigners. Kirsteen was tight, sleek, and thin as a swizzle stick, with an accent that fed fantasies. She could have had any ambassador's liaison officer in town. Pretty much any ambassador.

They'd met at the Corcoran Gallery, where Kirsteen led tours in French, German, Danish, and other minor languages. The day they met she was taking a Flemish-speaking Belgian group through an Annie Leibovitz retrospective. RC's tragic flaw was frequent urination, and he dealt with it by knowing every public-access restroom within ten miles of the White House. RC ran through Kirsteen's group—more or less ran over Kirsteen—without even a glance in her direction. She was not accustomed to men ignoring her, and RC's tunnel vision, before Europeans no less, excluded her in a way she took as a personal affront. She waited for RC to come out of the restroom like the spider stalking the proverbial fly. Theirs was a romance born in a pee emergency she mistook for a sleight. In RC's experience, more relationships start with a misunderstanding than end with them.

RC turned the thermostat up to sixty-five and closed the windows. He moved cautiously through the front room into the combination dinette/kitchen, bracing himself for booby traps. Kirsteen would not settle for freezing the apartment. There are women a man can sleep with a few times, even live with for a while, then after the split-up they turn into true friends for life; then there are women like Kirsteen. Kirsteen loathed every man she ever stopped sleeping with.

He found another sign of wrath on his computer screen. It was written in Carolina-blue lipstick: *I'm gone you røvhul. P.S. Look in the closet.*

RC wasn't sure what awaited in the bedroom—a dead animal, perhaps, or compost—but what he found was a closet full of mutilated clothes. She'd used pinking shears. The shirts had no sleeves;

the pants no legs. The crotch had been excised from both suits. He only owned four ties, and these were shredded to egg-noodle width. She'd split the underwear vertically and the socks at the toe. RC had to admire the thoroughness of the attack. And the inevitability. Only Kirsteen would think to punish a man through his wardrobe.

Honey sat in the alley in her Dodge Dart, stewing about her name. This kind of thing wouldn't happen if she were named Meredith or Jillian. Texas men just love strapping their daughters to names that force them into a lifetime of being *Daddy's Little Girl.* In Honey's senior class, back at Odessa Permian High, there had been three Missys, two Sugars, a Candy, a Brandy, a Pumpkin, an actual Baby, and countless PeggyMaryDebbiAlliePammyCindy Sues— enough Bleepy Sues to start a volleyball team. Nobody takes a woman named Sugar or Pumpkin seriously, and that is exactly why so many West Texas crackers name their daughters after high-caloric food. Honeys make wonderful cheerleaders, but what happens to them after the prom?

She'd tried switching to her middle name, Belle, at SMU, but that led to Honey B, which was way too much to live with. Being blonde and five-foot-three didn't help. Short blondes named Honey either grow up perky or commit suicide.

Honey chewed the black polish off her thumbnail and thought about her father. Winston. Winston made, lost, and made back three fortunes before he was reborn on the senior golf circuit. By Honey's third birthday she'd learned you have to flirt to get ahead in Texas. You must manipulate men by the systematic giving and taking back of favor. The men—the fathers, to begin with—leave the women with no choice. A girl has to sit on laps and talk baby talk and use her sex to get what she wants, because it isn't going to be given any other way. That's why Honey was a wreck. It was her daddy's fault.

Take the black fingernail polish. Honey did not look good in black fingernail polish, but she'd worn it when she applied for the job at Starbucks so she would portray a certain dignity. Black means, *I'm grounded. I am not an airhead, my name really isn't Honey.* Although, on her, black was often misinterpreted as, *I'm Goth.*

The assistant manager in the ponytail had scanned her application, then looked up at her, and oozed. "Well, *Honey,* do you have any experience with counter work?" And he winked. A definite won't-we-have-fun-in-the-storeroom wink.

Honey leaped to her feet and fled straight into the arms of the President.

Charles Franklin said, "Whoa." Honey knew who he was right off the bat. Until recently she'd held a position at the front desk at the Smithsonian Castle, a position she left after an episode that would not have happened had her name been Gwyneth. But for six months—before the episode—Honey stood eight hours a day facing the official portrait of our president that hung over the double front doors. She knew every crag in his craggy face, every gleam in his gleaming eyes, and even a fake mustache couldn't hide the bulb of scotch-swollen nose.

"What's the problem here, young woman?" the President asked. At least he got points for "young woman" instead of "little lady."

She tossed her blond hair toward Johnny Personnel with the ponytail. "I applied for a job, and he winked at me."

Franklin groaned, as if that were the worst insult he'd ever heard. He said, "No," and she said, "Just talking to him makes me want to take a shower."

He placed his hand under her arm and turned toward the winker. "Is this true? You winked at a job applicant?"

"I didn't wink, I swear. My eye has a twitch, I was born with it."

"Can you conceive what would happen if the Office of Economic Opportunity heard about your twitch?"

"It's not something I can control."

Honey wasn't sure if Ponytail knew he was dealing with the President or not. He was certainly fawning enough, but maybe the kid was a natural-born bootlicker.

"Don't you owe this young woman a certain something?"

Ponytail looked confused. "She didn't buy anything."

Franklin's grip tightened on Honey's arm. "An apology."

Honey and the assistant manager faced each other, waiting. He muttered, "I'm sorry."

"For what?" Honey asked.

"I'm sorry my eye twitched at you."

"Okay," Honey said. "You can keep your job."

The President insisted on buying Honey the beverage of her choice. She had a mocha Frappuccino; he had a triple espresso. He said his name was Franklin Charles, as if she didn't know it was Charles Franklin. She said her name was Honey and he said, "Is that so?" They talked about the difference between Odessa and Madison, Wisconsin, which is where he came from. They agreed it came down to humidity. The President asked her what church she belonged to and she said she was raised Nazarene but it was so long ago she thought it had worn off. He told her faith helped him through times of crisis and she said she relied more on money.

She told him about SMU and how she'd quit with only forty-seven credits to go before graduation. Charles was sympathetic. He encouraged her to try a junior college, or even a trade school.

He said, "Education is our youth's hope for the future."

Honey agreed, wondering how long before he would make his move. He seemed kind, and sweet, you could say gentle even though that wasn't normally a turn-on for her personally, and she hadn't yet decided what she would do when the time came to make choices.

After a while, he pried the top off a Tic Tac box and took out a pill. "My blood pressure medicine," he said.

"I know Viagra when I see it."

"My doctor prescribes it for low blood pressure."

"That's okay. I like it when you meet an old guy and the first thing he does is pop a Viagra. It means he can still dream."

Charles touched her inner wrist. "Do you have a car nearby?"

She glanced out the front window at the two men talking into their sleeves. Normally, Honey did not consider herself a starfucker. There was Farlow; he'd been an important football player when they met, but that was high school and he played on the defensive line. Hardly a star. At SMU she spent a weekend with a guy who claimed he was on *Dallas* for two seasons. He claimed a lot of things, including sterility, that turned out not true. She'd blown the drummer for a lead-in band for the Foo Fighters once. He at least knew some stars. But all in all, Honey was not a girl who humped fame. However, we're talking the President here. If she ever had grandchildren, it would be so cool to drop at the Thanksgiving dinner table. "Well, when I was your age I fucked the President."

He smiled at her—the smile that had seduced a nation.

She smiled back. "My car is in the parking lot, out back."


With a mighty *whomp* a beanbag chair containing the President landed in front of Honey's car. She got out, unlocked the trunk, and waited for Jimmy to work his way down from the fourth floor.

He dropped from the fire escape, walked over to the beanbag chair, and kicked it.

"Jesus, this sucker's heavy," he said. "I still don't understand why we're taking him with us."

Honey walked over to Jimmy and slapped him.

He yelped. "What's that for?"

"You hit me upstairs."

"That was before I knew who was down on you."

"No excuses. Don't ever hit me again."

Jimmy started to go Old World on her, but from the look in Honey's eyes, he knew better. "Help me get him in the car."

In Farlow's dream he was rolling a large ball made of spiderweb along a path by Monahans Draw. The mesquite was green, and it must have been during butterfly migration because monarchs flew from the ground like grasshoppers. k.d. lang sang a betrayal song somewhere nearby, and Farlow thought how pleasant it was to have a sound track. In the dream he knew he was dreaming, so nothing mattered and anything that went wrong could be taken back. Farlow liked that.

The monarch butterflies stuck to the spiderweb, and soon he was pushing an orange fluttery ball that buzzed. A beautiful boy with curly black hair and a Texas Tech football jersey rose from the river. The boy said, "Wake up, sleepyhead."

Farlow said, "I'm not ready yet," and just as the beautiful boy stripped off the jersey, a bright light flashed in Farlow's face.

"Wake up, sleepyhead."

Farlow shielded his eyes and looked through the bright light at Honey, standing beside his bed. He said, "I'm too tired for a wet dream."

Honey said, "This is no dream, Farlow."

Farlow blinked her face into focus. He'd known Honey for fifteen years, and she still had the nicest face he'd ever seen, male or female. He said, "Did your greasy boyfriend belt you?"

Jimmy's voice came from behind Honey, out of Farlow's view. "Why would a fag have a wet dream with a girl in it?"

Honey said, "Farlow swings both ways."

Which wasn't quite true. After Honey, there hadn't been much point in swinging from that side of the plate anymore. "What's he doing here?" Farlow asked.

"I'm the boyfriend and you're not."

Farlow smelled Jimmy's cigarette. He turned and saw Jimmy himself, slouched by the door like a moody teenager.

Honey nudged Farlow's shoulder. "Get up. Jimmy and I have something to show you."

"He's smoking in my house."

"Put out the cigarette," Honey said. "This is Farlow's house."

Jimmy dropped the cigarette on the sisal carpet and ground it out with his boot. Farlow propped himself up on his elbows to check the clock—five-thirty a.m. Honey did this thing where she hooks her hair behind her ear. Farlow knew it wouldn't stay back there for any length of time. He also knew it meant she was nervous.

She said, "It's a surprise—out in the garage."

"How'd you get into my garage? How'd you get into my house?"

"I have a key, silly. You said if I ever needed you again you'd still be here and not to hesitate to come."

"I didn't mean for you to bring the walking zit."

Jimmy growled, "Watch it, jock."

"Watch it yourself, bagman."

Honey pouted. "If you can't be nicer to my boyfriend I'll take my problem somewhere else."

It was the one threat she could make that would get him out of bed. Farlow knew the pout was self-conscious; he knew she didn't have anywhere else to take her problem. But he also knew that if his life had a higher mission, it was to rescue Honey.

He said, "Throw me some shorts."

While Honey rifled through his chest of drawers, Farlow sat up and swung his feet off the bed. "The thing in my garage, it's illegal, right?"

Honey discarded the top pairs of briefs as unbefitting the occasion. "Why do you always jump to the worst conclusion?"

"Your *boyfriend* is in a jam and you want me to save his butt. That's it, isn't it?"

Jimmy said, "For Chrissake, Honey, give him some clothes. He's naked over there."

Farlow stood up, flashing total frontal nudity at Jimmy. Nothing gives a straight man the willies like seeing a gay man's tool, and Farlow was a big gay man—six-five, three hundred pounds—with extremities proportionate to his height and weight. Jimmy shriveled up inside at the sight.

Farlow said, "I wouldn't put it past you two to have hauled a dead body into my garage."

Jimmy kind of froze. Farlow looked from Jimmy to Honey, who was also stuck in mid-motion.

Farlow said, "Oh, crap."

The sun didn't so much rise as the clouds changed from reflecting light below to filtering light from above. Silver to gray. Stonewall Jackson tapped the drum solo from "In-A-Gadda-Da-Vida" on the wheel, counterpointing the downbeats to the rhythm of Gamble's soft snore. It had been a long, eventless night. He'd balanced his checkbook, in his head, then counted the bones in his left hand and arm up to his elbow. After that, Jackson computed the exact number of hours before he could take early retirement and move to Spearfish, South Dakota, where he owned five acres and an Airstream. In South Dakota he would fish and pan gold and never read a newspaper again. If the news came on the radio, he would turn it off. He wouldn't even own a television. Jackson was one of the few people who knew the difference between what happened and what the news said happened, and no one with that knowledge could watch *60 Minutes* without screaming.

Gamble made a *snuff* sound and came to. He rubbed his face with his hand. "What time is it?"

Jackson checked his watch for the third time in ten minutes. "Six-fifteen."

"Doesn't he have a breakfast at seven-thirty? Youth in Recovery or somebody."

"Christian Stenographers of America."

"He should be out of there by now."

As if someone at Treasury heard them, the phone *buzz*ed. Jackson answered, listened wordlessly, and hung up.

"Time to get our boy out."

"Hell, we're not even certain which apartment he's in."

"Got to be that red light on the fourth floor. That's the only light came on after they went inside."

Gamble opened the door and stretched legs that had been bent for hours. "I hate when we have to yank him out."

"You can wait here if you want."

"Nah, if he's in love it might take both of us to get him out of bed."

As they walked toward the front door, Gamble said, "The little blonde's going to be mighty surprised to see us."

At the word "surprised," a chill ran down Jackson's spine.

"Unzip it."

"You unzip it."

"Jimmy, don't be a wharf rat."

So Jimmy unzipped the beanbag chair in the trunk of Honey's car. The first couple of feet of zipper zipped right along, but then he hung up on loose skin and had to force the last bit. He pulled the opening apart and brushed styrofoam pellets off the face.

Farlow said, "That's . . ."

Honey said, "Yep."

Jimmy whined. "It was an accident."

The tendency was for Farlow to think he was still dreaming. To hope. "Why is there a dead naked president in my garage?"

Honey pinched the President's arm, then let it go. The skin stayed pinched. Rena Mae, her next-door neighbor back in Odessa, had told her dead people's skin would do that, but Honey hadn't believed her. Rena Mae also claimed the hair kept growing for three days and if you put your fingers in a cadaver's mouth it would bite you.

Farlow said, "Honey?"

"We couldn't leave him behind."

Jimmy said, "I don't see why not."

Honey emitted that sigh women emit when they've explained something more than once to a male who doesn't get it. "Do you really want a body found in your apartment?"

Jimmy shrugged, not giving an inch.

"If they ask me, I'll say Charles and I chatted and he left by the back fire escape," Honey said. "That's almost true."

"Except he was dead when he left," Jimmy said.

Farlow studied the corpse, trying to decide which one of the hundred questions that came to mind he should ask first. The President's tongue had swollen some, giving his mouth a hillbilly look, and the eyes were nothing like the eyes of a dead person in the movies. These eyes were dead as peach pits.

"Why is he naked?" Farlow asked.

Jimmy jumped in. "Don't tell him."

"Oh, Jimmy, stop being macho. Farlow won't think less of you if he knows what the President was doing before you killed him."

"It's none of his business."

Farlow may have been a lineman, but he wasn't stupid. "You were screwing him."

"No she wasn't," Jimmy said.

Honey said, "Charles was tonguing my clit. I was about to get off too, if Jimmy hadn't jumped to the wrong conclusions."

"What conclusions were the right ones?" Jimmy asked.

Honey didn't answer, and Farlow didn't expect her to. Like most women he knew, she was adept at selective deafness. "What I'd like to know is what you're planning to do with him."

Honey stood close to Farlow and made eye contact. Since he was over a foot taller than her, it took some neck craning to pull off. "I was hoping to leave him with you for a little while."

"That's the worst idea I ever heard."

"Pretty please." She edged closer, her chin practically poking his sternum.

"Honey, I'm gay. This sexy begging act won't work with me."

"But you're my best friend. I can screw anybody, but I have only one best friend."

"Wait a minute," Jimmy said.

"He'll start to stink soon. I can't have a rotting corpse in my house. Do you have any idea how long it takes to get that smell out of the drapes?"

"No," Honey said. "Do you?"

Farlow tried to think. Things were going by too fast for him. He'd always prided himself on being one who firmly grasped each new fact before going on to the next one, and this was too many new facts to handle. "No, but I'll bet it's a long time."

"Don't you have a freezer?" Jimmy said.

Of course, Jimmy knew he had a freezer. It was standing over by the door into the house, humming its heart out.

"My freezer is full," Farlow said.

Honey stamped her sandaled foot. "Farlow, don't be such a spaz. This is hard on everybody."

Farlow crammed what food would fit into the kitchen freezer, and the rest went in the refrigerator or on the kitchen counter. He removed the shelving from the garage freezer and leaned it against the wall. Jimmy sat in the open passenger side of Honey's Dart and combed his hair. Honey decided to take a shower.

"His gobbledygook makes my tits sticky." She disappeared into the house.

Farlow grabbed the naked body by the armpits and pulled it from the beanbag chair, spilling styrofoam pellets onto the floor.

He threw the President over his shoulder and carried him to the freezer. Jimmy came over to offer advice.

"You think he'll fit?" Jimmy asked.

Farlow grunted. He didn't like being around Jimmy, and with Honey out of the room, he didn't have to pretend otherwise.

"You'll have to fold him in half," Jimmy said.

Farlow bent the knees up under the chin, but it didn't work. Franklin had been a big man, almost linebacker-sized.

"Another half-hour and he'll be too stiff," Farlow said.

"You better hurry, then."

They laid the body on its back on the concrete floor and pulled the legs up so it was bent at the waist instead of the knees. This made for only one fold, but Farlow had to sit on the legs to get them flush against the torso.

There was a soft *pop,* and Jimmy said, "I think you broke his legs."

"That was the hip joints."

Farlow picked Franklin up and slid him sideways into the freezer. Jimmy said, "The head's stuck."

"I know the head's stuck."

Farlow held the door partially closed while Jimmy launched himself against it. The head wedged farther in, but still not far enough.

"We have to cut off the head," Jimmy said.

"We're not cutting off the head."

Farlow stood back and studied the situation. The presidential penis was squeezed up against the freezer elements. It would probably stick, like your tongue sticks when you lick a bicycle rack in winter, and they'd end up tearing it off. Would serve the flaming heterosexual right. All this bother wouldn't have happened if the dork had kept his dick at home where it belonged.

Jimmy said, "You've got a power saw hanging on the wall over there. I could lop off the head and stick it in the space behind his butt."

"I don't think so," Farlow said. "What I'm worried about is later, after he's frozen. I don't see how we can get him back out."

"No need to take him out. We can throw the freezer in the Potomac with him in it."

"I'm not losing my freezer simply because you had to kill somebody."

Jimmy placed both palms on the President's nose and pushed with all his might. The head didn't budge. He reared back and punched. Then he flailed at the head till Farlow grabbed his arm in mid-flail.

"That's not helping."

Jimmy said, "I hate this jerk."

"Not his fault he won't fit in my freezer."

"I'm glad I didn't vote for him."

This was interesting. "You voted?"

"No, but if I had voted, it wouldn't have been for this cocksucker."

"If he sucked cocks, you wouldn't have killed him."

"You know what I mean."

Farlow wrapped his left arm around the side of the freezer with his hand braced against the back, and flattened his right hand on Franklin's forehead. Then he squeezed. He squeezed hard, with all the power of a professional athlete. His face turned stop-sign red and veins visibly pulsed in his temples. Suddenly, with a loud *crack,* Franklin's neck broke and the head popped into the freezer.

Jimmy said, "I could of done that."

Farlow closed the door and went into the house to make coffee.

The absolute worst way, to RC's thinking, that a man could be awakened was by having a phone go off like fireworks not two feet from his ear. If RC had his way, phones in the bedroom would be illegal, but that's a joke because RC had never had his way about anything that did or didn't go in the bedroom. He'd bought the Foggy Bottom condo as an allurement to entice Kirsteen into living with him, and the part of the lure that sealed the deal came when he promised her free rein on interior design. RC's job was to pay for her choices. He didn't mind so much, especially then, in the first flower of romance. He'd been living in your basic downtown dump since his divorce seven years ago, a dump so tawdry Kirsteen would not even ride with him through the neighborhood, much less enter the building, and all his possessions went back to the St. Vincent de Paul thrift store whence they had come. RC had no taste, and Kirsteen did; it only made sense for her to choose the furniture.

She chose Danish modern arranged by the principles of feng shui, which meant mirrors hung in weird places such as the bathroom ceiling so the energy could flow unimpeded in a counterclockwise direction. Kirsteen had a paranoiac fear of missing phone calls. There were phones on both ends of every stark couch and beside every black chair; phones next to the toilets; two phones in the kitchen. She installed a separate line on either side of the bed. They were rollover numbers, so if RC didn't answer the phone on his side by the third ring, the call was forwarded to her side. And vice versa. RC had known the honeymoon was over the day she picked up the ringing phone while they were making love. Caller ID said it was Condo Share Sales, International, but Kirsteen had stopped mid-passion to see what they wanted.

"What?" RC barked into the phone on Kirsteen's bedside table.

"You pissed in the beer again, RC."

RC pulled his head out from under the covers. "Alberta, is that you?"

"It's Ms. Chamberlain. Get your fanny down to my club."

"But I just got home three hours ago."

"The tennis courts in a half-hour. I want to do this in person."

RC said, "Do what?" but the line was already dead.

Eldon Bergstein perched on a high stool next to his grandfather, who was hunt-and-peck typing onto a Dell computer. Eldon didn't like spending time with his grandfather, Gino. The old man smelled of cigars and stale piss. His house was spooky. What's more, Eldon knew his grandfather didn't like spending time with him either, but they were stuck together one weekend a month on account of Eldon's mother read a book that said it was the thing to do. Eldon didn't buy the book-as-motivation line, though; his mom really wanted him out of the way so she could fly to New York City and buy stuff.

Saturday morning started out okay. His grandfather drank muddy coffee and read the newspaper while Eldon stared at a bowl of Froot Loops until the cereal became milk-logged and sank. After that came the bonding activity, which generally meant the old man teaching Eldon a skill that might have come in handy in Sicily in like 1922, such as stickball or this boring game his grandfather thought was a holy calling where you throw little bowling balls without finger holes across the yard. Today, however, Eldon's mother had decided a role reversal was in order. Eldon lacked confidence, and it would benefit the boy's self-image to teach his papaw basic Internet skills.

Only Papaw had the learning curve of a goat. "No!" Eldon shouted. "It's *H-T-T-P, colon, slash, slash, W-W-W.*"

"No one talks to me like that."

"Then get it right. Can't you tell a front slash from a back slash?"

"Slashes do not have a back and front."

"You'll never get anywhere if you don't type it right."

The door opened and a man of thirty or so entered. Eldon recognized him as Patrick, one of Papaw's protégés. That's what his mother called the men in suits and ties and shoulder holsters who hovered around Papaw like groupies on a rap star. Eldon may have been only twelve, but he could tell hoods from protégés, and he'd been in therapy since he was six, so he knew his mom was butt-deep in denial.

His grandfather growled. "I invented the goddamn slash."

Patrick stood with his hands folded in front of the third button of his dark suit. Papaw tapped a few more wrong keys, then glared up at him and said, "How often have I told you, don't bother me while I'm having quality time with Eldon."

Patrick said, "I'm sorry, Gino, but Jimmy didn't show up this morning."

Gino looked down at his hands on the keyboard. They were old-man hands, liver spots on yellow skin. The Mafia had gone to hell since he was Eldon's age. His papaw would have cut the nuts off any lieutenant who didn't call him Don Olivetti. Kids today knew nothing about tradition. Respect. Fear.

Eldon could no longer stand it. "Move over, Papaw. Let me do it."

Gino said, "I can do it. Keep your trousers on." To Patrick, he said, "So send somebody over to his place. Do I have to take care of everything?"

Patrick nodded, almost imperceptibly. "Should we scare him, or just bring him in?"

Gino rose from his stool and dug into his vest watch pocket. He pulled out a scruff of hair on a string. The scruff had a tail and two little feet. Patrick and Eldon rolled eyes at each other, the kind of eye roll where your eyes don't actually move but each of you knows what the other is doing.

"See this," Gino said.

Patrick said, "Yes, sir."

"This is the rat's ass I don't give what you do to Jimmy Sebastiano. Bring me my money."

Patrick said, "Yes, sir."

Eldon finally lost all patience. "*Colon, slash, slash.* How many times do I have to tell you?"

Gino thought to himself, *If that boy ever kills anybody, it will be for all the wrong reasons.*

RC stood by his car in the slanted early-morning light and watched Alberta Chamberlain attack the net. Attack the ball. Attack her water bottle between points. In a town filled with type A competitive males, Alberta was the most type A competitor RC had known. Alberta was worse than a congressman from Indiana.

The man across the net from her was deeply tanned and at least twenty years younger than Alberta. His shirt and shorts were crisply ironed. RC took him as a tennis gigolo, which, in RC's mind, meant he was in trouble. She would grind him up like horse meat at a dog food factory.

RC and Alberta Chamberlain had started at the *Daily News* at almost the same time. Back then, Alberta hadn't been quite so driven. She wasn't afraid to drink beer and tell dirty jokes about embassy wives. Alberta and RC covered wars together, and committee meetings so boring they lobotomized. They helped each other through their respective divorces, from which RC came out up to his neck in regrets and Alberta came out furious. There'd even been one night of drunken sympathy sex on a rubber floor-mat in the press room that RC wasn't sure Alberta remembered. Right about the time of the divorce was when she turned type A, but it didn't show so much until they made her an editor. Now Alberta would

snort fiberglass insulation before she'd admit a reporter could write
a decent headline.

Alberta ignored RC until the match was over and she'd won; then,
without speaking a word to her opponent, she walked over to a bench
and threw a Gucci warm-up jacket across her shoulders with the
sleeves hanging down like she was Zelda Fitzgerald at the yacht club.

As Alberta came off the court, RC fell in step beside her. "How'd
you find someone who'll play with you at the crack of dawn?"

Alberta had been raised in Louisiana, but in the last twenty years
she'd picked up a Boston accent. Sounded like a Kennedy with a
head cold. "I pay him a hundred and twenty dollars an hour—what
the hell happened in Paris?"

RC had trouble keeping up and talking at the same time. Alberta
seemed to be on a beeline for the locker room on the other side of
a putting green and several flower beds.

"It was amazing," RC said. "I got an exclusive interview with
Luis Del Arturo. He was between bomb plots and willing to talk.
He told me why he's dedicated his life to wiping out Spaniards.
Turns out Madrid policemen raped and mutilated his wife back
during the 'sixty-eight riots, and now the maniac thinks he's Mel
Gibson in *Braveheart*."

"You were sent to Europe to cover Tom Cruise's fifth divorce."

RC had to step this way and that to avoid balls on the putting
green. Alberta didn't even look down. RC said, "There's no story in
Tom Cruise. They mutually respect one another and will do what is
best for the children. So on, so forth. The usual movie-star drivel."

"You were sent to cover the drivel, not to interview second-rate
terrorists."

"Cruise's agent says what every agent in this situation has said
since the beginning of Hollywood history, and her agent answers
with the same line of lies. They must pay union writers to script the

shit, and they expect me to spew out garbage about the courage of
two billionaires going through the same problems everybody else
goes through every day."

"*I* expect you to write about Tom's courage. Not they. Me."

"I can't do it. You and I both know it's harder for a woman without money to leave her husband than a woman with a personal
staff, five houses, and a publicist. And Tom . . . Give me a break."

Alberta threw open the door to the locker room and strode in.

RC stopped at the threshold.

She wheeled on him. "Come on."

"That's a girls' locker room."

Alberta stared him in the face. "What's your point?"

"There's women dressing in there. They might not be comfortable with me in the room."

"God, RC, you are so cowboy."

She turned back again and left him standing at the door. There
was nothing for RC to do but follow.

RC had sneaked into the girls' locker room at Cody Middle
School once, during an Arbor Day assembly. About all he remembered of the experience was finding a bloody tampon in a trashcan,
and the showers smelled like fish. The locker room Alberta led him
into was high-end, carpeted, and laptop-connected, with Mozart
playing softly in the background and a black woman by the stalls to
hold a member's towel while she pissed. White females in various
stages of undress discussed power workouts and Kauai land prices
while trained masseuses paddled their bottoms into high definition.
As Alberta crossed the room, she stripped off her sweat-stained Izod
Lacoste tennis shirt and changed the subject.

"The *Post* has a front-page story this morning. Courtney Love
destroyed a hotel room at the Paris Hilton." She yanked a Fifth
Avenue sports bra off over her head. "You were at the Paris Hilton."

RC laughed. "The maid told me she put an alligator-skin boot through the television."

Alberta ripped open her locker. "The *Post* ran her on page one, and you were there?"

"Is that a Donna Karan suit? I never saw a Donna Karan in a locker before."

Alberta snarled. "You missed Courtney for a meaningless interview with a sheep fucker."

"That sheep fucker controls the Basque terrorist network."

Alberta's voice rose into a scream. *"Nobody gives a shit!"* This drew sullen stares from the massage tables. Alberta brought her voice under control. "RC, you have no news sense. You don't know what matters and what doesn't."

"I know the difference between news and publicity. Cruise and Love were photo ops. Luis Del Arturo kills people."

Alberta stepped out of her sweatpants and stuffed them into a gym bag. "Del Arturo never had a wife. He trots out that rape-and-mutilation bullshit whenever he meets a sucker." Alberta slammed her locker shut. "Courtney Love's boot through a TV is news. You're fired."

RC stared at Alberta, whose face was contorted into a spiteful glob. He could scarcely believe she'd fired him without the decency to cover her nipples. He said, "You're just mad because I'm the only one in the newsroom who remembers you before you were a flaming ball-breaker."

"Clear out your desk, Nash. We're finished."

Students with book bags on their backs and Walkmans in their ears swept in and out of the George Washington University library, reeking with confidence, ready and eager to take over the World Bank, the Pentagon, the White House, as if each one heard a voice inside saying, "I can't wait till it's my turn." RC felt like he had lost his turn. He sat in his car, watching the unimaginably young with their bicycles and baggy pants. They smiled at one another. They bounded up the steps two at a time.

How long had it been since RC bounded up steps two at a time? Had he ever reeked of confidence? Decades in the past, back at the University of Missouri journalism school, he had been idealistic. He remembered the idealism. The RC of then would be appalled to know the RC of now had been in Paris yesterday covering a movie star's divorce. But he couldn't remember having confidence. He'd always expected his grade school teacher from Cody to pop into his graduate seminar on ethics and tell the class he used to pick his nose. In social situations, he waited too late to check his zipper.

That's right—yesterday he had been in Paris. He had walked down the Boulevard Saint-Germain, secure in the knowledge that soon he would be in the arms of a beautiful Dane, the envy of friends and colleagues. Yesterday, he thought twenty-one years of seniority guaranteed his long-term prospects for steady employment. Twenty-one years in D.C. was the equivalent of eons in geological time. Younger reporters looked at him as an institution, like the Smithsonian.

What floored RC was how quickly it had gone. His divorce spanned two years of tears, trial separations, joint counseling, one-more-tries, let's-give-it-six-more-months. Hundreds of Frank Talks. Since the divorce, his dream had been to survive life without another Frank Talk. Well, his dream had come true with Kirsteen. Now you see her, now you don't. And the job—one day you're a vital cog, and the next you're out the door. *We're finished.*

The next stoplight left him staring into Edward R. Murrow Park. A black guy painted silver stood on a Coke crate, pretending to be a statue. His eyes and cheeks bugged out. He wore white gloves. RC knew that if pedestrians tossed money in his box, the silver black guy would move mechanically, like the puppets in a Swiss clock. While RC watched, none of the pedestrians gave the living statue a second glance. They were hardened urbanites. RC had turned into a hardened urbanite, and he hated himself for it, almost as much as hated himself for letting down Edward R. Murrow.

Maybe he would move back to Wyoming, find a weekly paper, and report on development scams and rodeos. Things that mattered, as opposed to Tom Cruise's fifth divorce. He would give up trips to Europe and skinny women with fifteen phones and a belly you could crack walnuts on. The night before their Heather Graham fight, Kirsteen had gone into an hour-long monologue on body wash, for Chrissake. In Wyoming, he might go years without a serious discussion of body wash. Out there, they cleaned themselves with soap.

The light turned green, and a millisecond later the car behind RC laid on its horn. He turned right, as slowly as possible, and drove past the World Bank, heading home for the simple reason that he had nowhere else to go.

His heart yearned for a land of soap. He found himself nauseated by diplomatic plates parked in front of fire hydrants, and bureaucrats hunched over Palm Pilots. He'd had it with hookers, panhandlers, and politicians.

As RC turned onto F, he felt a lightness in his head. It came on him suddenly—inappropriate happiness. Job termination wasn't nearly the death sentence it had been made out to be. Losing Kirsteen was not the same as heartbreak. Maybe he would sell his car and buy a motorcycle. To hell with Wyoming. Mexico was hot.

Four dark SUVs and the black Crown Victoria were parked in front of 2210. RC slowed down to study the cars. Men in sunglasses sat behind the steering wheels. On the corner, a guy in a green jumpsuit with a yellow wire coiling from his ear stood at parade rest, not crossing the street. RC pulled into a loading zone to watch the front entrance.

The back end of a District Cablevision van opened and Stonewall Jackson got out. He crossed the sidewalk quickly and went into the building. RC caught up in the foyer, which was decorated—floors and walls—in various shades of brown tile. He found Jackson talking to the building superintendent, saying, "And you don't know the girl's name?"

"I heard him call her Honey a couple of times, and Babe the once."

When Jackson saw RC in the doorway he snapped his notebook shut and said, "Get out of here, RC."

RC advanced into the dark foyer. It smelled like burnt matches. "Give me a scoop, Stonewall."

"There's no story, RC."

Jackson headed up the stairs with RC on his heels. RC said, "Right. The President gets lucky last night and big guys show up before nine today. They wouldn't come out this early for AIDS testing."

Jackson rounded the second-floor landing and kept climbing. He said, "It's nothing."

"Don't give me 'nothing.' I can print what I know so far and bring the networks down on you."

Jackson stopped and turned. "Somebody threatened Franklin."

"Here?"

Jackson shrugged. "That's all you get."

RC felt the hairs rise on his forearms. This could be the story he'd waited for for a lifetime. Jackson would not have told him that much unless there was a lot more to tell.

"So, is the President okay?"

Jackson wouldn't look at RC. He turned and started back up the steps. "Of course the President is okay."

RC said, "Have you seen him today?"

"I saw him this morning, he was fine."

"I'm a trained professional," RC said. "I know when government minions are lying."

They stopped at a door on the fourth floor. This floor smelled more like wet dog than burnt matches.

"I'm not lying," Jackson said, "But you have to leave." He knocked twice on the door. "Get lost, RC. You can't come in."

The door opened from inside and Jackson slipped through. RC followed. A crew cut on a square head looked RC over and RC said, "White House," which must have satisfied the crew cut because he nodded and stepped aside.

Jackson crossed the room and stood talking to Jonathan Weathers, head of the Secret Service. RC used the few seconds before they bounced his ass out to take stock of the situation. Besides Jackson and Weathers, there were four technicians in white lab coats and three agents in standard agent wear. Greg Gamble was on his knees next to a cast-iron flamingo, helping a technician scoop styrofoam pellets off the rug. They had every piece of high-tech spy equipment ever feared by western survivalists—big vacuums, little vacuums, infrared sperm indicators, spectroscopic fingerprint analyzers hooked up to computer modems for instant identification. RC didn't even know what most of the thingamajigs did.

The room itself was tacky. Domino's Pizza and Chinese takeout boxes cluttered a high-end entertainment center and low-end furniture. Besides the iron flamingo, RC saw a life-sized plastic penguin and an over-the-head gorilla mask. A supersized Rambo poster dominated one wall. There were also posters of Korn, the Beastie Boys, and *Godfather, Part III*. There was a framed photo of a Redskins football player, number 73, next to a Kurt Cobain poster, which one of the technicians was checking for fingerprints. Except for the contemporization of the posters, the room could have passed for RC's freshman dorm.

RC said, "Chief Weathers, do you have a statement for the press?"

Weathers's head snapped up. Jackson groaned. Gamble's face turned pink.

Weathers barked. "Who is this clown?"

No one spoke for a moment, then Jackson said, "RC Nash, sir, from the *Daily News*."

"Get him the hell out of here."

Crew Cut moved in on RC, taking his arm above the elbow in a grip like the jaws of a Rottweiler.

RC said, "Have you identified the woman the President slept with last night?"

Weathers raised his hand, stopping Crew Cut from getting violent with RC. Weathers turned to stare at Jackson, who stared at Kurt Cobain and said, "Mr. Nash walked past our position around four this morning. He came to certain conclusions."

RC watched Weathers's face. It was fascinating, like a psychotic wrestling with his dark shadow. Weathers said, "This wasn't in your report."

Gamble jumped in, temporarily shielding Jackson from the heat. "It didn't seem germane at the time, sir."

Weathers exploded. *"Germane!"*

The element of the frozen tableau that interested RC was the clueless look on the faces of the technicians and other agents. They didn't know any more what the hell was going on than RC did. What would make Weathers bring out the heavy equipment but not tell the investigators what they were investigating?

Weathers's voice fairly dribbled with sarcasm. "Besides you two bozos, who knew where Franklin was at oh-four-hundred hours?"

Gamble said, "The girl."

Jackson said, "And Nash."

Weathers stared at RC. "The only suspect we have, and it's not germane?"

"Suspect of what?" RC asked.

*Wham!* The door blew open, banging against the wall, and three punks dressed in black burst into the room, guns drawn.

The first punk, who was missing his top and bottom incisors, shouted, "Okay, Jimmy! This is it!"

As one, all five Secret Service agents drew their weapons. Midway between both sets of firearms, RC hit the floor.

The front punk, the one missing his teeth, looked at the five pistols pointed at his gut and said, "Uh-oh."

Weathers's voice was shrill. "Who the fuck are you?"

The punk to the right of the toothless one said, "We got the wrong apartment."

From his place on the floor, RC thought the punks held up well, considering they'd stumbled into a nightmare. They didn't piss their pants, anyway. Toothless, who appeared to be maybe nineteen and the leader, seemed to be thinking hard and fast. His confused gaze traveled from the guns to RC, then back to the guns.

"What apartment are we in?" he asked.

The third punk had skin so bad his neck came off as raw hamburger. He leaned out the door to check the number. "Four C."

The leader gave an apologetic shrug. "We wanted Four B," he said. "Sorry."

Weathers ordered, "Drop your weapons."

This made the punks nervous. It also made RC nervous because of the tendency dropped guns have to go off, and he was lying in the line of fire.

The front punk said, "You drop your weapons. We had ours out first."

Crew Cut sniggered. Weathers said, "You boys are in way over your heads. Throw the weapons down and place your hands behind your necks."

"We can't do that, sir"—RC could hardly believe the toothless wonder had called Weathers sir—"let us back away, and no one will get hurt. We'll call the deal even."

"Like hell," Weathers said. "You're going to get hurt bad if you don't surrender. *Now!*"

The leading punk's gun was shaking so badly RC was afraid he might start a bloodbath accidentally. The kid backed up slowly, but his cohorts stood frozen and he walked into them.

He whispered, "Back up."

The one without bad skin whispered, "Are you sure?"

"Sure I'm sure. Back the hell out of here."

Jerking their guns from one target to the next, trying to cover everyone at once, the three punks backed out in a huddle and slammed the door shut. As the sound of running feet receded down the hallway, RC exhaled for the first time since the door blew open.

Gamble said, "What was that?"

Weathers's fist came to his right ear and he spoke quietly into his cuff. RC stood, brushed off his pants, and walked to the window. Below him, he saw the three kids rush from the building, just as doors flew open on all four SUVs and the Cablevision van. More black Crown Victorias squealed around corners. Snipers arose as if from the concrete itself. In the blink of RC's eye, the punks had been thrown against cars, spread-eagled, and relieved of guns, knives, wallets, and combs. They must have thought they'd stepped into a SWAT team riot.

Greg Gamble stood beside RC, watching the action.

RC said, "I don't know."

Gamble said, "You don't know what?"

RC said, "What that was."

Twenty-five years ago Lonicera DeVries had been perky—the most sought-after Jazzercise instructor in Madison, Wisconsin. Her classes were packed, with waiting lists. Women in malls asked her advice on warm-up procedures and heart-rate targets. There was talk of local television and a video contract. Lonicera had been vibrant twenty-five years ago, but then she married Charles Franklin and it all went tits up.

No more vibrancy. No more video contract. These days, her past as an aerobics instructor was a deep, dark secret—a cause for embarrassment.

"Think what the Republicans would do with it if they found out," Charles said.

"At least I'm not a pill popper like Betty Ford," Lonicera said. "Or look at Nancy Reagan. If the Republicans can survive a dragon, you can handle a wife who takes care of herself."

"That's the point. No one ever imagined Nancy Reagan in Danskins. Healthy women are seen as shallow."

"Your secrets are black holes compared to mine."

Which didn't matter to Charles or the Democratic Party. The American public could accept a slick-talking pussy-hound president, but a former Jazzercise teacher as First Lady would be a laughing-stock.

So Lonicera danced alone now. She had converted Sarah Polk's old sewing-circle room into a studio with a gleaming hardwood floor and soundproof walls. There was a video screen in case she wanted to crank up *Buns of Steel,* but Lonicera didn't. She was too disappointed. She could have been Jane Fonda, and instead she had lowered her standards and married a future president.

On Saturday morning, Lonicera sat spread-legged on a mat and stretched her arms down along her right leg until her forehead kissed her knee. She was as flexible as ever, almost, anyway. She weighed three pounds more than the day she graduated from high school. Adulthood may have been a gyp, but by God, she hadn't let herself go.

She stood and walked, posture perfect, to the CD player, where she punched on Madonna's *Like a Virgin.* For Lonicera, the original Jazzercise sound tracks would always be the classics, beating the heck out of that noise-with-a-beat they pushed on late-night TV. Hip-hop. Fifties rock. Make me puke.

She warmed up to "Material Girl" with a set of Attitude Lifts interspersed with Flick Kicks. Jackie Kennedy in her prime couldn't pull off a decent Flick Kick. Lonicera went into Pendulum Lifts, then Heel Hops and Hip Rocks. The First Lady was in a zone. She loved Madonna, at least until 1986. After that it was all self-promotional commercial pabulum. But the old stuff . . . the old days. Only a woman married to Charles Franklin would yearn for the early eighties, when muscle tone was an end in itself and a woman's life revolved around her thighs. Lonicera jumped into lunges and pliés, working those legs, straining those lungs. God, this beat the hell out of state dinners.

But then the door opened and Claude Hammer slithered in. The buzz was ruined. Claude was the chief presidential advisor, and no one felt good about themselves in his presence. He was to self-confidence what slurry bombers are to a forest fire. Claude shut the door and stood with his arms crossed over his chest, watching her. Lonicera stalked to the player and punched Stop.

"What?"

He ignored her irritation. Claude's voice was slick as hair oil on a TV evangelist. "Mrs. Franklin, we have a problem."

"What is the Bess Truman first law of dealing with presidents' wives?"

"Never tell you anything you don't want to hear."

"Right." She reached for a towel to wipe the back of her neck.

"This one can't be avoided," he oozed. "It concerns the President."

"Tell Charles I will kiss the HIV kids and even eat off the floor next to that gremlin from Sumatra, but I refuse to do the photo op with the L.A. realtors. They give me hot flashes just looking at them."

Hammer cleared his throat. "We appear to have lost the President."

Lonicera dropped her towel. "What?"

"We cannot locate Charles. At the moment."

Lonicera turned to gather herself. As she popped *Like a Virgin* from the CD player, her hands trembled. "You can't simply lose the President. There's an entire agency whose job it is to follow him around."

Lonicera put the CD back in its case, then faced Hammer. "Is he hiding?"

"That's a possibility."

"Okay, Claude, what's going on?"

Hammer affected reticence, but Lonicera knew the embarrassed hesitation was a routine. The snake enjoyed spreading grief. "We have narrowed it down to three possible scenarios. Charles might have been kidnapped, or killed . . ."

"Or he could be shacked up with a bimbo," Lonicera said.

Hammer almost smiled. "That's the alternative we are hoping for."


Lonicera moved with the grace of a ballerina as she walked down the East Wing hallway, followed a pace behind by Claude Hammer. They passed between oil portraits of various presidents and their wives, not a smile in the bunch.

Lonicera said, "There's only been one First Lady whose time in the White House was not a living nightmare, and that was Harriet Lane. She was under thirty. You could have fun here if you were under thirty."

"I'm certain there was no President Lane," Hammer said.

"Harriet was Buchanan's niece. Buchanan was the bachelor president, the only gay President unless you count Chester Arthur, and he doesn't count in my book. Teddy Roosevelt was probably latent."

"Can a woman be First Lady and not married to the president?"

"Harriet was. It's not an awful life if you don't have to marry a man with an ego big enough to run for president. I sometimes wish I was Charles's niece instead of his wife," she said. She thought, He'd be more likely to sleep with me, but didn't say it out loud. "Julia Tyler was twenty-four when she married old John, after his first wife died. Do you know how many presidents' wives have died between marriage and the day their husband left office?"

She didn't give Hammer time to say, "How many?"

"Seven. Plus Abigail Fillmore, who died two weeks after Pierce's inauguration. Well over ten percent of the women in my situation didn't survive."

Claude smiled, exposing professionally whitened teeth. "I see what you are driving at."

"I doubt it." She stopped before the door to her suite. "My office is bugged so Charles can record his legacy for posterity," she said. "You'd better fill in the details here."

Hammer knew Lonicera's office was bugged, because he was the one who ordered it, but he hadn't known she knew. The President himself didn't know. Hammer had thought he was a loop of one.

"Charles was last seen going into an apartment in Foggy Bottom."

"With a bimbo?"

"With a young lady. They walked in around midnight. At six-fifteen this morning, our people initiated retrieval and could not find him. Every apartment in the building was searched, but he must have gone out a back exit."

Lonicera blew air straight up, lifting the bangs off her forehead. It was a thing she did to show exasperation. "The Secret Service is supposed to cover all exits."

"The President behaved as if he thought he'd lost the Secret Service, and it has never been his pattern to sneak back out once he reaches the copulation site. Therefore they didn't deem it necessary."

"Let me get this straight," Lonicera said. "He was trying to lose Jonathan's men, so they didn't deem it necessary to cover the exits."

Hammer shrugged.

Lonicera was torn between crying and spitting at Claude Hammer. The only way to avoid the fear was to keep herself royally pissed off. She said, "You know what I think. I think Chuck is nose-deep in muffin bread right now. I think he'll drag in here this afternoon and say he was getting in touch with the little people, and the staff will pretend to believe him. You and I will pretend to believe him."

"We hope so," Hammer said. "But he missed a breakfast meeting with the Christian Stenographers of America. He's never missed a meeting before."

"What did you tell the press pool?"

"Flu bug."

Lonicera opened the door to her suite, walked in, shut the door, then opened it again and walked out. "Where is our esteemed vice-president these days?"

"Fly-fishing in Montana."

"You'd better get ahold of him."

The Gallatin River trilled an autumnal melody, rippling over moss-covered rocks, slipping its course through groves of yellow cottonwood, golden aspen, and the dark cherry-red patch of bearberry. Midway between the banks of the river, clad in Orvis wool-lined chest waders, a Sundance chamois shirt, and the sort of hat favored by southern football coaches back in the sixties, stood Chip Allworth—Vice-President. Chip studied his #10 double humpy on a 5X tippet tied to a 4X leader by a professional fishing guide named Boots. Chip blew on the fly, which didn't appear to change in any way. He tore open the Velcro flap of his upper right vest pocket and pulled out a plastic bottle of Gink.

In Chip's mind, he was a hundred miles from the rat race, alone among the elements, living by his wits and skills in the unforgiving yet starkly beautiful natural world. He was the Man Called Horse. In reality, Chip was the bull's-eye of concentric circles made up of Boots and six other guides, a cadre of Secret Service agents, a personal secretary, a press secretary, assorted advisors, spokesmen, and gofers, an entire communications team manning satellite hook-ups and computers with wireless Internet access, a press pool that was freezing to death on the riverside, chefs, hairdressers, pilots and convoy drivers, and a man with a black suitcase that held the code for launching a nuclear attack. Two double-rotored Huey heli-copters *whock-whock*ed overhead, and above them, three F-16s kept the skies safe for fly-fishing. All together, it cost the taxpayers $100,000 an hour for the Vice-President to feel like he was alone in the wilderness.

Chip applied the Gink, then dropped the double humpy into the frigid water of the Gallatin. As the Vice-President let out line through a series of false casts, Boots said, "Drop her upstream from that rock there, and dead drift between it and the willows."

Chip frowned in irritation at Boots's imposition on the illusion of solitude.

Boots nodded to himself, certain of his value as a guide. He'd planted a couple of two-pound brook trout off that bank, behind the rock, and fed them a steady diet of double-humpy-shaped dog food for a week.

Chip's third false cast tangled up in a red willow along the bank. Boots nodded at two of his younger guides, who waded over and freed the fly.

Chip's next cast caught Lowell Panzer III of *The Philadelphia Inquirer* between the nostrils. The Vice-President's personal physician was brought down to the river to extract the hook from the bleeding reporter, who had never been off pavement in his life before today. This assignment had been punishment for faking an interview in which he quoted an orphan child as saying, "President Franklin's poverty bill will remove incentive for me to get off the streets."

Lowell stood rigid as a rock while the doctor fussed with the barbed hook through his septum. He swore to himself he would quit journalism tomorrow and take a job in telemarketing if he had to, anything so long as it was indoors in the Eastern Time Zone.

That was the historic moment when the red cell-phone in the Vice-President's limousine rang. His press secretary, Gary Pennington, answered, nodded twice, got out of the car, and walked down to the river's edge.

He shouted to the Vice-President: "There is a call on Red One," Red One being the line always left open for national emergencies.

Chip concentrated on holding his rod tip high while the doctor worked on Lowell. Chip was trying to keep an appropriately long face, but secretly he had dreamed of hooking a reporter—any reporter—and every now and then he twitched the tip, causing a yank on the line and a resulting scream.

"Can you take a message?"

Gary spoke into the phone, listened a moment, then shouted back. "It's Claude Hammer. He has to speak to you personally."

The Vice-President looked from the cell phone in Gary's hand to the doctor bent over Lowell's nose, and back to the cell phone. Now wasn't the time to walk away.

"Bring the phone out here."

So, holding the phone high over his head, Gary Pennington waded into the Gallatin. The freezing water sucked at his legs through his Brooks Brothers suit pants, and the moss-covered rocks on the bottom were slimier than a Florida Republican. He stumbled and fell in ice water up to his armpits, which made the Palm Pilot in his breast pocket go *zzit* and die. The pain in his Florsheim-shod feet was breathtaking.

Chip said, "Step on it."

After much struggle, Gary finally reached the Vice-President in the current. He handed the phone over, turned and sloshed for the bank, praying to make dry land before he passed out.

Chip held the phone to his ear. "Yes?"

The doctor snipped the barb; the double humpy flew back toward Chip, taking a piece of Lowell's nose with it. The fly dropped into the river between the willows and the rock, where it was instantly taken by a two-pound brook trout.

Chip's rod doubled over. The line pulsed through his free hand. He shouted, "Holy shit," and grabbed for the reel, dropping the phone into the Gallatin.

Back in Washington, Claude said, "Mr. Vice-President? . . . Chip?"

"Mind if I flip through your Yellow Pages?"

Leonard Levinson's morning replacement at Damien's was a dishwater blonde with deep frown lines running up from the inside edges of her eyebrows. To RC's reportorial eyes, she came off as an exhausted single mother with at least two kids, maybe three—definitely too anemic to give blood.

"Phone book is for customers only."

"I can live with that," RC said. "Give me two chocolate-covereds and the Yellow Pages. Please."

"Coffee."

"What?"

"You want coffee?"

"Only if I have to to get hold of the phone book."

A professional bean counter with a group of civil servants at the window table made a grunt sound of disapproval, as if RC was a typical male who would give a single mother with a crummy job a hard time. RC turned to stare at her and she stared back. No one at the table was more than a GS-11, which made her defiance somewhat rare. Washington bureaucrats generally don't stare back unless they're saying no in an official capacity.

RC said, "Okay, I'll take the coffee."

He carried his chocolate doughnuts, rank coffee, and the phone book down to the end of the counter, where the black homeless writer was still scribbling his heart out.

RC said, "Hey, Cranford, how's it going?"

Cranford said, "The tacos are cold."

RC looked in the Yellow Pages under sports teams, then punched the number into his cell phone. As he waited, he fished in his pocket for a dollar bill, which he put next to Cranford's little notebook. Cranford didn't look up from his writing. In fact, he kind of hunched his body over so RC couldn't see the words.

*"We're sorry, but you are calling from a closed account. Please contact your Verizon representative for further information."*

"Crap," RC said. "She only fired me an hour ago."

Cranford said, "Einstein is alive."

There was a rustling from the civil servants, as the word "fired" flowed through them like a breaking wave.

RC went back down to the cash register. "Mind if I use the phone?"

The worn-down single mother's right hand flew to the top button on her work shirt and twisted it viciously. "You can't do that No one can use the company phone."

RC looked at the phone on the wall, next to the sign that read, "If U ♥ NY, go back there." "Come on, I bought two doughnuts and a cup of coffee."

She thrust out her breasts. *"I* can't even use that phone."

"Why not?"

"It's the rules."

"What if I told you I'm a journalist and this is a national emergency?"

"You got fired. I heard you say so."

RC turned toward the GS-11s, who, even on their day off, came together out of colorless boredom. "You guys should hire this woman. She's a born bureaucrat." The tough woman's face hardened, and the others stared blankly, not quite processing the insult. Too late, RC realized he'd offended the very people who had what he needed most. "Any of you have a cell phone I could borrow? It really is important."

Their stares were without emotion, all except the angry woman. She glared from the moral high ground. The others had the look of fish in a tank.

"Give me a break here," RC said. "One of you must have a cell phone."

A fish said, "I need my minutes."

Cranford made a wheezy noise somewhat like a hawk from RC's childhood. He dug into a dirty paper bag and came out with the jelly center of a bismarck and a cell phone. He held them both toward RC.

RC said, "Jesus, Cranford, I'm touched."

Cranford said, "Lemongrass."

The phone was sticky, yet functional. By then RC had forgotten the number, but luckily he hadn't given back the phone book, so he didn't have to repeat the borrowing ordeal. As RC punched buttons he watched the counter woman haul a rack of doughnuts from the back to the front.

He said, "You never hear women called dishwater blondes nowadays. I wonder why that is."

Cranford said, "Nobody looks at dishwater anymore."

Cranford was right and RC was impressed. "You're pretty smart when you're not schizophrenic."

Cranford said, "Vote with your feet, vote from the street."

Whoever it was who answered the phone at Redskins head-quarters put RC through to Public Relations, and he went into the rap. "RC Nash here, with the *Daily News*. We're doing a series of articles on the less well known players on your team, you know, the common soldiers, fighting for their jobs every day, laboring there in the trenches, as opposed to the superstars."

The PR person said nothing; RC plowed on.

"We were hoping to focus on a special-teams player, Farlow Stubbs. Do you happen to know Farlow's home address?"

"Who is this?"

"RC Nash. *Daily News*."

"You're not a regular sportswriter for the *News*."

"I'm in editorial. This is more a feature story than sports per se." When RC said "per se," Cranford's head came up from his writing and he giggled the sort of high, knowing giggle you don't hear from people who sleep in beds. RC winked at him and went on.

"Whoever we throw the spotlight on will receive a nice career boost, and we're hoping for Stubbs, but if you don't know his address, I suppose we could try somebody else."

There was a long silence, then, "Give me a minute."

Honey sat on the diving board over Farlow's drained pool and dabbed black polish on her toenails, which were separated by Q-Tips plugged into the gap between each toe, all except the big thumb toes in the middle. She wouldn't admit it, but Honey was somewhat vain about her toes—men seemed almost compelled to stick them in their mouths—and Honey took care of her feet the way other girls take care of their hands.

"This black polish I found in your medicine cabinet is almost a perfect match for the polish on my fingers," she said. "Isn't it eerie how much we have in common?"

Farlow lay on his back on a weight bench, pushing barbells the circumference of hubcaps up and down over his chest.

"If we ever lived together we could share cosmetics," Honey said. From the board she could see across the low red-brick wall at the back of Farlow's property to the eighth fairway at the Prince George's Country Club. It was a par three with sand traps on either side of the green. Aging baby boomers in strangely patterned pants rode golf carts from the tee box to the green and on to the next tee box.

Honey said, "My daddy plays two rounds of golf a day, but I never saw the use. It's not exercise. At least with football you can vent your

latent homosexual aggression—maybe not so latent in your case—
but golf's nothing but a video game with sucky graphics."

Farlow let out a gasp and dropped his ton of weights onto a silver
bar thing that looked to Honey like a tall bike rack. He stood up,
shirtless in burgundy nylon trunks with the Redskins logo on the
thigh, and his muscles sweat-sparkled in the October sunlight,
sending a tingly shiver down Honey's spine.

She said, "Remember back sophomore year at Permian when I
was your Peppette and I had to carry your books and walk three
steps behind you in the halls? I knew even then that I would never
in my life behold a bottom as tight as yours. I used to go to class wet
enough to wring out."

"You were supposed to walk three steps behind me, but you
refused to," Farlow said. "And I don't recall you once carrying my
books. You were a terrible Peppette." He grabbed ninety-five pounds
in each hand and proceeded to curl the weights from his hips to his
chest and back.

Honey capped the polish and leaned back on her hands to let her
toes catch the light. "Farlow, do you ever think about us getting
back together?"

Farlow exhaled on the upbeat. "Nope."

"We had fun that year in high school. I think we might have set
a Texas record for most times in a toilet stall."

"When you dropped me I swore off women forever."

"That's sweet of you to say."

Farlow smiled up at her. "I'm a sweet guy."

The back door banged open and Jimmy came out, carrying the
attaché case and a revolver.

Honey sat up. "Where'd you get that gun?"

Jimmy twirled the revolver in his fingers, like Bat Masterson. He always felt optimistic with a gun in his hand. "Under the seat in your car."

"I don't carry a gun under my seat."

"I do."

Jimmy walked across the lawn to the red-brick wall and stood, watching golfers. He pointed the pistol at a doctor type practice-swinging a four iron up at the tee box. Jimmy fanned the cylinder and made the *p-shew* noise little boys use as the universal sound for gunfire.

*P-shew, p-shew.* "You could sit back here and pick off yuppie scum and they'd never know what hit them."

Honey dangled her legs off the side of the board. "Haven't you killed enough people for one day?"

"There's always room for more," Jimmy said, sighting along the barrel.

Calvin Straughn, who actually was a dermatologist, stepped up to the tee and addressed the ball. He tipped his head down, lined the inside of his left foot up with the ball, bent at the knees, shrugged at the shoulders, and twitched his weight into proper alignment. He counted to three on the back swing, brought the iron head level with his ear, then he swung through the ball, lofting it up, over the fairway, perfectly splitting the sand traps, and onto the green where it bounced once and rolled straight and true toward the flag.

Calvin held his breath—This is it, it's happening, the sweetest moment of my life is happening—when he heard a tiny pop, and three inches from the cup his ball snapped off a ninety-degree angle and shot into the left sand trap.

Calvin's golf partner, the internist Sonny Lingle, said, "What?" and Calvin said, "No." They both looked around, as if expecting an explanation from the air itself, but none came. No one was even in sight to witness the event, except for a thin man wearing sunglasses, standing behind a wall over by a house the other side of the rough. The man smiled and waved at them.

Sonny said, "You ever see anything like that before?" but Calvin was afraid to speak, for fear he might cry.

Jimmy Sebastiano turned to face the dry pool and empty barbecue pit. He smiled. "I love to shoot."

Honey stood and bounced the board twice, then backed down the three-rung ladder. Neither she nor Farlow had noticed the tiny pop. He'd been concentrating on blood pounding through his temples during the eighth rep, and she'd been concentrating on herself.

Honey walked barefoot over to the Crate & Barrel chaise lounge with matching web chairs and umbrella. She said, "Have you thought about where we should escape to, Jimmy? I was thinking of the Riviera."

Jimmy didn't get it. "Isn't that a car?"

Farlow sent Jimmy a disgusted look and plopped his hand weights on the rack. With some clueless people there's the inkling of suspicion that they're putting you on, but Farlow had no such inkling with Jimmy. Jimmy was as stupid as he acted.

Honey said, "It's a beach where civilized women go topless and it's no big deal. I lay out topless at SMU this one time and the Sigma Nus went bizarre. Acted like they'd never seen tits in their whole life."

Farlow sucked water from a bottle of Apollinaris. He unbuckled his lifting truss. "Do you have passports?"

Honey ignored the question, as he knew she would. She said, "Or maybe New Zealand. I saw a show on the Travel Channel about New Zealand. There's lots of sheep and it's green and cool. People are nice to each other. It's like the anti-Texas."

Farlow dropped his truss to the grass and lowered himself into a chair. This lowering isn't easy for big guys with bad knees. "Folks in Texas are nice to each other."

"Yeah, right. If you look, talk, and act exactly the way they expect you to. The man on the show said New Zealand is tolerant of eccentricity." She took the Apollinaris from Farlow before he was finished with it. "I'd like to be eccentric. Being what people want is exhausting."

Farlow let out a snort that translated as sardonic.

"I ought to take Gino his money," Jimmy said. He was standing by the baby end of the pool, holding the attaché case and the revolver the way people do who are weighing imaginary choices. Gun or money? Gun or money?

Honey said, "Don't be silly."

"You've never seen Rat's Ass when he's really pissed off, like I have."

"How can we escape without money, sugar booger?"

Farlow said, "You can't escape."

"Is that a threat?" Jimmy snapped.

"No, it's not a threat. It's a fact. You're screwed, Jimbo. You killed the big guy."

Jimmy fell back on toughness. "They'll never take us alive."

Farlow and Honey spoke simultaneously—"Us?"—which Honey saw as yet another example of their twin spirits.

That's when the doorbell rang.

It was a chime doorbell—the kind favored by gay Texans. Jimmy flinched like he'd been hot-shot. "Who's that?"

"How should I know?" Farlow said.

"I'll bet anything you're expecting company and you kept it a secret."

The doorbell chimed again, more insistently than the first time, if chimes can be described as insistent.

"Why would Farlow keep secrets from me?" Honey asked.

Farlow pushed himself up from his chair with both hands. To Honey, he seemed to have more trouble lifting himself than he had with a ton of deadweight.

He said, "It might be the recycling kid. He sorts my trash on Saturday afternoon."

"I didn't know you recycle," Honey said.

"I try to do my part."

The bell chimed a third time. Whoever was out there showed no inclination to give up and go away. Jimmy waved his gun toward the house.

"Get rid of him, for Chrissake."

Farlow went to answer the front door while Honey and Jimmy secreted themselves in what would have been the family room if Farlow had had a family, but was instead your typical gay jock's hang-loose room, which is surprisingly similar to a straight jock's hang-loose room, only it's clean and the trophy cabinet comes from the Ming dynasty. From the room, they had a fairly decent view through a crack in the window blinds at whoever was on the porch, and if Farlow left the door open between them and the hallway, they could hear whatever was said.

Farlow put his eye to the security hole in the door, but saw no one. He opened the door and still saw no one. He looked back at Honey and shrugged. She gave him a "Well, go on" eyebrow lift. Farlow stepped out onto his front porch with its hanging flower baskets and wicker porch swing. The yard was empty except for one of those East Coast squirrels that look more like rats with bushy tails than any squirrel he'd grown up with. The squirrel hopped from one red oak to another, oblivious of Farlow. As he turned to go back inside, his peripheral vision caught movement from the driveway. A man stood with his hands cupped around his face, peeping into the window on the garage door.

Farlow said, "Looking for someone?"

RC Nash flinched, caught in the act. His face showed a moment of guilt, then professionalism. He said, "Farlow Stubbs?"

Farlow nodded.

RC walked toward him with his hand out. "RC Nash, *Washington Daily News.*"

Farlow had a tendency immediately after lifting weights to find himself with unintentional, inappropriate erections. He thought it had more to do with trickling sweat and the cool whisper of nylon trunks over his thighs than any carnal need, but he'd learned long ago not to take risks, especially when it came to blatant heterosexuals, which this guy coming at him with his hand out obviously was. The upshot was that Farlow didn't touch RC for fear of embarrassment, which left RC with his hand in the air.

RC ignored the perceived snub. "I can't believe it's really you. Let me say, Mr. Stubbs, that I have always admired your work on the Redskins special teams. It is my strong personal opinion that without you they would be nothing but an empty shell."

"Laying it on a little thick, aren't you?" Farlow said.

RC laughed, sort of. "Sorry. My business is interviewing celebrities, and most of them are needy."

Behind RC, Farlow saw a flutter in the blinds. "What does your business have to do with peeking in my window?"

RC flicked his thumb toward the garage. "Nobody answered when I rang the bell, so I was looking to see if anyone was home. I thought you might be in the shower."

"I was in the backyard."

"Mind if I use your bathroom?"

Farlow hesitated. Not letting the reporter in might arouse suspicion, but letting him in would almost surely end in gunfire. "Now's not a good time."

RC shifted his weight from foot to foot. The toilet request had not been a ruse; he had to go. "I'll make this short," he said.

Farlow didn't say anything.

"You see, Mr. Stubbs, it's kind of embarrassing. I shared a taxi last night, from Dulles to Foggy Bottom, with a gentleman—a nice young man with chains around his neck." RC indicated where the chains had been. Farlow grunted. RC took the grunt as a sign to continue lying. "We seem to have traded briefcases."

"I'm not seeing what this has to do with me," Farlow said.

"The problem is, I don't know the gentleman's name or address or the first thing about him. All I know is he told me his girlfriend once spent time with you. In high school, I believe."

"The man with chains talked about me, specifically?"

RC nodded. "Would you recall if any of your old high school female friends now live in Foggy Bottom?"

Farlow said, "Not that I recall."

"The Redskins press kit says you're from West Texas. It seems like, if a girl you knew well in West Texas was living in the city, you'd know about it. The gentleman insinuated that you and the girl were quite close, at one time."

Farlow felt the beginning pulse of a stiffy. He knew it had nothing to do with this guy, who was probably lying—why would Jimmy tell a stranger about him?—but he was afraid of being misunderstood. Gay men are frequently misunderstood by straights.

"My briefcase had an interview with Luis Del Arturo in it. You know who Luis Del Arturo is?"

Farlow said, "Spanish."

"Basque."

"I never could tell the difference."

"There's not much difference unless you happen to be Basque.

It's an important interview, and I don't have to tell you how much trouble I'll be in with my boss if I don't get the briefcase back."

Farlow turned to face as far to the side as he could without being impolite, but this only accentuated the protrusion.

"Look, Mr. Nash," he said. "Lots of women claim they knew pro players in high school. I couldn't buy a date back then, but now there must be thirty girls who wouldn't look at me in high school all claiming I was their prom date. It's one of the strange by-products of my job."

"You think so?"

"My guess is this girl told her boyfriend she used to go with me, trying to make him jealous."

RC did his best to keep his eyes up where they were supposed to be, but he failed. "I'd hate to have my girlfriend making comparisons," he said.

When Farlow walked back inside, Honey met him at the door with his Apollinaris water. She said, "Looked like you were putting up a tent out there."

"It happens during cool-down after I lift. I can't help it."

"Yeah, well, the flagpole is dipping now."

Farlow sincerely wanted to move the subject away from his flagpole. He was one of those romantics who prefer "make love" to "do it" or "tasting his seed" to "sucking him off," which is what Honey called the act. Honey refused to allow romanticism into her sexual vocabulary.

"Where's Jimmy?" Farlow asked.

"He got a look on his face like a turtle'd bit his butt, and ran off out back."

They found Jimmy on the patio up to his elbows in hundred-dollar bills in his attaché case. "It's all here," he said.

Farlow had never seen so much cash. "Who'd you rob?"

Jimmy snapped the case shut and twirled the combination lock, but his hands shook, as if he'd survived a near-disaster. "The cocksucker was lying. Why would the cocksucker lie?"

Honey walked to the diving board, where she'd left her sandals. "I had a good look at the guy, and he didn't strike me as a cocksucker."

"Definitely not," Farlow said. "The man reeked of testosterone."

Honey stepped into her sandals, right one first, the way her mother had taught her as a child. "How can you tell, definitely?"

"The way he held his hands. Those hands have never touched a penis that wasn't his own."

"Will you two shut up? I don't care if he's a fag or not."

"I do," Honey said.

"We have to figure out why he was here, feeding Farlow all that garbage about switched briefcases."

Farlow smiled. "I'm flattered that you discuss me with strangers in cabs, Jimmy."

Jimmy's face flushed the color of a Redskins home uniform—the same color as Farlow's shorts. He fought to find wording, but before he could launch into a denial, there came a crash from inside, like a coat rack avalanche.

Honey looked at Farlow. "Do you have a cat?"


They found RC in the garage, his mouth open, staring into the freezer. The crash had been caused by freezer shelves falling to the concrete floor beside the zipped-open beanbag chair.

RC turned to the group in the doorway. "He's dead."

Honey was the only one of the three who met his eyes. She said, "No shit, Sherlock."

The computer skills class had gone from bad to gruesome. Eldon had taken to stomping his foot. Gino no longer saw Eldon as his grandson; now it was more along the lines of a rival out to make a fool of him within the Sicilian community.

"Okay," Eldon said. "Show me the Mafia home page."

Gino puffed a cigar, which was something he had promised his daughter he wouldn't do in front of the boy, because Eldon had stress- and smoke-triggered asthma. "The Mafia doesn't have a home page."

"Everyone has a home page," Eldon said. He spoke slowly, with exaggerated lip movements. "First you go to Yahoo."

"Yahoo."

"Or Google."

"Which is it? How can I learn if you keep giving me conflicting messages?" "Conflicting messages" was a term Gino had picked up from watching Mafia shows on HBO. He watched Mafia shows whenever possible, in hopes of someday being asked to consult.

Gino tapped the keyboard, then hit Return, and a sign appeared in a box on the screen—Fatal Error #61. Eldon slapped himself on the forehead.

"No, Papaw! What are you—attention deficient?"

"I'll show you attention deficient."

Patrick Diprisco entered and crossed the room as quietly as he would have had the floor been carpeted. Eldon thought maybe Patrick had rug scraps glued to the bottom of his shoes. Nothing else could explain how the protégé came in and out silent as a sunbeam.

Patrick bent toward Gino and murmured, "Excuse me, Mr. Olivetti." Then he mumbled into Gino's ear while Eldon set about fixing the latest crash. It wasn't easy. His papaw had managed to burn down a firewall.

"The Secret Service took them?" Gino said.

Patrick nodded. "We can't even get a lawyer in to find out what the charges are. I've never seen anything like it."

"What's the Secret Service got to do with Jimmy Sebastiano?"

"I don't know. Maybe we ought to leave it alone until we know what we're dealing with."

Gino stood up. He held out his hand. "Give me your piece."

Patrick said, "Sir?"

"Your piece. I pay you good money to provide me with a piece when I want one, and I want one now."

Patrick reached under his jacket into his shoulder holster and withdrew a .38 S&W Special. For his part, Eldon ignored the gangster rituals. He was more interested in rebooting the network.

Gino took the pistol from Patrick, checked the chamber, then popped three bullets into the monitor.

"There," Gino said. "I'm not deficient anymore."

Bits of glass and metal sprayed across the work station, much of it landing on Eldon's shirt and lap. The boy was aghast in every sense of the word. And deaf in one ear. He'd known, without being told, that his grandfather was a brutal man, but to shoot a Dell computer . . .

Gino handed the .38 back to Patrick. "You find Jimmy Sebastiano and you get my money."

"What about the Secret Service?"

"I don't give a rat's ass about the Secret Service. Shake down Jimmy's mother, shake down the whole damn family. All his friends. That boy doesn't have the brains to hide somewhere he hasn't been before."

"Yes, sir."

Gino growled. "Bring me that punk's dick on a plate."

Patrick turned to go, but as he reached the door, Gino snapped his fingers. "Last year Jimmy had a fight with that slash he calls a girlfriend. She was spending his money on catalogue trash like lawn birds and spice racks and shit."

Patrick nodded. They had all thought it hysterical that Jimmy, who acted like Mr. Godfather, Part II, couldn't control his own fuckee. He was such a wimp about it he couldn't even hit her.

"The girl ran off to an old boyfriend," Gino said. "Football player or something. Check him out too."

Eldon stared at his grandfather, for the first time seeing the old man for what he really was. Eldon now knew that someday he would destroy his papaw, throw him out of the house, out of the business, out of America herself. Anyone stupid enough to think he'd killed a computer when he'd shot the monitor instead of the hard drive was too stupid to run a modern crime machine. Monitors could be replaced for a hundred dollars. Eldon saw the future—he would own this bastard.

Honey, Farlow, and RC trooped back through the kitchen door and into the house with Jimmy bringing up the rear, brandishing his revolver, making certain everyone knew he was armed and they weren't.

"We'll lock him in the sauna," Jimmy said.

As RC passed Honey, he introduced himself. "RC Nash."

She flashed a smile. "Honey DuPont. I'm not related to those other DuPonts."

"That's too bad. Mind if I use your bathroom?"

"I mind," Jimmy said.

"Don't pay any attention to Jimmy," Farlow said. "Go right ahead. It's my bathroom."

By then they were gathered in the living room, where the lamps were steel tubes and the end tables were glass tops on black marble bases, not unlike Kirsteen's lamps and end tables. RC counted three nude women and two nude men among the paintings, engravings, and statuary. There was a full-length mirror, and a glass fruit bowl with kiwis and melon. Straight football players do not keep kiwis in their fruit bowls.

"There's a window in the bathroom," Jimmy said. "He can escape."

Honey did this thing to RC where she looks in the guy's eyes and fires off a direct challenge. Her eyes were a bright, dark blue, like those waterproof tarps you buy at Kmart, and as RC fell deeper into them, he saw glints of what he had always understood to be hazel.

"Are you planning to escape?" Honey asked.

"I wouldn't think of it."

"See," she said to Jimmy. "He doesn't even want to escape."

"He might be jiving."

She turned her gaze back to RC, like a poacher turning a spotlight on a mule deer. "Mr. Nash would not jive. He's a gentleman."

RC peed, then washed his hands, then peed again. The prospect of being locked in a sauna made him wary, not so much from a claustrophobic as a bladder point of view. He stared at himself in the mirror, realizing he'd just seen the dead President of the United States. Several times in his life he'd been in incredible situations where he said to himself, God, I hope this is a dream, and sure enough, it was. Conversely, he'd had wonderful, romantic experiences in which he said, I really hope I'm not asleep, only to awaken to disappointment. But this time, it was real.

This was a news story the likes of which break only a couple times a century. A Pulitzer Prize waiting to be typed up. Bigger than a Pulitzer—a National Book Award. Oprah would start reading again. And it was his story, alone. No single reporter had ever owned a story this big. If that idiot with the gun didn't kill him, and the Secret Service didn't kill him, and whoever sent the gunslinging teenagers busting into Jimmy's apartment didn't kill him, RC would come out of this the most famous journalist in America. Dan Rather would look like a copyboy.

After checking the medicine cabinet for steroids and counting the candles around Farlow's black bathtub, RC joined the others in the weight room for a lively discussion on the mechanics involved in locking the sauna with RC in it.

"We shouldn't lock him in at all," Farlow said. "Someone might turn on the heat and he'd bake."

"Nobody's going to turn on the heat," Honey said, giving Jimmy a look that said she meant it.

Jimmy diverted the look by studying the wooden handle on the sauna door. It was half-loop-shaped, making a natural eye for something long and thin to act as a hook. "A broom handle might do it," he said.

"Broom handle's too thick," Farlow said as RC approached.

RC double-checked his fly. "Your pistol barrel would be a perfect fit. Brace it against the door frame there with the trigger against the glass, I'd be stuck till Doomsday or somebody lets me out, whichever comes first."

Jimmy didn't fall for the giving-up-his-gun ploy. "You'd best not mouth off. There's no taxi driver to protect you now." Then he left for the kitchen to search out a proper locking object.

Honey said, "I'm sorry about Jimmy. He's usually a sweet guy."

RC said, "What?"

"Okay, you're right. Jimmy isn't sweet, but most of the time he's civil, more or less. Ever since he killed the President he's been kind of jerky."

From the kitchen, they heard a crash, like a cast-iron skillet bouncing off the stove and falling to the floor, and Jimmy called, "Farlow!"

"I better go help. He might break my stuff," Farlow said.

Left by themselves, RC and Honey stood silently for a moment, both embarrassed about the prisoner thing. RC was acutely aware of the downy hair on Honey's forearms. The hair seemed, to him, to vibrate slightly. To shimmer.

"So Jimmy killed the President?" RC asked.

"Sort of."

"I was hoping it was a heart attack, in the heat of the moment. Assassinations are traumatic for the country."

"It was more an accident than an assassination. Charles fell down and hit his head."

RC nodded. That was fairly close to the way he had it figured. "Jimmy pushed him?"

"The President was running and his thong got caught around his ankles."

"Then it wasn't Jimmy's fault. You can just call the White House and say, 'Oops.'"

"Jimmy threw a knife. And they were fighting before that. At least, Jimmy was fighting. The last thing Charles did was lick my clit, before he died." She cocked her head, like a wren. "I guess that's not a bad way for an old guy to go."

"Beats cancer," RC said.

"I would like to think so."

"So where are his clothes?"

"We threw them in the river."

Jimmy came back from the kitchen carrying a steel rod that Farlow had purchased from Sur La Table for the purpose of sharpening knives. He said, "Into the sauna, smart guy."

RC opened the door and looked at the benches and heater. Two benches were low, and one higher. The floor was wooden slats.

"You got anything to read?" he asked Farlow, who had followed Jimmy from the kitchen.

"There's a magazine I read while I exercycle." Farlow crossed to the Exercycle and brought back the magazine—*Out*. It wasn't a subject RC had much interest in, but he was one of those people who must read at all down times—instructions in Spanish on a Kotex box, Jehovah's Witnesses' comic books, stock market stats even though he didn't own any stock. Being locked up with nothing to read was more frightening to RC than being locked up with nothing to pee into.

As he carried his *Out* into the sauna, Honey said, "It was nice meeting you, Mr. Nash."

"Nice meeting you too, Honey."

Jimmy said, "Jesus Christ," and shut the door.

A stack of maybe a dozen frozen pizzas lay melting on the granite kitchen counter next to the stainless-steel refrigerator. While Farlow went back to his room to shower and dress, Jimmy popped a pepperoni and an Italian sausage into the oven, which was also stainless steel. They weren't Tombstone either; these were deli department pizzas. Farlow's standards had risen since he left Odessa.

Jimmy ate only one slice of pepperoni before the urge to smoke and fret overcame the urge to eat. Honey sat on the Victorian settee and pretty much consumed the Italian sausage, all except the crusts. Honey never was the type to fret away her appetite.

"Look at the goiter on this guy." She nodded toward the *Ricki Lake* show on Farlow's plasma flat-screen TV. The screen was about five feet high and six feet wide, which made the man's goiter the size and color of a soccer ball. He was on the show defending his right to be simultaneously married to three fat teenagers. The fat teenagers sat together on the right side of the stage, expressing their love for the man with the goiter while the audience hissed.

"She had a show on necrophilia last week." Honey bit the tip off the last piece of pizza. The tip bite gave her the greatest pleasure; the rest was just food. "There was a panel of three men in ties and sports coats discussing the pros and cons of screwing dead people."

Jimmy flipped ashes onto the remains of the pepperoni pizza. He said, "Human beings are disgusting."

Honey said, "One man was bisexual."

Farlow came in from the bedroom, wearing Redskin-red sweats and carrying a sports duffel. He looked at the man with the goiter and three wives and said, "Which would you rather screw, Jimmy— a dead girl or a live boy?"

"I'm no fag. A dead girl."

Honey put her bare feet up on the marble table. "The way you screw, you wouldn't know she was dead."

"Fuck you, Honey," Jimmy said.

Farlow smiled. He enjoyed watching Honey and Jimmy give each other grief. Honey would get in a couple of zingers and Jimmy would try to keep up, but in the end he always fell back on "Fuck you, Honey."

"I'm off to work. You two hold down the fort."

Jimmy did his combination laugh-sneer. "Work? You *play* football. You don't work it."

"Better than playing bagman."

"Will you buy water while you're out?" Honey asked. "There's no water in the house, and I drink sixty ounces a day."

"Try the tap marked C," Farlow said.

"That's not water you drink."

After Farlow left, Jimmy drifted over to the front window and pretended to shoot the tires of the receding BMW SUV. "Better than playing bagman," he said in an ugly voice. "Someday I'm going to pop that queer."

Honey was watching a commercial for a pill that made women lose weight. "If you want to pop somebody, you should pop the swindlers who make these commercials," she said.

The commercial ended, and the show picked up with all three

fat girls crying. "And don't make jokes about killing Farlow," Honey said.

"As soon as your precious Farlow starts to think, he's going to call the police on us. He'll say he's doing it for our own good. I hate it when people fuck me over for my own good."

"He took a chance letting us stash the President in his freezer."

"Yeah, well, us and Pres better be gone when Farlow gets back."

Honey hit the mute button on the remote. Whimpering women irritated her. "I like it here," she said.

Jimmy paced. That was another thing that was starting to irritate Honey. It seemed like all Jimmy did anymore was smoke and pace. When they first met, Jimmy had never stressed out over anything. She liked a boy who was free of fret. He'd always been sort of a jerk, but he'd been a fun jerk. Now he was turning into an anal jerk.

"If that bozo in the sauna can find us, so can Gino Olivetti," Jimmy said.

"Don't forget the Secret Service."

"How could I forget the Secret Service."

One of the fat teenagers started beating the snot out of the man with the goiter. At first, the other two tried to stop her, but then they joined in, kicking him with their chubby legs until he fell on the floor. Ricki Lake watched impassively.

"This is better with the sound off," Honey said.

Jimmy pulled the steel knife-sharpener from the sauna handle and opened the door to reveal RC reading.

"Hey, bozo, how did you know to snoop around Farlow's garage?"

RC marked his place with his finger. "The beanbag chair. There were beanbag pellets on the floor at your apartment, and when I looked through the window and saw the chair, it didn't take a genius to catch the deal."

Jimmy nodded and shut the door. Then he opened it again. "What were you doing in my apartment?"

"The place was crawling with Feds. I just followed the crowd."

"I hate strangers in my apartment. I'll bet anything they were touching my stuff."

"Do you know three punk kids who might want to do you harm? They kicked in the door while I was there." RC gestured toward his mouth and neck. "One with no front teeth, another with skin looked like Hamburger Helper."

Jimmy's face drained of blood.

"They seemed put out that you weren't home."

Jimmy relocked the door and returned to the family room, where Honey sat watching a commercial about the heartbreak of psoriasis. The sound was still muted.

"We'll take the body to my mama's house," Jimmy said. "Then plan how to get out of the country."

"I'm not taking any dead body to your mama's."

"Why not? The food here stinks."

Honey hit the remote off. She wasn't interested in heartbreak or glorified dandruff. "Your mama will act like it's my fault the President is dead."

"It is your fault."

"Besides, where's the first place Rat's Ass is going to look? Your mama's house."

Jimmy beelined for his skinny brown cigarettes. He clicked on his lighter, lit a cigarette, and inhaled deeply. "We've got to move him someplace."

Surprisingly, RC found a lot more of interest in *Out* magazine than he thought he would. He sat in the sauna, on the upper bench, reading an article on the never-ending affair gay men have with *I Love Lucy*. The writer of the article thought it had to do with Lucy's red hair which made her the romantic outsider gays could relate to. RC was more of the opinion that Lucy Ricardo's mannerisms, voice inflections, and the "Wah!" thing she did when she was unhappy were the mannerisms, inflections, and "Wah!" of a gay male. It would explain why gays and redheads are both referred to as flaming. That and the hots for Cubans.

Someone knocked at the door, and RC heard the steel sliding out of the handle. Had to be Honey or Farlow; Jimmy wouldn't knock. She came in barefoot, in a pink dress shirt from Farlow's closet that reached all the way down to her ankles. She was carrying a Yoplait strawberry-kiwi yogurt and a spoon. With the door open, RC heard a buzz off in the distance.

"Jimmy's trying to get the President out of the freezer," Honey said.

"With a drill?"

"Power saw." She offered the strawberry-kiwi yogurt and spoon. "I thought you might be hungry."

RC said, "Thanks." He opened the yogurt and checked under the lid to see if he'd won a prize, but all it said was, Sorry, try again.

Honey sat on the lower bench with her knees under her chin and her arms wrapped around her shins. She seemed content to sit and watch RC eat.

He pointed with the spoon. "What's that on your ankle?"

Honey looked down, as if she'd forgotten. "An armadillo. It's an animal in Texas."

"I know, they're like roly-polies only a million times bigger. Why do you have an armadillo tattooed on your ankle?"

"Back in high school a bunch of us went to Del Rio for mescal and peyote, and I woke up with a toothless Mexican must have been eighty years old and a tattoo." She ran her finger over the tattoo. "I was lucky. Most the other girls and all the boys but Farlow got the clap."

RC wondered how a girl with her track record could come across as innocent. It was like meeting a hooker who thought men were nice.

"I don't mean to be personal," RC said. "But you're a winner and Jimmy is a loser."

"You think so?"

"He's the most obvious loser I ever met."

"I don't mean Jimmy. Do you really think I'm a winner?"

RC looked at Honey over his poised spoon—blonde, pert, wide awake—her body language was a cry to be fathered or fucked. The style worked because she seemed unaware that it existed.

"You look like a girl who always lands on her feet."

"And landing on your feet is the same as being a winner?"

"It's a sign you don't give up the first time life punches you in the face. Far as I can tell, surviving is the hardest step toward winning." Jesus, RC thought to himself, I'm beginning to sound like television.

Honey was staring at her feet, running her index finger in and out between each toe. RC noticed that the toe and fingernail polish almost, but not quite, matched. The toes were a lighter black, more like dark brown.

"So why are you with him?"

Her eyes grew misty, thinking back. "When I met Jimmy he could pour a beer down his throat without swallowing. I thought that was sexy."

"I've had relationships based on less," RC said.

"Jimmy came across as the anti-Farlow. Which I guess I needed then." Honey mused. RC watched. After a bit, she looked across at him. "Do you have a girlfriend?"

RC finished the yogurt and licked the spoon dry. "I used to, but we split up."

"That's sad. How long ago?"

He looked at his watch. "About eight hours."

Honey's eyes widened. It was a neat thing to see, as if he suddenly had her attention. "You must be at the depths of your grief," she said.

Jimmy's voice came from outside the sauna. "Honey, where are you?"

Honey sighed, annoyed by the interruption. RC saw this as a good sign. She called out, "In here."

Jimmy walked in and Honey said, "Jimmy," with something like horror in her voice. It didn't take RC long to figure out why. Jimmy stood in the doorway, holding President Franklin's head.

He lifted it up by the hair. "I power-sawed the sucker loose."

The eyes were the color of raw biscuits, and the front teeth had been knocked out. The neck had not been sliced so much as ripped off the body. RC and Honey heard little plops as it dripped onto the wooden slats.

Jimmy suddenly realized how cozy things had been in the sauna before his arrival. "What are you two up to in here?"

Honey straightened her legs. "He was hungry and I brought him a yogurt."

RC held up the yogurt carton as proof of her statement.

Jimmy said, "Don't get too friendly. We have to kill him before we take off."

RC looked at Honey, who was looking at him. Neither one was happy.

A four-car caravan eased away from the White House, turned left onto Pennsylvania, and headed west. The first, third, and fourth cars were your standard Ford Crown Victorias, but the second was a black Cadillac Fleetwood limousine containing Claude Hammer, Jonathan Weathers, and Lonicera Franklin. Soon after passing the Renwick Gallery intersection, the convoy picked up a fifth and a sixth unit—the fifth a fairly late-model Oldsmobile Cutlass with a "Charlton Heston Is My President" bumper sticker, and the sixth another Crown Victoria.

Presidential advisor Claude Hammer sat with his back to the privacy panel that cut the passengers off from the driver, facing the First Lady and the head of the Secret Service, who were as far apart as two people can be on a limo seat. Although Claude's face appeared paralyzed by a sneer, as always, his heart raced in his chest. He was tempted to check his own pulse, and probably would have had he not been afraid it would affect his reputation.

If the President was dead, or even had run off with another woman, this could be Claude's golden window of opportunity. Combining perfect timing and bold purpose, he might press the advantage with Lonicera, and the love that he felt certain they had kept buried for the sake of Charles and the nation might burst into sunlight.

"Are you feeling up to this, Mrs. Franklin?" he asked.

"Cut the patronizing tone, Claude. We're going to the apartment."

That was how they spoke to each other, even when alone, yet Claude knew it was only a ruse. He knew in his heart that Lonicera saw through the cold mantle he was forced to wear; that she and she alone truly understood his vulnerability.

Jonathan snapped open a briefcase and withdrew papers. "The lease is under a false name, but the prints match those of James 'Jimmy' Sebastiano. The building superintendent ID'ed a mug shot of him, and the men we arrested at the scene this morning admit they were sent to escort Jimmy in to Gino Olivetti."

"Rat's Ass Olivetti?" Claude asked. He could not pry his eyes away from the lips that he craved to touch. And her nose, perfect, small, yet the nostrils flared with such passion. He dared not gaze into her green eyes, lest Jonathan should discover their desire.

"That's the one," Weathers said. "Seems Jimmy was supposed to bring Rat's Ass last week's Miami gambling bag and he never showed up. We have Olivetti's phone bugged and he's staked out, but at the moment he's looking for Jimmy as hard as we are."

Jonathan turned to peer through the smoked bulletproof rear window. "His men are three cars back of us."

Claude tore his eyes from Lonicera long enough to check out the Cutlass. "Aren't those your people following them?"

Jonathan emitted a low, mean chuckle. "And I wouldn't be surprised if they have men following us following them."

"So who is this girl Charles found true love with?" Lonicera asked.

Jonathan and Claude exchanged a glance. They were about to enter territory everyone in the administration knew existed but no one had the balls to talk about, until now. Jonathan read from his papers, although Claude knew he didn't have to.

Jonathan said, "The neighbors estimate Jimmy Sebastiano's girlfriend as somewhere between seventeen and twenty."

Claude risked a look at Lonicera's eyes. They were hard as glass. How he longed to hold her in his arms and murmur into her ear, "That ingrate doesn't deserve a woman as fine as you," and she would whisper, "You are so wonderful, Claude," as warm tears fell against his neck.

"One of the neighbors said Jimmy called her honey," Jonathan said.

"Half the men in the country call their women honey," Claude said.

Weathers cleared his throat. It was a thing he did when he wanted his listeners to pay attention. "When we go in, remember our team thinks the President was physically threatened while in the apartment, but he is unhurt and recovering at the White House. No one but the two agents with him last night are in the loop—disappearance-wise."

"How are we handling the two agents?" Claude asked.

Jonathan lifted the top sheet of paper to check a note on page two. "Gamble and Jackson are maintaining silence, but if this plays out as a worst-case scenario, they will either have to be promoted or terminated."

Lonicera's voice was dry. "By terminated, I take it you don't mean fired."

An awkward silence fell over the backseat. Claude loathed Jonathan for exposing Lonicera to the grimy side of government.

He wanted to protect his little flower. And even though he knew beyond doubt that she appreciated all he did to spare her pain, sometimes in that dark hour before dawn when he should have been sleeping but wasn't, a dull fear lodged in Claude's belly, a fear that the sham of shared contempt he and the First Lady showed the world was not necessarily a sham on her end. They were both so good at hiding their true feelings, what if the adoration he saw behind the wall was an illusion? The thought made him tremble, but then the morning came and Claude's wife made coffee while he showered and put on his suit, tied his tie, checked his messages. By the time Claude left for the White House he was once again certain that his and Lonicera's love was strong and whole and real.

"Gentlemen," Lonicera said. "The President did not disappear while screwing a seventeen-to-twenty-year-old called Honey."

Her voice was fierce. Direct. Claude saw that Lonicera suffered from no second thoughts. "Charles will be the joke of the Free World if this gets out," she said. "His poverty bill will fail. Health reform will die forever. The Democratic Party may well cease to exist. The entire government could fall."

Jonathan looked dubious, but Claude's eyes shone with faith in his First Lady. He had known she would take command in a crisis, but this was beyond his dreams. She was sending him a message now—a message saying, "We must wait a little longer, my darling. We must see America through her time of need, but then you and I shall be together."

Lonicera stared straight into Claude's eyes. "You are to do whatever it takes to protect the presidency."

Breathlessly, Claude said, "Yes, Lonicera. I hear you."

The closet was a nightmare. Tiny cotton tops with corporate logos stretched across the tits, skirts meant for draping over pubic hair, a pink baby-doll dress, two black leather jackets—one sequined, one bomber—calf-high boots on fuck-me heels. Half the shirts were on the floor instead of hangers.

Lonicera slammed the door, but it bounced off an Abs Roller. "She dresses like a hooker doing a Britney Spears fantasy."

"I guess that's what Charles likes," Claude Hammer said.

The look she shot Claude should have peeled flesh, but as usual, he misinterpreted.

Lonicera circled the room, counterclockwise, inspecting the not-quite-empty takeout boxes, the clumps of dry makeup in front of the vanity mirror, male and female underclothes—not a bra in sight—on the only chair, an unlit but chewed-on cheap cigar on the floor. She stayed away from the unmade bed.

"What do your crackerjack technicians make of the crime scene?" she asked.

The only technician in the room sent a questioning look to Claude, who nodded.

"Tell Mrs. Franklin what you have, Dolf."

"Are you certain—"

"Dolf." Lonicera's voice said she was not to be toyed with.

Dolf stood with his back to the door, keeping his eyes away from Lonicera. "The President attained two spermal emissions. One in the front room, where we found the styrofoam pellets, and the other at the foot of the bed there. Where you are standing."

Lonicera stepped to the side.

"He did not use protection," Dolf said.

Lonicera muttered, "Of course not."

"There appears to be a spot of blood on the floor in the front room, there by the stork."

"Flamingo," Claude said.

Dolf blinked, not understanding the difference. "We should know later this afternoon if it came from the President."

"You know the sperm came from Charles, but you're not sure about the blood?" Lonicera said.

Dolf stared at the floor.

"Explain it to her," Claude said.

"Over the last couple of years, we've become accustomed to the makeup of the presidential sperm—under the microscope. He has a high percentage of two-headed gametes. We know less about his blood than his . . ." Dolf drifted off.

Lonicera said, "Jizz."

Claude filled the silence. "Were there any signs of a struggle, other than the drop of possible blood?"

Dolf scanned the mess of what may or may not have been trash in the room. "That is hard to ascertain," he said. "I would have to know what the place looked like, pre–presidential entry."

Lonicera used the toe of her right shoe to lift a Hawaiian-print bikini brief, cut low in front and high at the sides, off the floor. She said, "I find it hard to believe that even Charles would sleep with any woman who would wear this."

"Evidently, he did," Claude said.

Lonicera knew gloating when she heard it. "I guarantee he did not fall in love with her and run away to Temptation Island."

Back in the living room–kitchen, a cadre of agents and technicians were finishing up the fine-tooth-comb search while a photographer worked his way down the Kurt Cobain poster wall. Lonicera easily separated the girl's bad tastes from Jimmy Sebastiano's bad tastes. The animals—iron flamingo, stuffed pregnant penguin, cut-glass unicorn, fuzzy donkey—belonged to the girl. The *Cracked* magazine and the Sony PlayStation with the Leisure Suit Larry game were Jimmy's.

Jonathan Weathers and Stonewall Jackson worked on refrigerator inventory.

"We'll have to test the mold," Jonathan said.

"It's old food," Stonewall said.

"Has to be tested anyway."

Claude walked over to check out the furry lunch meat Jackson was bagging. "What's this I hear about a reporter poking around?" Claude asked.

Stonewall sniffed at a carton of milk. "God, I hope they didn't feed the President."

Claude said, "Jonathan?"

Weathers did not, as a rule, give information to civilians, and Claude was a civilian, but Lonicera had taken an interest in the question, which meant there wasn't much choice but to answer. "RC Nash of the *Daily News* spotted our men last night. He deduced that the President was here."

Lonicera stepped closer. "What else did Mr. Nash deduce?"

"He observed heightened activity in the building this morning, which raised his suspicions, but all he has are suspicions."

"What are you planning to do about him?" Claude asked.

"Whatever it takes."

Stonewall and Greg Gamble traded a quick look. They both had been with the Service long enough to know that "Whatever it takes" also applied to them. They were two men at a crossroads, with fairly equal odds of moving way up or all the way down and out. Stonewall could feel his dream of an Airstream in Spearfish, South Dakota, slipping into the fog.

Lonicera stood before the Farlow photo. "Except for this picture, is there anything in the apartment that would lead you to believe these two are sports fans?"

Claude looked at Jonathan, who looked at Stonewall. Various agents and technicians shrugged.

Greg Gamble said, "No."

"This photograph means something the tacky posters and junk art don't," Lonicera said. "Charles dragged me to enough Redskins games, even I know this guy isn't a star. He's somebody's brother or a friend or something. This one is personal."

Greg was reaching for his cell phone even as Jonathan spoke. "Gamble, call the Redskins and find out who's number seventy-three."

"I'm on it." Greg disappeared into the bedroom.

While they waited, Lonicera stared at a Noise Addict poster. To Stonewall, the expression on her face was one of bitter disappointment. He understood what she felt; a cheating spouse was bad enough, but when your spouse cheats with a Noise Addict fan, especially if the spouse is president, it must be a hard pill to choke down.

Her attention moved on to an Atlantic City ashtray overflowing with thin brown butts. She said, "No man who smokes brown cigarettes calls his woman honey. It's babe or bitch, depending on his sex drive."

The male contingent was impressed, although they did their best to hide it.

"Honey is her real name," Lonicera said. "Or a nickname her precious daddy gave her when she was two and a half, and no one's called her anything else since."

Gamble returned, snapping his cell phone shut. "Seventy-three is Farlow Stubbs. He's special teams and third-string defensive end. Played college ball at SMU."

Jonathan already had his people tracking Jimmy's family, friends, and co-workers, and this football player seemed like a long-shot lead, but it was Lonicera's lead, so it had to be moved up to the top of the list.

"Take a couple men, find out if he knows a girl named Honey. And pick up a search warrant on the way. We don't have time to dick around."

Gamble didn't hop to it the way he normally would have. Instead, he stood in the bedroom door, looking slightly ill. Lonicera was the only one who noticed.

"All right," she said. "What else did the Redskins office tell you?"

"I'm the second person to ask about Stubbs today."

Weathers said, "Rat's Ass?"

Greg shook his head no. "RC Nash."

RC Nash sat at the kitchen table, scribbling into a little red notebook he'd found in the top drawer of a Louis XIV escritoire in the dining room, next to the china cabinet. The notebook was the same size as the one Cranford Nix, the homeless man with a cell phone, wrote in at Damien's. RC wondered where Cranford hid his stash of daily notebooks. He was certain a homeless black schizophrenic would have interesting insights into the human plight.

RC's notes were of a journalistic nature. The body was here; the head was there. I entered the garage at 12:10 p.m. Facts that wouldn't have been that interesting, standing alone, had the body and head not belonged to the President.

Jimmy Sebastiano came in from the garage, carrying the attaché case and a Redskins workout bag. He looked at RC and said, "How'd you escape?"

"Honey let me out."

"Don't think I've forgotten that you threw my cigarette out the cab window."

"I didn't think that for a minute."

Jimmy set the case and bag on the floor by the dishwasher and walked back into the garage.

RC's release had been easier than anticipated. He'd read the *Out* from cover to cover, even the weird ads at the back, then he banged on the door until Honey opened it.

"I have to pee," RC said.

"You peed before, when we came in from the garage."

"This is something you should know about me if we're going to be friends. Whenever I don't have anything else to do, I have to pee."

She cocked her head and did the thing where she hooks hair behind her right ear. "Is that on account of you being so old?"

"It's on account of a nervous prostate."

She followed him into the bathroom and stood at the mirror, inspecting her teeth, while RC took his leak. He carefully cupped himself, hiding what should be hidden, and aimed for a rim shot so the piss wouldn't sound like a horse going on a cow pie.

"The President was older than you, even," Honey said. "But he didn't pee the whole time I knew him."

"That's a politician's skill. They have to sit in meetings that last for hours and hours, and it would be embarrassing to be going in and out all the time."

"I've never been to a meeting," Honey said.

RC shook off the final drip and flushed.

Honey perched on the sink counter. She seemed in no hurry to go anywhere. "I think Charles made a good president."

That statement amazed RC more than the one about never having been to a meeting. As usual, with women, Honey knew what he was thinking.

"You think just because I'm blonde that I don't read newspapers."

"It's not that."

"I can't stand TV news, but I read papers every day. I've read your stuff. The story you did about the courage of the Backstreet Boys was dynamite."

RC didn't want to think about his squandered talent as a writer. Instead, he put both toilet lids down and sat on them. "Why do you think Franklin was a good president?"

Honey swung her legs like a little girl. "He cared what happened to people. None of the other presidents cared. Course I haven't been around for that many presidents, but most of them look at running the country as a game where they win or lose."

"Is that why you invited him home with you?"

"I invited him home because he was lonely. I thought I could help him feel better."


What Honey said about Charles being a good president bothered RC. No one causes bigger conundrums for a journalist than a politician who cares. All politicians have scandals in the past, and most of them have scandals going on as we speak, which is fine when it comes to the ninety-five percent who deserve to be dragged through the slop and horsewhipped, but every now and then you find a good person who happened to snort coke in college, or stole a car—said "nigger" when he was six years old.

RC knew there wasn't a reporter worth calling professional who wouldn't destroy any man or woman in America for a front-page byline below the fold; Alberta Chamberlain would do it to plug a hole on page ten, which was maybe the reason Alberta Chamberlain was an editor and RC Nash wrote puff pieces on the courage of the Backstreet Boys.

However—the big however—in six years Charles Franklin had cut crime, unemployment, and the national debt, raised health benefits for the poor and old, raised the literacy rate, all that shit you look for in a leader. And now he would go down in history as the president who died with his underwear wrapped around his ankles.

Jimmy backed through the doorway from the garage, dragging the beanbag chair into the house. RC watched him grunt and strain until he got the chair halfway through the door, where it seemed to hang up on something.

Jimmy said, "I'll let you walk around free till we're ready to go, if you give me a hand here."

RC took a corner of the bag and lifted while Jimmy pulled, and the chair popped through the door in a rush, dumping Jimmy on the floor.

"Where we taking him?" RC asked.

Jimmy stood up, dusting off his pants. "Back to your sauna. Farlow will come home and see his freezer empty and think we took him with us. It'll be days before the stink gives it away."

"Unless Farlow takes a sauna."

"By the time he finds the body and calls the police, Honey and I will be in a new country. Pick up your end again."

RC didn't pick up his end. "Where will I be in your plan?"

"You'll be in the sauna too. My papa always said two bodies are as easy to hide as one."

Honey blew into the room, wearing designer jeans, a red pullover sweater, and see-through jelly sandals. She carried a silver lamé purse that, as RC understood it, was called a clutch.

She said, "I'm ready to take off, but we're not killing RC."

Jimmy spoke without looking away from the beanbag chair. "We have to kill him, or he'll tell on us."

"Tell on us? What is this, grade school?"

"Where'd you get the clothes?" RC asked.

"I left them last time I lived here, while Jimmy and I were working out issues." Honey walked up beside RC. He liked the way she smelled. She said, "And we can't leave Charles in Farlow's sauna. He's coming with us."

Jimmy said, "Like hell."

"Don't be a dope," Honey said. "We need time to get away, and our best chance is if the Secret Service thinks Charles and I ran off together, on purpose."

"No one will believe the President ran off with a girl like you," Jimmy said.

"What a terrible thing to say." She appealed to RC. "Be honest. Do you think the President would have run away with me for romantic reasons, or was he only using my body for oral sex?"

RC couldn't come up with an inoffensive answer, so he did the next-best thing: he agreed with the statement that had brought on the trick question. He said, "You can't leave him here. You'll need the body to cut a deal."

"What kind of deal?" Jimmy asked.

"Whenever a president dies, it's important that they have a body. Without it, the country turns to chaos."

Jimmy said, "I don't care if the country turns to chaos."

"Yes, but the government does. If they get hold of the body, they'll probably charge you with murder, or even kill you on sight. If you have the body, you can negotiate your future."

"That's what I said before," Honey said. "Charles is our bargaining tool."

Jimmy said, "That is not what you said before. First you said you were going to tell them you chatted and he left by the fire escape, then you said you wanted them to think you and the Tongue Man ran off for romantic reasons. You didn't say a word about bargaining tools."

Honey said, "I did so. You never listen to a word I say."

Jimmy had been looking forward to surprising Farlow with two dead guys in the sauna, and now that he couldn't, he was in no mood for a raft of shit from Honey.

He said, "Shut up, cunt."

Honey reacted as if she'd been slapped. "Don't call me that."

"I'll call you whatever I feel like. Cunt."

RC said, "I've found women are hardly ever charmed by guys who use that word."

"Nobody asked you," Jimmy said.

Honey drew herself up to her entire five feet, three inches. "You owe me an apology."

Jimmy got right in Honey's face and said, "Cunt."

Honey swung at him, but he'd been expecting it and caught her wrist before her fist smacked him. She swung with the other hand and connected this time, but she was in too close to pack much power.

Jimmy sang to the tune of "Jingle Bells." "Cunt-cunt-cunt, cunt-cunt-cunt, cunt-cunt-cunt-cunt-cunt."

No one but RC saw two men with guns walk in the door from the garage.

The taller one, Patrick Diprisco, said, "The geek is right, Jimmy. You'll never impress a girl that way."

Jimmy stopped mid-"cunt," let go of Honey's wrist, and said, "Boy, am I glad to see you."

Patrick nodded as a third man with a gun came from the backyard, through the utility room. RC knew reporters who could look at a pistol and say, "Ten-millimeter Glock," or "Thirty-eight airweight," and almost all fictional detectives can name caliber and brand on sight, but to RC a pistol is an object that can kill you personally and the size doesn't mean squat when it's pointed your way. He'd had seven guns pointed his way today, not counting a bunch of Secret Service guns pointed through him at targets on the other side, and frankly, he was sick of it.

Patrick did the Al Pacino quiet-menace thing where you frighten people without moving your face. "Gino wants his money, Jimmy. What happened to Gino's money?"

Jimmy tried not to look at the attaché case. "We had a little accident, and I couldn't make it to Gino's this morning. I was hoping you would show up and give us a hand."

"My socks are turning brown, Jimmy. Don't bullshit me."

"I'm not bullshitting you. Tell him, Honey."

Appealing to Honey was a bad idea on account of "Jingle Bells."

"I didn't have anything to do with ripping off Rat's Ass. Jimmy made me do it."

"He'll talk if I shoot his kneecap off," the hood over by the utility room said. He was the youngest of the invasion force, and to RC's practiced eye, the one most likely to have been awake three days on an amphetamine binge. The third hood, behind Patrick, was calmer and dressed better. Looked like a poster boy for the Big 'n' Tall Shop.

Patrick waved his pistol vaguely in RC's direction. "Who's your friend here?"

"He's RC Nash," Honey said. "RC, meet Patrick Diprisco. That's Francis with him. Vincent's the one wants to kneecap Jimmy."

"Pleased to meet you," RC said.

Patrick smiled without smiling. "What's your part in the fiasco?"

"I'm a reporter for the *Daily News.*"

"A reporter?" Jimmy turned on RC. "You didn't tell me you're a reporter."

"Honey knew. You should have asked her."

To Honey, Jimmy said, "I told you we should have killed him right away."

Patrick said, "Jimmy. The money."

Vincent said, "Let me break his legs."

"Only if he won't tell us where the money is," Patrick said.

He walked over and picked up the gym bag. "Is it in here?" Patrick unzipped the bag and reached in and pulled out Charles Franklin's head.

He recoiled. "Jesus."

Jimmy whined, "I told you there was an accident."

Patrick turned to RC. "That's—"

RC said, "Yep."

Patrick ran a hand across his face. "I said to Rat's Ass, 'We should back off,' but he never listens. It's all Sicilian honor to him. 'Nobody takes my money!' Crap."

Francis and Vincent crowded forward to look at the head. It'd lost a couple more teeth since RC last saw it, and the eyes seemed to be sinking into flesh. Francis said, "That don't look accidental."

Then the doorbell chimed.

RC said, "I'll get it."

Patrick said, "No you won't."

"We ordered a pizza," RC said, kind of stupidly, since ten pizzas lay melting on the counter.

"It's the recycling kid," Honey said. "He comes on Saturday."

The doorbell chimed again—four notes, three up, one down.

"Whoever it is will go away," Patrick said.

RC said, "They'll see my car and know someone's home."

Patrick's eyes moved from RC to Jimmy to the President's head. The skin was starting to draw up on the skull, making it look like an editorial-page cartoon of the President. The big jaw was the only part that hadn't shrunk.

Patrick said, "Get rid of them fast."


RC led the parade out of the kitchen, through the family room, and on to the living room and the front door. Patrick made Vincent wait in the family room with Jimmy and Honey—a gesture RC appreciated. He felt better opening the door with Patrick behind it and Francis out of sight along the wall than he would have with Vincent the Nervous twitching at his side.

The bell chimed again and Patrick said, "Nothing cute, now. You hear?"

RC nodded. He opened the door to find Greg Gamble with his finger on the chime button. Behind Greg, out in the yard, stood Stonewall Jackson and an agent whose name RC thought might be Parker Somebody-or-other.

Greg said, "RC."

RC said, "Gamble."

"Are Sebastiano and the girl here?"

RC could feel Patrick breathing behind the door. It wasn't a time for frankness. "No."

"How about Farlow Stubbs?"

"He left for football practice."

Greg nodded. He looked back at Stonewall, who was looking at RC with an odd expression on his face, as if trying to understand why everyone was calm. The third agent drifted over by the garage.

RC said, "I'm waiting in case Sebastiano shows up, but I think he'd be here by now if he was coming."

Greg nodded again. "We have to come in, RC."

"You got a search warrant?"

Stonewall spoke from the yard. "Now RC, you don't have to be like that. It's not even your house."

"I promised Farlow I wouldn't let anybody in unless they had a warrant."

"Why?" Stonewall asked.

RC couldn't think of an answer.

Greg said, "The warrant's in the car." He nodded to the agent whose name might have been Parker, who walked down the driveway toward the agency Crown Victoria.

Greg's eyes went to something behind RC. "Who's this?"

Then Francis shot Greg in the head. RC leaped to the side just as Stonewall fired. Francis looked down at a hole in his sternum.

Another hole appeared higher in his chest, and one in the neck, and he fell back as Patrick slammed the door shut.

"That was stupid," RC said.

Patrick said, "No shit."

A hail of bullets smacked into the door and the side of the house. RC heard glass breaking in the family room. He took a quick look out the window to see Stonewall and the third agent scrambling for cover while Vincent opened fire.

RC said, "I was hoping this wouldn't happen."

Patrick duck-walked to RC's window, but there was no need to break the glass with his pistol barrel, because it shattered from the outside, spraying shards over both of them.

"I cannot believe Jimmy killed the President," Patrick said. "What an asshole." He raised up and snapped off a shot that wasn't aimed at anything.

He said, "I'll kill that asshole."

RC jumped across Francis's body and hustled into the family room, where things weren't any better. Vincent had produced a second, smaller gun and was double-fisted firing through gaps in the horizontal blinds. Honey crouched behind the Victorian settee while Jimmy crawled on his hands and knees for the kitchen, where he'd left his pistol on the microwave.

As RC entered the room, Vincent spotted Jimmy making his getaway. The unfairness of it all infuriated Vincent, that the cause of all this noise was sneaking off while he had to stay and shoot it out with the Secret Service.

Vincent aimed his gun at Jimmy and said, "Time's up, dickwad," but just as he squeezed the trigger, RC nailed him in the arm with a Texas Class 5A State Football Most Valuable Defensive Lineman trophy. The bullet took out the fruit bowl and two kiwis, and the gun flew across the room and slid under the settee. Vincent tried bringing his other gun to bear, but RC grabbed him by the collar and belt and threw him through the blinds and out the window.

There was an amazing crash as more glass came down, and before Vincent even hit the lawn, Stonewall put three bullets in him. Stonewall stood up from his crouch position behind the Crown Victoria and shot Vincent a fourth time, on general principle.

Honey said, "That was so cool."

RC could not believe what he had done. "It was, wasn't it."

Jimmy sat on the floor, staring at the broken window where he'd last seen Vincent. Apparently, the events had gotten the best of Jimmy, putting him temporarily in shock. Patrick must have had extra ammunition, or maybe he got hold of Francis's pistol, because a veritable fusillade of gunfire was pouring out of the next room.

"Stonewall's calling for backup," RC said. "We better move along."

In the kitchen Jimmy pointed his gun at RC. He said, "It's time for me to shoot you now."

Honey was outraged. "RC just saved your life."

"What's that got to do with anything?"

"Can you carry the body alone?" RC asked.

Jimmy considered the beanbag. "Maybe," he said.

"You couldn't lift it from the ground to the trunk of my car without help," Honey said.

"He was heavier when he had a head."

Jimmy soon realized the wisdom of letting RC carry one end of the beanbag chair while he carried the other and Honey followed with the workout bag and her silver clutch. At first Jimmy insisted on holding the gun and the attaché case in his right hand and carrying the chair with his left, but by the time they reached the wall, he could see the plan was impractical.

"You'll have to take the head and the case," he said to Honey.

"Only if you ask nice."

They threw the beanbag across the brick wall and, when no one shot it, jumped over themselves.

Two golfers named Rex and Duff watched from their cart on the ninth-hole tee box as RC, Honey, and Jimmy lumbered with their loads across the fairway.

"Sounds like gunfire," Duff said.

"Must be negras," Rex said.

Jimmy grabbed Duff by the shoulder and yanked. "Out of the cart, asshole," but Duff hung on to the cart frame until Jimmy whacked him across the knuckles with the revolver barrel. "Didn't you hear me?"

With Duff's grip on the frame gone, he found himself thrown to the turf. Rex was a plastic surgeon and, as such, resented authority, but Jimmy came across as a madman with a gun, so Rex got out of the cart. But slowly. With dignity. He didn't want Jimmy thinking he was timid.

"Lay down," Jimmy ordered.

Meanwhile, RC tore open the straps holding the golf bags to the back end. He dumped the clubs and replaced them with the bean-bag chair.

From the ground, Duff said, "This cart is a rental."

Honey slid into the passenger's seat. "Don't you worry. We know how to treat other people's property." The score card clipped to the console showed Duff had shot a seven on the par-three eighth hole. Rex had par, but Honey didn't believe it. She knew a cheater by his pants.

Jimmy signaled with his gun. "I told you. Get down by that other asshole."

Rex said, "I will not."

Jimmy put a bullet in Rex's foot. The plastic surgeon dropped like he'd been shot out of the sky.

"Any objections from you?" Jimmy asked Duff, who buried his face in the grass and didn't look up.

Honey said, "Christ, Jimmy. You're so tough when you've got a gun and everybody else doesn't."

Jimmy said, "Shut up."

RC climbed into the driver's seat. "Let's talk about this later."

Jimmy jumped onto the back bumper bar. He said, "I'm a crack shot. If either one of you moves while we're in sight, I'll nail his ass."

Duff nodded. Rex writhed.

RC drove the golf cart into an alley behind the Sam's Club discount store, and they unloaded the head and body bags next to some dumpsters, then moved off fifty feet or so to reassess the situation. That way, if they got caught with a hot golf cart, at least they wouldn't lose the corpse.

"What now?" Honey asked.

"You wait here and I'll be back." Jimmy climbed into the driver's seat.

"Where you going?"

"I wasn't always an interstate courier."

As Jimmy rode off in the golf cart, Honey sat on the curb and took off her jelly sandals. RC noticed Jimmy had kept the attaché case. If the President's head and body were in bags, RC wondered what that left in the case.

"What'd he mean?" RC asked.

"Before Jimmy was a bagman, he used to steal cars."

RC said, "Oh," and sat down next to Honey. He leaned back on his palms to soak in the sunlight reflecting off the wall of the huge shopping warehouse. Some guys down the way were wrestling a forklift through a garage door. RC typed in his head. *The President's coquette and I waited, desperately aware that any moment might bring the full wrath of the American government crashing down upon our heads. I couldn't help but stop for a moment and consider the chain of events that had brought me to the point of hiding with the dead body of our President behind this, the finest symbol of capitalism on display.* That would never do: he'd used "President" twice.

Honey said, "Jimmy thinks he's such hot stuff whenever he shoots people, but anyone can pull a trigger. What you did when you threw that hood out the window was really daring."

RC cut the brain typing. It sucked anyway, even for a first draft. "If you'd known me before today, you wouldn't think I was capable of throwing a person out a window."

"But you did."

Honey gazed at RC thoughtfully. He felt she was assessing him, the way she would a salad bar.

"How old are you?" Honey asked.

RC said, "Forty," lying by two years. "How old are you?"

She said, "Twenty-one," lying by one. "What was your girlfriend like?"

RC tried to picture Kirsteen. "Thin, in every sense of the word. And she wore black, always, even to bed, and if I watched a basketball game on television she treated me like the autistic child of a sister she didn't like."

"She sounds nice."

"You think so?"

"Why did you two break up?"

RC considered the question. "Kirsteen and I started leading separate lives a while back. I guess now we'll lead them from different places."

Honey hooked her hair behind her right ear. RC was growing fond of the gesture. It meant she was thinking.

"You know how I tell when the romance has gone out of a relationship?" Honey asked.

RC skipped Kirsteen and went way back to his marriage. He'd known the romance was gone from that relationship when Catherine started wearing Breathe Right nasal strips to bed.

"Kissing," Honey said. "Everyone says it's oral sex, but that's not true. I've blown guys just to get them to shut up and go to sleep, but when a couple stops making out, that's the beginning of the end, romantically."

RC could not remember the last time he and Kirsteen had made out. When they first met, they'd kissed so long and hard his lips tingled the next day. But lately the closest they'd come to necking had been air kisses and a couple of X's at the bottom of a note saying she'd gone out. They'd continued having sex twice a week with orals on birthdays and major holidays, but kissing? He could not recall when they'd last kissed.

"I guess you're right," RC said.

"Of course I'm right. It goes in two stages. First you stop kissing except as foreplay. I firmly believe, and you can write it in your story, that every single kiss does not have to be followed by an orgasm."

"Write it in my story? What story?"

"That's why you're here, isn't it? You didn't lug Charles's body across a golf course as a favor to Jimmy. And second—"

"Second what?"

"The second stage. You start fucking without even bothering to kiss at all. The guy touches you here, you touch him there, he plugs in, everybody comes, and you both go to sleep. The romance is gone and you've turned into mutual masturbation machines."

"That's kind of harsh, isn't it?"

"It may be harsh, but it's true."

RC had to admit it was. Through trial and error, he'd learned the precise sequence of movements that could get Kirsteen—and before her, Catherine—off in the shortest period of time. Variations brought criticism.

"And another way to tell the romance is dead—when touching his dick gives you the creeps. Recently, I've found Jimmy's penis disgusting. It feels like a wet 7 Up bottle. I don't mind him sticking it in, but for Chrissake keep it away from my fingers."

This was going places RC did not care to go. "How did you find the presidential penis?"

Honey thought, a light smile on her face. RC enjoyed watching that smile. It was internal, like a memory.

"I found it small."

RC nodded. In the press room, the common myth was that every president had a tiny penis. They ran for office to compensate.

"He was better with his tongue than with his peter," Honey said. She thought a moment and said, "Most men are."

Honey used a twig to draw figure eights in the dirt along the curb while RC tried to figure out how long a frozen body and partially thawed head could lie in the sun before they started to stink. He was certain there was a mathematical formula for it somewhere. Probably in Boston.

Without looking up, Honey said, "Do you believe love is a chemical reaction between two people?"

RC considered Kirsteen, and Catherine. "At first it is. Then, theoretically, it grows into something more. Or dies."

Honey touched RC's hand—the outside edge of his right little finger. To him, it was the most startling thing that had happened all day.

She said, "I'm finding myself chemically attracted to you. Isn't that funny?"

RC said, "Funny." He reminded himself she was half his age, living with a psycho killer, and had sucked off the President last night. None of it mattered.

"Let's try this," he said. He leaned into Honey and kissed her. It was good—soft, sweet, fresh as clean air. No bells or whistles, but it must have been romantic, because RC found himself nauseous.

"That's nice," Honey murmured.

They heard an overrevved engine, then Jimmy ripped around the corner driving a brand-new Ford Explorer. Honey gave RC a tiny smile before she turned to watch Jimmy squeal to a stop.

Jimmy rolled down the window and threw out an antitheft device called The Club. He said, "You better not be seducing my girlfriend."

RC's face wasn't as innocent as Honey's, but God knows he tried. He said, "Wouldn't think of it."

Jimmy grinned. "Last guy did that lost his head."

Farlow's knees hurt. So did his ankles, shoulders, neck, and right elbow. Those were the joints. He didn't know the names of the muscles that were killing him, or the bones under the muscles. He was twenty-two years old and setting himself up for a life ruled by arthritis.

A hand grabbed his arm and spun him around. Special-teams coach Mal Czeneck was in a fury. Foam spittled at the corners of his mouth. His ears flamed red, and tiny blood vessels pulsed in his nose like varicose veins on a Denny's waitress.

Ream time in Dixie—"What the shit were you pulling out there, Stubbs? Nobody can cover punts with their head up their ass!"

They were stopped in a stream of players at the head of the tunnel leading to the locker room—smell of big-man sweat; *clack-clack* of rubber cleats on concrete—but none of the worn-out players so much as glanced at Mal or Farlow. They'd all heard coach fits a thousand times before, and if this one registered at all, it was with relief that it was aimed at someone else.

"How many times did you get yourself blindsided on coverage?"

Farlow didn't know, but his ribs said a lot.

"You ran like a queer out there today, Stubbs. A goddamn dick-sucking pussy. Do you have any reason why your brain was in fairyland? If there's an excuse I would love to hear it."

Farlow shrugged and kept his eyes on the feet moving up the tunnel. He'd been playing competitive sports all his life, all the life he remembered anyway, and he knew better than to offer excuses. *I didn't sleep much last night. I have a dead president in the freezer.* Nothing justified letting himself be blocked on his ass on a punt.

"No excuse."

Mal stepped in front of Farlow—chest to face. "Let me tell you what will happen to you if you don't shape up, *Mr.* Stubbs. Before you can take a crap you'll be back pulling your pud in Amarillo—"

"Odessa."

"*I don't give a fuck.* Listen to me. The only job you're fit for outside football is bouncer at the bar in a Holiday Inn. And that's where I will put you if you don't wake up, right quick."

Even though the terrible metaphors were spewing from a homophobic alcoholic with bad breath and a restraining order signed by his wife, Farlow knew the jerk was right. Old quarterbacks ran for office, and running backs sold cars, but there wasn't much for an ex-lineman other than bouncer, bodyguard, or pro wrestler, and he hated pro wrestling. He'd rather rob banks.

"Shape up by Sunday, Stubbs, or you're out of here."

Farlow stripped at his locker, wrapped a towel around his waist, and headed for the training room. From peewee to pro, when a coach feels the need to humiliate his players, he calls them either "girls" or "fags"—the two lowest forms of life. "Girl" is usually used in sarcasm— "You girls ready to run laps?" And "fag" in anger—"Get up, you fucking faggot! You're not hurt. I'll tell you when you're hurt!"

Farlow had the self-image of a walking fuse. It was only a matter of time before a coach screamed, "You play football like a queer!" and he screamed back, "That's because I am a queer, you dickhead!" Then he would quit, but not before he'd kicked the living daylights out of whatever coach represented the last straw.

But not yet. He wasn't ready to embark on the bouncer career quite yet.

*L*ike feed stores and muffler shops, the training room is one of those bonding temples men love and women hate. Naked giants swilling soda pop in whirlpools; black, glistening Adonises being rubbed, taped, or untaped by the American equivalent of eunuchs. Many, including Farlow, lay about on tables encased in ice; a few were taking injections straight into joints. Conversation revolved around Internet porno sites, women, and violence. And money, of course.

One wall-mounted television showed a silent lumberjack competition on ESPN2, and the other, an equally silent *Dance with Danielle* exercise program on a local station. Practically everyone but the linebackers watched Danielle and her two hard-as-space-age-plastic assistants bounce up and down, the smiles seemingly spot-welded to their faces. It was just the sort of show Lonicera Franklin had given up to marry the future president.

*Dance with Danielle* was a tradition in the Redskins training room. The point was to watch closely and theorize on the sexual proclivities of Danielle and her assistants.

"I heard Trudy there can crack a coconut with her thighs."

"Bullshit."

"My cousin got killed by a falling coconut."

"Jeez, look at the quads on Danielle."

From his table, Farlow looked at the quads on Danielle. The girl had no breasts at all, but her quadriceps looked like footballs stuffed in tights.

"If she sat on your face, she'd break your nose."

"If I could get past the smell, I'd sure enjoy the taste."

Jocks consider themselves the wittiest profession, but Farlow hadn't heard a new line since SMU.

A wiry little man everyone called Kid even though he was seventy-three stepped over to check the ice collars on Farlow's knees. "You want them tighter?"

"Sure," Farlow said. "I can still feel my legs."

Kid turned a dial that pumped the slush-filled cuffs tighter around Farlow's scarred knees. Even freezing body parts had gone high-tech.

Danielle and the Bouncing Anorexics were abruptly preempted by a helicopter shot of what appeared to be a suburban war zone. Police cars, ambulances, vans filled with equipment for both ending and recording armed standoffs flew haphazardly up and down streets. Sharpshooters crouched behind cars and on rooftops, their high-powered rifles focused on a house backed up to a golf course. The moving banner across the bottom of the screen read: ONE FEDERAL AGENT DEAD IN SIEGE IN COLUMBIA PARK NEAR LANDOVER. POLICE SAY HOSTAGES FEARED DEAD.

Around Farlow, injured men booed the loss of Danielle. Nobody wanted to see a television station justify its helicopter budget.

Kid pinched Farlow's toes to see if he'd cut off the blood supply. "Don't you live over in Columbia Park?"

Farlow watched as what appeared to be National Guardsmen tumbled out of the back of a truck. That couldn't be right. "Yeah, I do."

"Think that's anywhere near your house?"

Farlow blinked. "It is my house."

The general chaos of SWAT-team mania raged on the street as Stonewall Jackson slid around a WRC-TV news van and, crouching, sprinted across the neighbor's yard for the far side of Farlow's garage. He'd walked out on a heated jurisdictional debate as to who was in charge here. The Prince George's County Sheriff's Department had a unit trained in this stuff. They couldn't understand why the Secret Service was even on site, and none of the agents who'd arrived since the shooting began could tell them, because the agents themselves didn't know. Only Stonewall knew, and he wasn't talking. Neither group seemed in any hurry to charge the house, even though it was obvious to Stonewall there was only one shooter left.

He tried to recall exactly what he'd seen: RC Nash at the door, then someone behind him, shooting Greg. The door slammed shut, although neither RC nor the man Stonewall was in the process of blasting had touched it. That meant three, at least, inside, with one down, and a possible fourth who had jumped out the window and was also down. It was conceivable the dead gentleman in the yard had shut the door, but that left RC as the shooter and that didn't seem likely. RC had looked as amazed as anyone when Greg flew back off the porch.

The sight of Greg Gamble sprawled on the red-brick walkway with a hole in his head had a major effect on Stonewall. It was not the suddenness or the finality of death that affected him. He'd known since he joined the Service that oblivion was one bad decision away; it was the utter nonchalance with which Greg's death would be greeted by the men at the top—Jonathan Weathers and Claude Hammer, for instance. Whoever else knew secrets deemed too dangerous for the public to handle.

Stonewall wasn't paranoid. He didn't think he and Greg had been set up, or even sent on a mission where an agent's getting killed was looked on as a bonus to the main objective. That could, probably would, come later. What chilled Stonewall's psyche and brought on an epiphany that would change his life was the shrug he knew Jonathan would give when informed of the casualty. One less problem checked off the list. Stonewall didn't mind dying so much, but he did mind his death being viewed as convenient. For almost thirty years, through five presidents, he had bought the Secret Service directive of All for One, and the One Is in the White House. As he crouched behind the Crown Victoria, looking across the hood at his partner's body, Stonewall's number one shifted. It was not a decision so much as sudden knowledge. Stonewall Jackson was out of the sacrificial lamb business.

So when a jerk with a pistol came crashing out the window, Stonewall shot him three times. Then he stood up and shot the body.

Twenty minutes later, with the house surrounded and helicopters *whock*ing overhead, Stonewall stepped through the side door to the garage. It was quiet inside, compared with the scene on the street, and cool. He heard a siren in the distance and some reporter with a bullhorn trying to interview the shooter. *"What are your issues?"* A low pop came from inside the house, but it sounded several rooms away.

Stonewall worked his way around an older Dodge Dart with the trunk open. The door of a cabinet freezer along the wall also hung open, and freezer racks lay scattered across the concrete floor. He knelt and picked up a styrofoam pellet, same size that'd been on the floor at the apartment.

Another shot was fired from the house. How much ammunition could this guy have, anyway? Stonewall was about to move on, when he noticed one of the pellets was shaped like a tooth, and when he ran it between his fingers, he discovered it was a tooth. By brushing his hand this way and that through the styrofoam, he found two more. First pellets and now teeth, tech support would have a field day.

Stonewall squatted on his haunches, staring at the teeth in his hand—one capped incisor and two molars. They were unnaturally white. Politician white. Even the roots weren't the brownish yellow you usually associate with pulled teeth. Stonewall had no clue as to how they came to be where they were, but he was certain they belonged to Charles Franklin and they would be important to the Service. So—to hell with tech support—he pocketed the teeth.

Stonewall crept to the door that led inside and held the knob, listening. Wouldn't do to charge into an unknown quantity. He'd hate to get himself killed only twenty minutes after deciding not to.

He let the door swing open, waited, then slipped in. He stayed low and near the wall, with his eyes on the entry into the main part of the house. He knew the other door, leading to the backyard, was covered from outside, but he couldn't relax about that direction either. Friendly fire killed just as dead as the unfriendly kind, and in his position there were those who might jump at the chance to create an accident.

Stonewall stopped next to a pile of frozen pizzas leaking onto the countertop. Were they planning a party, or what? A whispered *"Fuck this shit"* came from the main part of the house, then Patrick Diprisco walked through the door. Their eyes met, two guns came up, and at the same moment, they each pulled the trigger.

Luckily for Stonewall, his gun was the loaded one.

This was a day for dreams to come true. Claude said, "Keep me posted," hung up the phone, rose from his desk, and walked out of his office, all the while maintaining stoicism in front of his secretary. Walking down the hallway to the family dining room, he rehearsed what he would say and what she would say and so forth, which was something he often did before meeting Lonicera, only so far he'd never gotten it up to saying the words themselves, so he wasn't sure if she would have stuck to her lines or not. He imagined she would. What kind of woman upon hearing "I love you" doesn't return with "I love you too"?

He would say, "It's over. Three Mafia dead and one of ours," and she would say, "Did they find Charles?" and he would silently shake his head no. Strong and silent always beat eloquent in the movies. No reason to think real life is different.

He would wait calmly for her emotionalism to ebb, then he would say, "It's looking unlikely that Charles disappeared by his own choice."

A single tear would appear at the corner of her eye. She would murmur, "Comfort me, Claude," and he would take her into his strong arms. He wasn't certain what would happen then. Would they make love there in the dining room, or later? The waiter came in and out of the dining room, and that weird busboy with the ponytail. Maybe it would be better to wait.

He stopped at the dining room door and braced himself. Under his breath, he muttered, "Mr. President, I hope you rot in hell."

Claude found Lonicera at the bois d'arc table given to Martin Van Buren by the French in 1841. It was a long, incredibly heavy table, and it made Lonicera look alone and vulnerable up there at the end, where she sat in front of her chicken cordon bleu with asparagus tips and a crystal glass of Pinot Blanc. At the moment, Claude loved her more than life itself.

"What?" Lonicera said.

"I'm sorry to interrupt your lunch."

"You have your breaking-bad-news face on, Claude. What is it you have to break this time?"

He walked down the long table toward her. "It's over. Three Mafia dead, one of ours."

"Did they find Charles?"

He shook his head and waited, keeping his eyes focused on her hands. If she was going to tremble, it would start in her hands.

Instead, Lonicera drank from her wineglass. "Who was the one of ours?"

Claude stopped to think. She wasn't supposed to ask that. "Greg Gumble. He's one of the two who know Charles is missing, so it's probably for the best."

"You are saying it is for the best that a man is dead?"

Claude shrugged. "I'm saying that if someone had to die, it's for the best that it was a man we would have had to deal with later."

"It is not *for the best,* Claude, that four people are dead because my husband couldn't keep his cock in his pants."

Claude waited, embarrassed. His flower must be truly distraught for her to use so tawdry a word as "cock." He imagined the intense strain Lonicera was under and what an inner battle she must be waging to maintain this hard exterior through such utter humiliation. His heart cried out to her.

Finally he said, "Would you like some comfort, Mrs. Franklin?"

She gave him a look he did not understand. "Get out of here, Claude."

"Yes, Mrs. Franklin."

Out in the hallway, Claude leaned his back against the door and closed his eyes. Sweat trickled from his hairline. At last, he had declared himself. He offered comfort and Lonicera did not say no. His dream was alive.

"Gotta hit the john," Chip Allworth said, rising out of the padded captain's chair.

Gary Pennington looked up worriedly from his laptop computer. Pennington was always worried. He considered it a career choice. "We land in twenty minutes."

"Gotcha."

Chip made his way toward the *Air Force Two* bathroom, which was half the size of the *Air Force One* bathroom, a fact Chip deeply resented. Who'd decided the Vice-President needed less room to take a crap than the President?

Out the window, he could see the silver flash of his F-16 fighter jet escort off to the north. Another jet he couldn't see flew alongside, to the south. Fifteen men and women inside the plane, not counting the flight crew, revolved around Chip like electrons on a nucleus. Sometimes all the attention felt like a great weight on his shoulders. Other times, it was kind of cool.

He shut and locked the bathroom door, then leaned into the mirror to check himself. Last month, *Us* magazine had named him Best Male Hair in America. Julia Roberts won Best Female Hair. Chip thought maybe he should give Julia a call, to congratulate her.

He'd have Gary find out her relationship status, which changed too often for Chip to keep up.

He opened his Banana Republic billfold and took out a folded slip of paper the size of a stick of gum. He started to close the billfold, then remembered—*Careless me*—to withdraw a five-dollar bill. Abraham Lincoln. Someday, there would be a picture of Chip Allworth on money. People the world over would snort across his face.

As Chip unfolded the paper, he hummed "Brown-Eyed Girl" on account of Julia. Hell, if Charles Franklin really was dead, that meant Chip was president and it might not matter if Julia was in a relationship or not. If there was one lesson Charles had drilled into Chip, it was this: Power attracts pussy, even more than money. Women will always love the top dog.

President Chip Allworth, imagine that. The first thing he planned to do was fly back to Pacific Palisades Day School and tell his algebra II teacher where to stick it. *You said I would never amount to squat, Mr. Singleton, well, you can call me Mr. President now, penis head. And oh, by the way, you're being audited.*

Chip said the words aloud to hear how they sounded. "Mr. President . . . Right this way, President Allworth . . . Good morning, Mr. President. Did we sleep well?"

The paper—technically called a bindle—had been given to him by the mayor of Lima, as a token of esteem from the Peruvian people. Nice guy, the mayor, although he would never make it in American politics with those teeth.

As Chip rolled his five-dollar bill into a cylinder, he daydreamed of tomorrow, when he would be president of the United States. Leader of the Free World. By God, he'd have the power to make dry fly-fishing an Olympic sport. He just might proclaim Jerry Garcia's birthday a national holiday. He could do that.

*Air Force Two* hit a bad air pocket over the Shenandoah Mountains, which threw Chip forward so that his arm hit the bindle on the back of the sink, flipping it into the steel toilet.

"Oh my God."

He reached into the toilet and snapped up the paper, but too late—the flaky powder he loved so much had fallen out. Chip muttered, "Why do these things always happen to me?"

He stared into the toilet at the little white pile down there, beckoning him. Time to think like a leader. What would Abraham Lincoln do? Abe would say, "Keep your fucking powder dry." Airplane toilets aren't filled with water, and they're flat on the bottom. There was hope.

Chip dropped to his knees and stuck his head in the commode. Bad plan. Snorting is a two-handed affair, and neither hand fit. He pulled his head out and inserted the rolled five-dollar bill deep into his right nostril. He gave a practice snort to see if it worked, and it didn't, because of the collateral passage. He tore off two sheets of toilet paper, rolled them tightly, and stuffed them into his left nostril. Chip looked in the mirror again. Not exactly glamorous, but American ingenuity was ugly more often than not.

As Chip stuck his head back into the commode, a knock came at the door. "Mr. Vice-President. We're on approach."

"Just a minute."

"What's that, sir?"

He pulled his head up. "I said, 'Just a minute.' You can't rush these things."

There was a pause, then Gary said, "Right."

Chip had to bend way over and tip his head way up, but soon the far end of the rolled five-dollar bill hovered over the pile of powder. He snorted hard, and loud.

"Mr. Vice-President. Is everything okay?"

Chip rocked back on his calves. A glow spread across his face. That nice Chloraseptic drip leaked down his throat. His ears buzzed.

"I am okay."

"I'm going back to my seat," Gary said.

Chip reached over and pushed the flush button. Bluish water swirled clockwise down the steel toilet basin, the bottom plate dropped open, and the powder residue drained away. Chip watched in fascination. Airplane toilet water is always blue and the blues are what you feel when you'd like to be flushed down the toilet and no one in the history of mankind ever made the connection. That's why they called it the blues. He was the first to see the truth, and being first made the whole thing twice as intense. He had thought an idea that no one had ever thought before. He was astounding.

Chip stood up and checked his hair in the mirror. Finest in America. He would have Gary research Jerry Garcia's birthday. He might have to deep-six Columbus Day, but politically, it would be brilliant. A hell of a lot more voters were named Garcia than Columbus. Chip smiled. He was going to enjoy being president.

When Farlow came out of the locker room he found RC Nash leaning against the hood of his BMW SUV. RC was reading an advertising supplement called *The Thrifty Nickel.* He looked like he'd been waiting awhile and would have waited a lot longer if he had to. He was that settled in.

RC said, "There's some great deals in here."

"Is Honey alive?"

RC nodded. "They dropped me off here and went to ditch the car Jimmy stole. We're supposed to pick them up in front of the Barnes and Noble in the Bowie Town Center. I hope you know where it is, because I'm lost out here in the 'burbs."

Farlow fought back tears. "I thought she was dead. The TV news said the hostages were killed."

RC folded the newspaper neatly in case he needed reading material later. "Never believe anything you hear on the news."

RC had been in some swank cars, even a limo or two when he was profiling movie stars, but he'd never been in any car as swank as Farlow's.

"I like my beater truck back in Texas better," Farlow said as he pulled out of the parking lot. "This gas guzzler is nothing but an affectation."

"Really?" RC looked at the horde of readouts showing the outside temperature, inside temperature, tire pressure, and the number of miles they could go before running out of gas. "Would you call it a gay affectation or a pro jock affectation?"

Farlow glanced over to see if RC was being a jerk or was just interested, and decided RC was just interested. "Jock," he said. "I actually hate it, but it's one of those things that can't be helped when you live a lie."

"Then your teammates don't know . . ."

"Only the gay ones. You'd be amazed how many gay men are in the NFL, but we have to stay far, far back in the closet." Farlow pulled right onto Fort Totten Road, thinking. "It's probably on account of the group showers."

"What is?"

"Why we have to stay in the closet. That, and the coaches tend to be pigs."

"Oh." RC watched their progress on the global positioning screen between the seats. It disturbed him, somewhat, that the car knew where they were but he didn't.

"Is this saving-Honey thing a pattern with you two?" RC asked.

Farlow almost smiled. "You noticed, huh?"

"Hard to miss."

"It started in the sixth grade. Honey's mom found lipstick in her school book bag. They were Freewill Baptists, and lipstick was a sin until high school, when the girls made up for lost time."

"It was the same in Cody, only with drinking."

"Honey's parents grounded her until I went over and confessed that the lipstick was mine."

"Was it?"

"Of course not. It was this completely gross shade of cooked liver. I wouldn't have been caught dead in it, and Honey's mother should have known that, but she was willing to believe anything so long as it proved Honey was innocent. Honey had her parents wrapped around her finger. Wrapping people around her finger is Honey's gift."

RC considered that statement in light of the recent kiss.

Farlow continued. "We went steady one fall in high school, but right before state playoffs we both fell in love with Arthur Putnam. He was the quarterback. Girls always go for quarterbacks."

At a stoplight, a police car with its siren blasting and lights flashing blew past them on the left and ran the red light and clipped a black limo with diplomat plates. The police car spun a 180 and slammed into the stoplight pole. The limo drove away.

"Which one of you got him?" RC asked.

"Who do you think? But then Arthur bragged about banging her in the locker room—those were his words, 'Guess what whore I banged in the locker room?'—and I broke his arm. We lost the playoff game, and everyone in town blamed Honey and me."

Farlow eased around the smashed police car. The policemen stood out on the sidewalk, looking bewildered.

RC said, "The two of you probably weren't popular that week."

"We got death threats. You wouldn't believe how important high school football is in Texas. They make the Redskins' Hawgs look apathetic."

A block later they discovered where the police car had been going in such a hurry. Jimmy and Honey had abandoned the Ford Explorer in a McDonald's drive-thru lane, where it was surrounded by a SWAT team.

"The Panthers wouldn't have even been in the playoffs if it weren't for me," Farlow said. "Arthur Putnam couldn't throw a rock over twenty yards. I don't know what I ever saw in him."

"Did you and Honey get back together?"

"Nah, I realized I was definitely gay instead of bi, and she went through a string of hideous boyfriends. We stayed close, though. She followed me to SMU, then when I got drafted, she came up here. Every boyfriend she's had the last three years has hit her or stolen from her or cheated on her or something awful. Jimmy's actually above the average."

"Maybe getting in trouble over and over and needing your help is her way of saying she still loves you."

Farlow groaned. "I wouldn't have let you in the car if I thought you were going to analyze me and Honey."

"Well, it makes sense."

"Honey simply gets turned on by bad men. I know guys like that. Loving assholes is not gender-specific. There she is."

Honey was sitting at an outdoor table in front of Barnes & Noble, although it was cool for drinking coffee outside. She said, "We lost the body."

RC pulled up a wrought-iron chair while Farlow stood with his arms crossed, looking off over the parking lot at a mountain of pumpkins in front of the Food Lion. Honey was dipping a biscotti in her coffee, then kind of sucking on the soggy end. The workout bag sat on the ground beside her chair.

"I've got the head, but some old lady and a little kid took the body away in a shopping cart."

"How could you two have lost the body?" RC asked.

"Don't start criticizing me. We don't know each other well enough for you to be critical."

Farlow had been dealing with Honey longer than RC had. He knew how to word questions. "How did Jimmy lose the body?"

Honey bit off a piece of biscotti. "We hid it down by those dumpsters." She pointed to a pair of dumpsters behind the God-father's Pizza on the outside corner of the shopping center parking lot. "Just like we did at Sam's Club. It was your idea." She stared at RC with some reproach. "If it's anybody's fault Charles is gone, it's yours."

"I didn't want the police finding us and the body at the same time," RC said. "I said we should stay close enough to keep anything from happening to the beanbag chair but far enough not to be arrested with it."

"Yeah, well, you didn't think about old ladies and little boys with shopping carts out searching dumpsters for free furniture. Jimmy wanted to run over and threaten them with his gun but all these people were around. It's bizarre how many people have nothing better to do than lurk in shopping center parking lots."

"So where's Jimmy now?" Farlow asked.

"He followed the old lady. I waited here for you two, and you took your sweet time about coming to get me. I've had three lattes already, and that much coffee makes me impatient."

Honey did seem peevish. Maybe it was caffeine overdose, or the night without beauty sleep had caught up with her, but she wasn't as delectable as she'd been behind Sam's Club.

"I need to use the restroom," RC said. "Then we'll drive around and look for Jimmy."

Honey said, "Have you ever thought about a catheter?"

No one in the SUV was in a blissful mood as they cruised the residential area where Jimmy was last seen following the woman and boy with the shopping cart containing the dead president—no one except maybe Farlow. RC hadn't spent much time with Farlow, and he wasn't confident of his sensitivity toward male moods anyway. He had little experience. However, it didn't take a sensitive man to tell Honey was on the surly side, and RC didn't feel all that peppy himself. He felt unappreciated. When Honey and Jimmy had let him off at the Redskins practice complex, he could have caught a taxi and gone home to bed. But no, he had stayed. He'd waited for Farlow, and together they had gone back to look for Honey and Jimmy and the body parts. He wanted credit.

As if she read his mind, Honey said, "Don't worry, you'll still get your precious story."

"I'm here for you," RC said.

"If you have to pick between the story and keeping me out of prison, what's your choice going to be?"

RC was so surprised by the question he didn't answer.

Honey said, "That's what I thought."

Farlow crept through an intersection, craning his thick neck right and left. "What's the old lady look like?"

"She was wearing a dark blue Kmart pullover from the Jaclyn Smith Collection that I would swear she bought at a garage sale because no one has worn them that long since my mother pledged Tri Delt, and red stretch pants, the kind with the loop that goes under your foot so they don't ride up your leg."

"Laura Petrie wears those on *Dick Van Dyke Show* reruns," Farlow said. "They're sexy."

"On a woman under seventy—maybe. She was also wearing red tennis shoes. Keds."

"Was she white or black?" Farlow asked.

"I don't remember. That's not the sort of thing I notice."

"I would save you before the story," RC said. "But I think I can save both."

"You do that," Honey said. She pointed down an elm-shaded block. "I see Jimmy over that way."

Jimmy was holding a black kid—short khaki pants, filthy sweatshirt—by the ear. RC had never actually seen one person hold another by the ear, although he had heard of it often enough, mostly back in Wyoming, from elderly teachers making threats accompanied by rulers across knuckles.

The kid, who could have passed for anywhere from nine to fourteen, flailed his fists wildly while Jimmy held him out at arm's length, so mostly the kid threw air punches. Jimmy stood straddling the attaché case with his gun in his left hand, aimed at the boy, who ignored it. The tussle was taking place behind a juniper hedge that hid Jimmy and the kid from a white frame house across the street, but practically no one else.

"Put your gun in your pocket," Honey told Jimmy as she, RC, and Farlow piled out of the SUV. "I'm tired of you waving that thing in the face of everybody we meet."

"I'm going to trade him for my beanbag chair," Jimmy said.

"That's *my* beanbag chair!" The boy tried a drop kick, but Jimmy twisted his ear and the karate *eee-oww* turned into an "*Oww!*" of pain.

The boy stopped struggling and held his right hand over Jimmy's fingers on his sore ear. "My grandma's going to get you. She don't allow child abuse on me."

"Your grandmother sounds like a fine woman," Farlow said.

The boy said, "Fuck you, fag."

"He and the old lady took the chair in there." Jimmy pointed his revolver at the frame house across the street. It had a dirt yard and a smog-colored divan on the porch. "I snatched this one when he snuck out here to smoke a cigarette."

"You're too young to smoke. You'll grow up impotent," RC said.

The boy fell back on, "Fuck you too."

Jimmy gave the ear a twist. "When he calms down we'll take him over there and offer Grandma a deal."

"If I was his grandma, I'd keep the chair," Honey said.

The boy grinned at Honey—smitten. RC didn't get it. She hadn't shown the slightest encouraging body language, and her tone had been neither teasing nor ironic, yet the kid was charmed. How did Honey do that?

RC said, "Why not just explain to her there was a mistake? She might voluntarily return the beanbag chair."

Jimmy smirked, which was RC's least favorite facial expression. "You can't let people do things *voluntarily.* You've got to scare the piss out of them, then they do what you want."

"Not my grandma," the kid said.

A scream ripped through the air. RC and Honey looked at each other, Farlow turned toward the house, and Jimmy fell on his attaché case, pulling the boy down with him. Another scream followed, if possible more high-pitched than the first one. A black woman dressed as Honey had described crashed through the screen door and ran out onto the porch, screaming all the way. She looked left toward our group, then took off running the other way with her hands up at shoulder level. She cut across two yards and ran to a house that looked like her own, only with tricycles on the porch instead of a couch, and without knocking, she ran inside.

Jimmy stood back up. "Where's she going?"

"That's my aunt Enid's," the boy said. "Grandma's going to call the cops, and they're going to come stick you with their stun guns."

RC said, "I hate stun guns."

Farlow tossed Honey the keys. "Drive around back and meet us in the alley." To RC he said, "Let's go."

Jimmy looked from the house to the SUV to the kid, whose ear he still held. "What do I do?"

"You let the boy go, apologize, and give him twenty dollars for his grandma's chair," Farlow said.

Jimmy turned the boy loose and picked up the attaché case. "I don't have any cash on me."

Farlow and RC sprinted across the street, up the porch, and into the house, which was nicer inside than RC had expected from racially profiling the woman based on the lack of grass and the couch on the porch. Granted, the decor was IKEA, but it was clean IKEA. The walls were papered with a yellow rose design and the floor was waxed hardwood with area rugs. The dining table was littered with supermarket coupons and a pair of fingernail scissors. The beanbag chair lay on the floor in front of a television turned louder than RC would have liked—cubic zirconiums on QVC.

The beanbag chair was partially unzipped and a dead arm had flopped out.

"I'd scream too if I sat on that," Farlow said.

A siren sounded off in the distance.

"We better go," RC said.


RC and Farlow hauled the bag across the backyard and through a gate into another backyard, which belonged to a house with blue aluminum siding.

"Honey was supposed to pick us up in the alley," Farlow said.

RC said, "What alley?"

The only way out was through the blue house. The back door led into the kitchen, then, as they passed a dark hall, a skinny-legged white man with a three-day beard and an appendicitis scar stood in a bedroom doorway, wearing a pair of corn-dog-colored boxer shorts. The man had obviously just awakened from a deep sleep.

He scratched his scar and said, "I heard a yell."

RC said, "You were having a bad dream. Go back to sleep."

The man blinked and nodded and shut the door.


Later, with both the body and head safe in Farlow's SUV, Honey drove through the McDonald's drive-up. As they pulled in, they passed a tow truck pulling the Ford Explorer out. Honey ordered cheeseburgers, fries, malts, and Chicken McNuggets all around, with extra of everything for Farlow, then they sat in the McDonald's lot, eating and watching children romp in the plastic-bubble playground.

Honey turned to RC and Farlow in the rear seat. "What now?"

Jimmy said, "We can still go to my mama's."

Honey said, "We can't go to your mama's, Jimmy. We can't go anywhere anyone might look for us, which, so far as I can tell, is everywhere."

Farlow took in half a cheeseburger with a single bite. Chewing, he said, "I know a place they won't look."

Farlow parked in the concessionaire parking zone, threw the beanbag chair across his shoulder, and led them around to the south end of FedEx Field, to a tunnel wide enough to allow a limousine through if it backed out. The tunnel had an alcove in the middle before leading onto the field level.

"This is where they bring the true VIPs," Farlow said. "That elevator goes up to the best of the luxury suites."

"You're hiding us in a luxury suite?" Jimmy said. "I've heard they come with fully stocked bars and a cocktail waitress who puts out."

Farlow said, "You wish. We're headed the other way." He turned and backed through a door that led to a concrete-block landing and narrow steps descending into near-darkness. He started down, followed by Jimmy with the attaché case, RC with the workout bag, and Honey with her clutch.

"I don't see how we can hide in the stadium," RC said. "There's a game tomorrow."

Farlow said, "Haven't you ever seen *Phantom of the Opera*?"

Honey said, "Movie or live show?"

Farlow said, "They both have the same plot."

Honey said, "I saw the movie on all-night TV, but someone told me the live show is a musical. I don't do musicals. Not since *Seven*

*Brides for Seven Brothers* came to Odessa and my parents made me go on a night I was supposed to have a date with Buzz Fontaine."

"Buzz Fontaine was a pig," Farlow said.

RC wasn't thrilled about hiding in the bowels of a football stadium. He was ready to write the story, and for that, he needed a computer, or at least a typewriter, and a phone, and probably an Internet connection. He'd have to check some facts. This stairwell did not look as if it led to an Internet connection.

They dropped two flights before Honey said, "So what?" which RC took as a comment on Buzz Fontaine, but it could have applied to anything. It might have been a "So what?" dropped into space without any relationship to other language.

At the base of the third flight, Farlow turned into a narrow hallway lit by battery-pack security lights. He made two right turns, went through a fire door, and down another flight of steps to a much wider hallway that was full of junk.

"It's an underground flea market," RC said.

Farlow said, "Storage."

They passed abandoned popcorn machines, temporary bleachers, rolled-up hoses, rakes and shovels, and a Porta Potti. Behind the junk piles, next to the wall, shoulder-high plywood bins held more perishable goods such as beer cups, straws, and toilet paper.

"That pitching machine came over from RFK when they shut it down," Farlow said. "The Washington Senators used it."

Jimmy said, "Who?"

Farlow stopped before a five-man blocking sled shoved sideways against a storage bin and said, "This is the place."

Honey said, "I don't get it."

Farlow crouched in a three-point stance before the middle padded upright and dug in. He slammed a shoulder into the pad and, face red as a cherry Twizzler, slowly slid the sled across the concrete floor. After a moment, RC took the outside pad, to show Honey the contrast between himself and Jimmy.

Five feet was enough. Farlow stopped, straightened, and opened his billfold to extract a key.

"Where's the door?" Jimmy asked.

There was no knob or handle, just a key hole in the siding. Even without the sled blocking the view, it would have been a trick to find. Farlow stuck in the key, turned it, then popped the board a good one with the heel of his hand. A door opened.

Honey said, "That's cool."

"There are only two keys," Farlow said. "I put the lock in myself." He ducked low and crawled into the storage bin while the others bent to look on. Farlow crawled over to another door in the cinder block and opened it into a room lit up a semi-ghostly blue.

He called back. "It's so dark here I leave this security pack on so I can find the light switch." He crawled into the inner room and stood to flip on a light. "Come on through."

As RC pulled himself through the inner door, he felt Honey's hand on the small of his back, steadying herself. RC read way more significance into the touch than Honey intended.

Farlow said, "It has electricity but no water. There's a slop bucket around the corner there if you need to pee." The room was L-shaped, and tastefully arranged with a corner love seat, a dorm-sized refrigerator, an espresso machine, Japanese erotica on the walls, two cases of Evian water, and a weight bench but no weights. Around the corner, in the bottom of the L, besides the slop bucket—slop jar if you were raised in Wyoming—with its tight-fitting lid, RC also found a double bed covered by silk sheets and a double-wedding-ring-pattern quilt. Purple candles sat on the bedside tables.

Jimmy was amazed. "Farlow, you old pervert. You've made yourself a love nest."

"This is wonderful." Honey's mouth turned up a bit on the right side, in a kind of half-smile. "Why didn't you show me your secret room before?"

"It's somewhat personal," Farlow said.

"Who has the second key?"

Farlow blushed, both shy and proud. "A placekicker from Dallas."

Jimmy mock-whistled and said, "And you call me sleazy."

RC walked back to check out the seam where the inner door met the cinder-block wall. The fit into the frame was tight, to the point of making air supply a question, soon answered when he discovered a pair of vents in the ceiling.

"Even if they know we're in the stadium, it'll take days to find us," RC said.

Farlow said, "Once I move the car, they won't know you're in the stadium."

"You guys mind staying on this end a minute?" RC said. "I need to use the slop jar."

Honey put both hands on her hips, thumbs forward. "How old are you, anyway?"

*Air Force Two* banked gently over the vast Pentagon parking lot and eased in against the breeze for a one-bounce landing at Andrews Air Force Base. The staircase was wheeled alongside, the door popped open from inside, and Vice-President Chip Allworth paused at the head of the steps on the off chance that photographers hovered in the foreground.

He said, "Gary, do you know what today is?"

Behind Chip, Gary Pennington consulted his Rolex. "October twenty-third. Saturday."

"It's the first day of the rest of our lives."

"I've heard that, sir," Gary said.

"It's the dawn of a new epoch."

Actually, it was sunset, but Gary didn't keep his job by pointing out the obvious. He said, "I would feel more confident if you told me why we cut short the fishing retreat."

Chip smiled. "My country needs me."

"It never did before."

Chip was disappointed at the lack of media coverage. As usual, no one cared where he went to or came from. The only person waiting—other than the regular contingent of Secret Service and air support—was Claude Hammer, who glared across the runway from the open back window of the White House's second-best limo. Chip thought Claude could profit from a Peruvian uplift, but on second thought, to hell with him. Coke makes the mean of spirit only meaner.

Chip asked, "Who was it who said, 'I am the man'?"

"I think Churchill, but let me check." Gary the literalist reached for his laptop, where he had *Bartlett's Familiar Quotations* on file, ready for instant speechwriting.

"I was speaking rhetorically," Chip said.

"What?"

"That means I asked a question I didn't want you to answer. I can create my own quote." Chip closed his eyes, more to avoid staring into the sunset than in pursuit of inspiration. Inspiration came from his nose. His lips moved, working out the word choice. He opened his eyes and said, "I started the day as an appendage, but now I am the man."

His eyes fixed on the future, Chip stepped forward and missed the stairs. His body pitched right and bounced off the guardrail, which he lurched for but missed. His left foot almost caught step number two, but instead he slipped onto his butt and back and bounced down to the tarmac, where he came to a rest.

"We found a power saw with traces of blood and skin in the teeth. Forensics is running it, but I predict they will discover the blood came from the President."

Chip Allworth gazed out the deeply smoked window at snarled traffic on the Beltway. The southwest-bound lanes were moving at a second-gear crawl, while across the median, traffic to the 'burbs had gone gridlock.

Chip said, "Charles was a good sport. I'd hate to find out he's dead."

Claude Hammer stared straight ahead at his own reflection in the privacy panel. He didn't care what traffic in the other lanes did. He'd lived in the District long enough to realize there was no point in looking outside.

"Jonathan Weathers is taking the power saw as a sign the President may be alive. It's his theory the kidnappers will messenger us a couple of fingers or an ear and demand a ransom. He can't see any other reason for cutting up the President."

Chip thought of various reasons one might cut up a president. "Did you ever watch *Texas Chainsaw Massacre*? We used to run the video nonstop at the Psi Upsilon house."

Claude had a firm policy of ignoring Chip's comments. He viewed any response as sinking to the Vice-President's level. He said, "Nash and Sebastiano stashed a leather bag on the back of the stolen golf cart, where the clubs go. At first we thought the President might be in the bag, but Jonathan made some measurements and proved Charles couldn't have fit in the space provided."

Chip turned to look at Claude. "Did you ever wonder why airplane toilet water is blue? I have a theory—"

"I've called a meeting for ten a.m. tomorrow. I'm afraid if President Franklin can't be accounted for by then, we may have to go public."

Claude had a small black mole on his cheek, where the dimple would have been if he had had a dimple. Chip fought off a nearly irresistible urge to take out a pen and poke the mole. He always had the same urge when he was near Claude, and so far he'd always fought it off. If he was president, he might be able to get away with a poke.

Chip said, "This means I'm in charge, right?"

The mole twitched. "I wouldn't go that far."

"My guide on the Gallatin River there in Montana was named Boots—that's his real name—and Boots has wonderful ideas about international relations. I'd like him to talk to the Cabinet. He says that if we offer Havana a National League baseball franchise in exchange for kicking out the commies, Castro will be gone in a heartbeat."

Claude blinked several times in a row. He turned from the view of himself in the privacy panel to stare at Chip. "Chip," Claude said, "you do understand why Charles and I chose you to be vice-president?"

Chip thought. "I read in *TV Guide* that it was my boyish charm."

"Polls show seventeen percent of female voters and eight percent of males make their decision based on the candidate's teeth, while fully ten percent will vote for any man from their home state, no matter who it is. You were chosen because you are from California and your teeth are capped."

Chip grasped for a pithy reply, but the best he could do was, "*TV Guide* would not lie."

Claude made a piglike *grunt* sound. "My personal reason was that you're so stupid I figured you as assassination insurance."

Now in spite of all anecdotal evidence, Chip Allworth wasn't stupid. Early in life he had taken on a distracted persona in order to avoid unpleasantness—not unlike girls with food names in Texas—and there were coke-induced gaps in the frontal lobe synapses, but Chip was not stupid. He knew when he was being underestimated; he just wasn't sure what to do about it.

Chip said, "At least people voted for me. You don't have the social skills to run for county coroner."

The mole in what would have been Claude's dimple but wasn't started to glow and faintly pulsate. He said, "Let's get this straight, Chip. By tomorrow you may be president, but that doesn't mean you are in charge of squat."

Lonicera shampooed her hair in the shower, then worked in conditioner and let it set while she brushed her teeth. After rinsing the conditioner out, she shaved her left leg. Lonicera shaved one leg each shower because shaving both every day was ridiculous, even for a public figure. She didn't wear leg-revealing clothes much anyway, but still, if *The New Yorker* ever spotted inappropriate hair she would never hear the end of it.

She stood with her face in the shower stream and turned the water as hot as she could bear, which was pretty damn hot because she'd been gradually increasing the temperature for six years, ever since Charles got himself elected president the first time. The pain purified her. It was the high point of her day. After thirty seconds under scorching water she turned the hot off and cranked the cold. This was her secret regimen for clear skin. In a recent *Cosmo* reader poll, Lonicera's skin had been chosen as her finest feature by thirty-nine percent of the respondents, eight percent more than her compassion and fifteen percent more than her intelligence. Fuck 'em, Lonicera thought. At least I have more to do with my life than fill out reader polls.

After the shower she rubbed Johnson's baby oil on her arms, legs, and nipples. That was another beauty tip *Cosmo* wouldn't get.

She squeezed moisturizer into her hands and walked into the bedroom, still wet and glistening. If Lonicera had time, she enjoyed air drying without a towel. She liked the feel of walking around the bedroom with water dripping from her hair and down her legs. Charles had liked her that way too, back when they shared a bedroom. Now the only Charles in her room was a framed eight-by-ten on the bedside table. In the photograph, he was wearing a cardigan sweater and Dockers and throwing a Frisbee for Pluto, the Australian shepherd Claude Hammer had bullied them into pretending to own because a president without a dog might lose a few votes in some key state like Minnesota. The name Pluto had been chosen by a focus group. Lonicera wanted Max, but Claude vetoed the name as being anti-Semitic, although Lonicera found out later he'd swung a product placement deal with Disney. She kind of liked Pluto; he was all feet and ears and had terrible eye-to-paw coordination, and she would have enjoyed playing with him more, but the trainer said she couldn't unless photographers were close by. The dog was for photo ops only.

Charles had given her the framed eight-by-ten on their twentieth anniversary. In the picture, he was smiling and relaxed. He seemed at ease with himself—happy. It was a look he'd spent decades developing.

He had signed the photo: With love from your husband—President Charles Franklin.

When they met back in Madison, Charles had come on with the determination of a hurricane. She didn't even like him so much on their first date, but he eventually won her over by the sheer strength of his desire. God, he had wanted her then. Charles had a way of making her feel like she was the only person he cared for on the planet. Like she was the center of his being. It took her four years to discover he made everyone feel that way. The man had an insatiable need to be loved. He wasn't so much a sex addict as a love addict.

Lonicera stood before the full-length mirror that was her closet door and examined herself closely. What did a twenty-year-old called Honey have that she didn't have? Lonicera would bet cash her body was harder than the little girl who wore baby-doll dresses. And more flexible. She hadn't lost a single sexual position since college. She thought. It had been years since Charles wanted to try the more complex Kama Sutra stuff. He probably played pretzels with the little girls. With her it was chore sex.

She leaned toward the mirror. Perfect skin, as *Cosmo* said, shining hair, clear eyes. She still had a chin. Most senators' wives didn't, or if they did, everyone knew why. No scalpel had touched Lonicera's body, except for bunionectomies on both feet that had hurt like hell and made her swear off elective surgery.

In the mirror, she saw a woman with the posture of a dancer. A woman old enough to be good but young enough to be enthusiastic. She was everything a man could want. Why didn't Charles want her?

Lonicera turned to the photograph of Charles and the dog everyone thought he loved but he didn't, and quietly, she said, "Dickhead."

She opened the closet door and took her nightgown off the hook. It was white cotton flannel with a notched collar and a flounced hem that dropped to her ankles. It made her feel virginal and old at the same time—like Emily Dickinson. As Lonicera slid the nightgown over her head, she decided what she would do if she ever became president. The first legislation she would push through Congress would be a law making it a felony for a character to describe herself by looking in a mirror.

With the body taken out, the beanbag chair was surprisingly comfortable. For all that zipping and unzipping, it had lost only a moderate number of styrofoam pellets, and except for a smudge of sticky blood on the cover, it was good as new.

RC nested with his head on a cross-stitch pillow that read, "Placekickers stick it between the uprights," listening to the light snore of Farlow sleeping on his back on the weight bench. In the dim shadows cast by Farlow's blue lightbulb, RC could make out the headless body propped up next to the espresso machine. The legs had stiffened in the position Farlow had frozen them, so he looked more like a folded futon than anything that once was alive. There was a faint smell, like green olives on the edge of going bad.

On the lower leg of the L, back out of RC's sight but not his hearing, Jimmy and Honey were fucking. To RC's untrained ear, it sounded as if Jimmy was on top in a straight missionary deal, but RC had never listened to other people fuck much. A roommate back in college with a thing for nursing majors, and a couple of soft-porn films he'd watched on pay-per-view in motels in places like Nebraska and Delaware where the alternative entertainments were too depressing to think about. Even then, RC wasn't sure if soft-porn sex was real. They could be faking it and laying down the *Faster, harder* track later.

Kirsteen had taped them doing it once, without telling RC. She wanted to prove to RC that her orgasms were not inappropriately high-pitched. He had teased her, saying she sounded like a mouse caught in a sticky trap, and naturally, she had taken offense. On the tape, she had screamed a Danish word she later said meant "boring," but RC said it didn't count since she'd known they were bugged. RC was struck by the whininess of his own orgasm. He sounded like he'd stepped on broken glass.

By now, Kirsteen would no doubt be holed up in her sister's antebellum eyesore over in Kalorama, because that's where she ran whenever RC didn't live up to her standards. Equally no doubt, Kirsteen was not sleeping alone tonight. She believed relationships were sporting events with winners and losers, and when an event came to an end the combatants were compelled to rush out and immediately get laid or society would label them as victims. Kirsteen spent much energy ensuring no one ever saw her as a victim, which in her Danish-to-English mind translated as "loser."

RC himself didn't care if he was perceived as a victim. He wanted to be thought of as a professional journalist.

Honey kind of yelped and said, "You're pulling my pubes," then the kids shifted to a new position. RC's mind saw it as Stuck Dog. Honey made a *squeal* sound, then the bed banged into the wall and Jimmy gasped "Bitch," then the pattern started again at the *squeal*. RC wondered how long this was going to continue, and if she was thinking of him.

Doubtful. Honey didn't seem to waste time thinking about imaginary sensations. RC thought about the kiss behind Sam's Club and what it meant. Maybe when this was all over he and Honey could rent a cabin at Old Faithful in Yellowstone Park and he'd be the top dog. He wouldn't grunt "Bitch." He would be gentle and stroke her hair and show her real men don't simulate rape.

RC rolled over, covered his free ear with his arm, and tried to figure out what he felt for this girl. He was confused. Here he should be mid-grief for Kirsteen, but instead he was fantasizing about running away to Old Faithful with a woman-child who wasn't proving herself romantically focused. The very best, highest possible outcome he could envision with Honey involved a few weeks or maybe even months of living life for the first time, followed by her wandering off with the next guy who passed through her circle of awareness, leaving him to grovel in dust. Not to mention the monogamy issue. Asking Honey to be monogamous would be like sticking a free-running gazelle in a zoo. It would be an immoral request.

Back to the bottom line: Why was he sleeping in a room with the beheaded body of the President, anyway? The story was one of the four or five most important and exclusive in the history of news, and taking risks to get it was noble, brave even. However, if it wasn't the story, if he was wading through a crap storm to be near a girl, he ought to have his head examined. Lying here planning his future around Honey while listening to her being humped on by a sociopathic sleazewad was ludicrous. Yet he couldn't think of anything that mattered more.

sunday

Eldon knew perfectly well how to tie a tie, but he pretended he didn't so he could go to his grandfather's bedroom and find out if anyone had killed the courier and his girlfriend yet. Eldon had to know how the business worked if he was going to take over and bounce Papaw back to Sicily. Besides, Eldon was still young enough to get away with walking in on grown-ups while they were dressing but old enough to know he was seeing something he wasn't supposed to see. Papaw's new wife, Louise, was only twenty-five, which made her closer to Eldon's age than Rat's Ass's, but she viewed Eldon as a child, and flashing underwear around a child is a confirmation of innocence.

Memaw, Gino's first wife and Eldon's mother's mother, cooked pasta and prayed for Gino for thirty-seven years, then died of lung cancer, even though, as she repeated over and over on her deathbed, Gino was the one in the house who smoked, not her. Two weeks after his wife's funeral, Gino married Louise, who was the granddaughter of Gino's bitterest enemy in the D.C. area, the theory being that of a royal wedding between opposing nations. It didn't work. At the reception, Gino kissed Louise's grandfather on the mouth.

Louise sat in front of her makeup mirror in her half-slip and push-up bra, layering on eye shadow. Eldon was disappointed. He could see more flesh than that at Toys "Я" Us. Louise's eyebrows and lids were permanently darkened by cosmetic tattoos, but she put on eye makeup every day anyway. At twenty-five, she was afraid Rat's Ass would dump her for someone younger.

"Are you ready for mass?" she asked Eldon.

"I need help with my tie."

He looked to his grandfather, who was watching CNN. The Olivettis had TVs in every room in the house, including the bathrooms, so Gino wouldn't miss anything. He had TV speakers in the shower, but no screen.

"Gino," Louise said, "help Eldie with his tie."

Gino glanced from the TV to Eldon, standing at the end of the bed. Eldon looked helpless. Pretending he couldn't do things he could do was about the only way Eldon ever got to spend time with his dad. He had perfected the helpless look. He plumped out his lower lip and hung his head at a bit of an angle. He'd learned the stance from a documentary on wolf puppies on the Discovery Channel.

"Ace, tie Eldon's tie for him."

Eldon hadn't noticed Ace Columbus standing over by the breakfast cart. Ace seemed to have ascended into Patrick Diprisco's position since yesterday.

"I can't do it facing the wrong way," Ace said. "I'll have to stand behind you and pretend it's on me."

The TV was showing a tape of yesterday's shoot-out. There was a lot of smoke, and people in uniforms rushing forward and back. The story cut from helicopter shots to a woman with a strange mouth standing in front of a tree, telling us what had happened.

She said, "Although Farlow Stubbs was at football practice when the siege occurred, he has since disappeared."

A Redskins publicity photo of Farlow in his home uniform came on the screen.

The woman said, "President Franklin issued a statement today commending Greg Gamble and extending sympathy to both his family and colleagues at the Secret Service. In spite of his recent bout with the flu, Franklin is reported to have said, 'Let me make this perfectly clear. We will leave no stone unturned in our search for the cause of this horrid calamity.'"

Louise said, "Patrick was such a polite boy. I'll miss him."

CNN switched to President Franklin's Sunday radio address, which was a plea for passage of his education bill. The President said it was the most important piece of legislation since the Civil Rights Act. His voice cracked with emotion when talking about children growing up in America unable to write or read.

"Stop wriggling," Ace said.

Eldon said, "You're the one with the twitches."

Gino hit the off button on the TV. He said, "Bullshit."

Louise looked at him in the mirror. "Gino, there's children in the room."

Gino ignored her and spoke to Ace. "I'll tie the damn tie. You call Sleet. Wake him up."

Eldon felt a tremor in the fingers at his neck. Ace said, "Sleet gives me the creeps."

Gino said, "Sleet gives everybody the creeps. Get him over here. And find me a picture of Jimmy and the slash."

Louise corrected him. "We no longer refer to girls as 'slash,' Gino."

Gino said, "You're right. Get me a picture of the cunt."

The man called Sleet slept on his back on top of the fully made twin bed in a cardboard-colored box of a room on the sixth floor of the Downtowner Hotel. Sleet slept in plaid Bermuda shorts, plastic sandals from Hurricane Hattie's in Honolulu, and a Phnom Penh Hard Rock Cafe T-shirt with the sleeves cut off. He slept with his eyes open, which is actually possible although you have to be born with the ability. It's not learnable, even by hit men.

Sleet had been staying in the cardboard-colored room for five months, and he still had not pulled down the bedspread and used the sheets. The maids who cleaned the room twice a week marveled at this. Sleet had also been diagnosed with dream deprivation disorder, or DDD, which means he did not dream, ever. It wasn't that he forgot his dreams; he'd been tested at the University of Cincinnati Sleep Unit and they verified the fact: The man lived without dreaming.

Sleet's mother, Sylvia, firmly believed that DDD had adversely affected Sleet's personality.

Sleet caught the phone midway through the first ring.

He didn't speak.

From the other end of the line, Ace Columbus said, "Rat's Ass wants to see you. He's sending a car."

Sleet hung up.

He swung his legs off the bed, braced himself with both hands, and stood. Sleet walked with the posture of a Chinese gymnast to the sink in his kitchenette. He soaked a hotel washcloth in cold water, then held the cloth over his eyes.

He positioned the washcloth back on the rack at exactly the same spot it had been in when he picked it up, and turned, without glancing in the mirror, to walk to the room's only window, where he had arranged a stiff-backed chair, a Harris S-series bipod, and a Bravo-51 7.62-caliber sniper rifle broken down in a velvet-lined case.

Sleet did not blame DDD for his personality. He blamed a seventh-grade gym teacher and his father, who had been a hod carrier in Paterson, New Jersey. In the seventh grade, back when Sleet was named Ivan Greene, he had been afraid to take showers in front of other boys, so he didn't shower after gym class, and when Mr. Steckyl the gym teacher found out, he called the class down to the locker room and made them watch Ivan shower. The mortified Ivan faced the wall, but Mr. Steckyl walked into the shower and pinned his arms behind his back and twisted him around to face the class. Mr. Steckyl was pressed against Ivan's back, holding his arms, and boys were laughing and Mr. Steckyl had breath to kill a cockroach and the upshot was, Ivan peed himself.

It's not a unique American story. Not reason enough for a life spent killing people. Thousands, if not hundreds of thousands, of boys have been permanently scarred by gym teachers.

But Ivan went home and told his father the hod carrier what had happened and his father whipped him with the pull cord off a snowblower and said no son of his was going to grow up to be a pussy. That was the word he used. Pussy.

Ivan ran away. In the Paterson, New Jersey, bus station a one-legged Vietnam vet morphine addict told him, "Some people love rain and some people love snow, but never in my days have I met a person who likes sleet." So Ivan Greene changed his name to Sleet.

On this morning, many years and miles later, Sleet stood looking down from his open window at the early joggers in their high-tech shoes; the tai chi practitioners exercising in slow motion; professional dog walkers hauling eleven dogs of various breeds on leashes; a black schizophrenic named Cranford, who had been a noted forthcoming poet until Jonathan Yardley of *The Washington Post* publicly trashed him, crawling into the dry culvert where he slept; and a work detail of District prisoners in orange jumpsuits who were supposed to be picking up trash but instead were field-stripping cigarette butts.

Sleet eased into his chair, and eyes on the park, he assembled the Bravo-51—McHale stock, wide bolt, threaded twenty-inch barrel, Leupold Mark 4 M3 scope, clip. The pieces clicked together with the firm precision of Bill Buckley's mind. As Sleet screwed on the six-inch noise suppressant he had invented himself, he focused down on two strawberry-haired girls, ages four and eight, walking a beagle puppy. The younger girl, in a sky-blue pinafore, dragged the puppy by an extralong white shoelace tied to its collar. Across the lawn, their mother gossiped with two women who had that look of congressional aides living the full life of mother, wife, and career woman while maintaining perfect health and style.

Sleet leaned into the Eagle cheek piece and pressed his right eye to the scope. He brought the puppy into the crosshairs and tracked it, bouncing along beside the girls' ankles. A skateboarder passed between Sleet and the puppy, then three nuns in old-fashioned black-and-white habits. The girls and the puppy continued on to a water fountain, where the little one stood tiptoe to drink while the older one held the puppy by the shoestring leash. The puppy stood on its back legs, trying to climb the water fountain.

Sleet smiled.

His eye still pressed to the scope, Sleet swiveled the rifle on the bipod, tracking along the sidewalk, back to the three nuns power walking, talking with great arm-flapping motions. Two wore glasses. The middle one didn't. Sleet nailed the one who didn't right in the sternum.

She went down like she'd been cracked by God's own lightning bolt. Reaction from the nuns with glasses was about what you'd expect.

Methodically, Sleet inspected the Bravo-51 for wear as he broke it down and fit the pieces into the case. His mind was clear. He was ready for Rat's Ass.

Honey found a peach silk bathrobe that she assumed must belong to the Dallas placekicker as opposed to Farlow since it was only five sizes too big for her instead of ten. She scooted the weight bench across the floor and sat watching RC sleep in the beanbag chair in his trim-line blue boxer shorts with white stripes up the sides. A touch of drool hung from the corner of his mouth, next to the cross-stitch pillow. After fifteen minutes of her silently watching him, he developed an erection in his sleep, what is usually called a morning boner.

RC blinked slowly awake and looked at Honey and smiled, then he realized his penis was poking out, which embarrassed him because he came from the last generation that embarrassed at the unintentional genital flash. Honey wasn't looking down that way, anyway. Even though RC was embarrassed, he still would have preferred it if she took a peek. It felt odd that this girl would rather look at his eyes than his dick.

She said, "You didn't answer my question."

RC blinked a couple more times and admired the freckles on either side of her nose. He would have enjoyed connecting them dot-to-dot with a felt-tip pen. In his fantasy, he would discover the meaning of life spread across her cheekbones.

"How old are you, really?" Honey asked.

RC tried to remember what he had told her yesterday. "Forty-two. How old are you, really?"

"Twenty." She bit the edge of her lower lip and studied him closely.

To avoid the intensity of inspection, RC glanced around the room. They appeared to be alone.

"Where's hotshot?"

"Jimmy went to buy cigarettes. And Farlow wanted to see what was left of his house. They slid that blocking thing back in front of the door, so we're locked in, and if they get arrested or killed you and I are stuck here until the next home game, against Dallas. That's sometime next month."

RC said, "I guess they had to do it that way, to make certain we aren't found."

"I guess." A conclusion formed in Honey's eyes. They shifted, as if she had stepped across a line. She said, "I decided I like you better than I like Jimmy."

RC woke up.

"He's immature," Honey said.

"I thought girls your age liked immature boys," RC said. "Why else would you sleep with a person because they can drink a beer without swallowing?"

"That was last year, but I've grown since then and he hasn't." Honey looked down at her hands in her lap. It was her first sign of demureness, and RC was charmed no end. "It's weird," she went on, "I know Jimmy and I have a personal commitment, but you have depth and he doesn't. Being around you excites me so much I can't even think about being with anyone else."

RC sat up, casually arranging his shorts. "Didn't sound that way last night."

She raised her eyes to his. "You heard us?"

RC shrugged and spoke in a higher tone. "'Ouch. You're pulling my pubes.'"

"Jimmy was jealous, after he saw how attracted we were to each other in the sauna. When I told him you kissed me behind Sam's Club he was all hot to shoot you, until I let him ball me. Jimmy is Italian, he thinks you can make a girl love you by giving her a good fuck."

RC glanced over at the headless President folded against the wall. RC was from Wyoming and had been taught the same thing.

"Do you think you could take a woman twenty years younger than you seriously?" Honey asked.

"Twenty-two."

"Not to mention I sucked off the President."

"You'd have to promise, no more sex with politicians."

"I promise." Honey did the cross-my-heart-and-hope-to-die gesture. "I only took Charles home because he was so needy. He was the neediest man I ever met, even more than you."

Honey's face went contemplative, another mood for RC to explore. "And to be truthful, which I try to be, when I can, I thought it would make a cool story to tell my grandkids."

RC said, "You have to have kids before you can have grandkids."

Her eyes snapped back from contemplation, alive and in the moment. "I want bunches of kids. I have for months now, only I had trouble seeing Jimmy as a father who nurtures."

They both imagined what Jimmy would be like as a father. Although their mental pictures were different, neither was flattering to Jimmy.

"I'd rather have my babies with you," Honey said.

"That's nice."

"You're not latently gay, are you? Farlow's the only other guy I've felt romantic love for, before you, and he turned out homosexual."

"I'm not gay," RC said.

She smiled. "It's settled, then. We'll be together and have babies."

Honey leaned down and kissed RC, whose head was spinning like dehydration on top of an inner-ear infection. Babies? His wildest dream had been a weekend in a cabin at Old Faithful. Honey slipped her tongue into the equation, and her hand was creeping down his bare chest toward the area where RC's morning boner had returned with a fury, when, from outside, they heard the scraping of a five-man blocking sled.

Honey gave RC's penis a friendly squeeze. "Let's keep this our little secret for now."

RC nodded, numb.

By the time Jimmy crawled through the door, Honey was in the back of the L, brushing her teeth with the placekicker's toothbrush.

The reason Honey had time enough to squeeze Rembrandt whitener onto the placekicker's toothbrush was that before Jimmy crawled in the door, he pushed through a large cardboard cutout of Bullwinkle the Moose wearing a notch-tailed tuxedo with the right sleeve torn off and his bare right arm stuck in a magician's top hat. Under Bullwinkle's feet—which had toes instead of your normal hoof—a sign read: "Frostbite Falls Lager."

To RC's whacked-out sense of the last two days, a cardboard moose coming into the room seemed perfectly predictable.

Jimmy's voice preceded him. "You should see the neat junk they've got out here. It's like a free yard sale."

Jimmy himself slunk in and stood with his hand proudly perched on Bullwinkle's swiveled shoulder. There was a six-volt battery on the back of the sign, but the connections hung loose. He said, "Check this out."

Honey came around the L with the toothbrush in her mouth. She'd taken off the bathrobe and was wearing a white T-shirt and blue panties. Since she wasn't wearing a bra, her nipples were visibly forward. Her breasts were fairly small, but RC like them that way. He'd always been more interested in nipples than breasts.

"What's it do?" Honey asked.

Jimmy talked as he fiddled with the red and blue wires. "Do? It's art. It'll look great in the apartment."

"Not in my apartment, it won't. There's no room."

"We can throw out the stupid flamingo."

"I'm not giving up my flamingo for a tacky moose."

A green trunk that barely fit through the door came shooting into the room, followed by Farlow.

Farlow said, "Neither of you kids is ever going to see that apartment again."

RC said, "May as well face it. The flamingo is history."

Jimmy stopped fiddling. Honey looked profoundly depressed, which is kind of an awkward look for a small blonde wearing a T-shirt and panties. She said, "My stuff is there."

In the silence, Farlow opened the trunk and ran his hands around the nylon liner. He lifted the President's body and stuffed it in the trunk. There was plenty of room. They could have fit two bodies, if they were short or one didn't have a head.

RC kept his attention on Honey, without actually looking at her, as he stood on one foot and slid his pants on. The fact that nothing would be the way it used to be seemed to be working down through the layers of denial, and RC was concerned about what would happen when Honey faced raw truth. She might not want to have babies with him anymore. And where the hell did that leave the story of the century?

Farlow said, "This should give us eight or ten hours on the odor problem, but I don't see that we have that long." He took a *Daily News* out of his back pocket and dropped it on the weight bench. "There's people looking for me and I have a game at one."

The story of the shoot-out at Farlow's house was on the front page, below the fold. Alberta had led with Greg Gamble, which is what RC would have done. The murder of a Secret Serviceman was more important than a shot-up house or three dead Mafia grunts. The second paragraph was a quote from Rex, the plastic surgeon Jimmy drilled in the foot. His descriptions of Jimmy, RC, and Honey were all screwy—among other things, he said Jimmy was Hispanic—and the story said the police had no clue as to the names of the three fugitives, which meant that either the police were lying to the press or the Secret Service was lying to the police.

"Did you see your house?" RC asked.

"I couldn't get close on account of the yellow tape and police cars, but I can tell every window is broken, and the tear gas smelled from a block away. I'll never get the stench out of the carpets."

"You guys don't have any money we could borrow?" Jimmy asked.

Honey said, "Jimmy."

He looked at her. "If your boyfriends would give us some cash, we could steal a car and hit the road."

Honey gave a pointed look at the attaché case, which RC caught but Jimmy didn't.

Farlow reached his exasperation limit. "Get a clue, for God's sake. Thousands of people are looking for you, Jimmy. Did you see that jumpy clerk at the Zippy Mart? I'll lay you five-to-one odds he called the Feds before we were out of the parking lot."

RC shut his eyes and ran his hands over the lids. He thought, *The story matters more than I do. Be a professional.* When he opened his eyes, Honey was looking at him.

She said, "What?"

RC said, "Running is dumb. Your only chance is a pardon. No charges and a trip out of here in exchange for the body."

Farlow said, "This yahoo *killed* the President."

"Not really," RC said. "Jimmy's innocent."

Jimmy had gone back to working on Bullwinkle. He said, "Of course I am. What are you talking about?"

"It was an accident. Could have happened to anyone."

"Not me," Farlow said.

"The longer they pretend Franklin is alive and dandy, the more they'll eventually need that body. If we think about this from the White House point of view, they're in more trouble than we are."

Honey said, "That's a comfort."

"Yeah, well, I have to play football this afternoon," Farlow said.

RC snapped his top fly snap. "Then we better make a deal this morning."

Jimmy said, "Got it," and flipped a switch. A warbly tape voice said, *"Watch me pull a rabbit out of my hat,"* then the bare arm in the hat swung upward, but instead of a rabbit it held a squirrel wearing diapers and an aviator helmet.

The squirrel said, *"Oops. Wrong hat."* Then the arm and squirrel dropped back into the hat.

RC said, "I like it."

Stonewall Jackson drove to a curb market he frequented in Berwyn Heights called The Git Shit and bought a tin of Altoids and a minipack of tampons. From there, he drove to a nameless suburban park with a belt swing set and a tetherball pole but no tetherball and parked next to a trashcan. He put one Altoid in his mouth and dumped the rest into the trashcan, keeping the tin on his lap.

The sun shone more brightly out here than it did in the District. The grass was bright green. In D.C., the grass was more of a dark pine-needle color than grassy. Except for cherry blossom season, the town had a murky feel—colorwise. Therefore, since thought follows color, it was natural that once a person crossed the federal line into D.C., that person's thoughts turned murky, and Stonewall could not afford murky thoughts. He had come to a decision point. By Stonewall's reckoning, most people never make a real decision, and the few who do make only two or three in a lifetime.

He could either flee from the beast or leap headlong into its belly—South Dakota or hell—and he had no idea yet which it was to be. The only thing he knew for certain was that his days of waiting in a cold car for someone to finish getting laid were over.

Stonewall used the little pocketknife on his keychain to cut open a tampon. He cut a square of filler to fit the empty Altoids tin. What he was doing went against his many years of training. The Secret Service was founded on the agent's willingness to take a bullet for others. Without this willingness, a Secret Serviceman is no longer a Secret Serviceman, which is how Stonewall felt. He'd lost the basic drive. Now what he was doing was covering his ass. He'd taken on the philosophy of a bureaucrat.

He drove over to the Brentwood Postal Facility, the only post office anywhere near Washington that is open on Sunday. Stonewall knew this trivial piece of information because he'd been on duty the day President Franklin cut the ribbon reopening Brentwood after it had been closed for years by the anthrax attack. Secret Servicemen are not supposed to listen to the speeches. They are supposed to stay alert for unforeseen scenarios, but ribbon-cutting is so boring Stonewall could not avoid listening and learning.

At the Brentwood Facility he stood in line with others who for some reason needed stamps on Sunday. When he bought the padded mailer, the clerk said, "Have a nice morning," and Stonewall said, "I'll try."

He walked to a table and took out the Altoids tin, and the teeth he had found in Farlow's garage. He decided to mail the molars and hold on to the incisor. That should keep his ass covered.

As Stonewall flipped though the Zip Code Finder for Spearfish's zip code, his cell phone rang. It was Parker Swindell.

"You said to call if I came across any unusual police reports," Parker said.

Stonewall held the phone to his left ear and wrote Spearfish, South Dakota's zip code on the envelope with his right hand. "And you did?"

"Yesterday afternoon a woman in Landover reported a dead body in her living room, but when the investigating officers arrived, the body had disappeared. The officers think it was a passed-out addict who woke up and left."

"What do you think?" Stonewall finished addressing the envelope. It was going to a rural route box.

Parker said, "I'm here at the house now. The woman is understandably upset, but she's not hysterical. She doesn't seem the type to mistake a dead body for a live one."

"Ask her if the body was in a beanbag chair," Stonewall said.

While Stonewall waited, he arranged the molars in the tin. They looked like a pair of earrings. Parker came back and said, "Amazing. How did you know?"

"Just a guess. The disappearing body in a beanbag chair is an urban myth. You hear it every now and then."

Parker was quiet a moment. He obviously hadn't heard the one about the body in a beanbag. "You think it might be related to those people who threatened Franklin?" he said.

Stonewall said, "No."

"I heard Sebastiano and Nash stuffed something in the back of the golf cart. Maybe it was a beanbag."

"I'm certain there's no connection. Disappearing bodies are a dime a dozen in Landover."

Stonewall hung up the phone and went to mail his package. He got the same clerk but the clerk didn't recognize him. The clerk had been working in the post office so long he'd turned into a blind drone.

Stonewall said, "Will this be postmarked today?" and the clerk said, "You're mailing it today, aren't you?"

Stonewall said, "Right," and the clerk said, "Have a nice morning."

"Tell the fuckers not to bring guns." Jimmy shouted so as to be heard in the back of the L, above the piss drizzling into the half-full—or half-empty, depending on your view—slop bucket. "I see one gun and the deal is off."

Honey said, "It's not fair for you to have the only gun, Jimmy."

"Fair?"

RC shook and tucked. He fit the lid tightly on the bucket and walked to the front. Jimmy was still tinkering with Bullwinkle, Honey was reading the *Daily News* from cover to cover, including the classified section and the real estate ads, and Farlow sat on the concrete floor with his legs crossed, his eyes closed, and his forefingers and thumbs formed into O's. Every now and then he breathed, "Om," to which Jimmy muttered, "Hairy Krispy," or something equally offensive. Farlow ignored the distraction. It was game day, and he was preparing for battle.

"Wish me luck," RC said.

Jimmy said, "Yeah, right."

"When they ask where you want to go, what do I tell them?"

Honey said, "New Zealand. The south island. I want to rent a house on a sheep ranch and bake bread and chase fireflies. I've heard they circle the opposite way as Texas fireflies."

Jimmy sulked. "I want Sicily."

Honey used her little finger to mark her place in "Dear Abby." It was an interesting letter from a girl whose mother-in-law had threatened to kill her for fixing cornbread with jalapeños. "We talked this over yesterday till I was blue in the face. We're escaping to New Zealand."

Jimmy said, "We always go where you want, never where I want." He appealed to RC as the only other true male in the room. "I like McDonald's, but *no,* Miss Holy Pants has to have Wendy's."

RC thought but didn't say, *Holy Pants?*

Farlow spoke without opening his eyes. "She was the other way around in high school. We lived an entire summer on Coke and Chicken McNuggets."

To himself, RC thanked God the few people in a small room without windows or running water wasn't long-term. Another day and he'd be the one capable of murder.

So he did what western boys are taught to do when their impulse is strangulation. He faked good humor. "All right, then! Two tickets to New Zealand!"

Honey said, "Three. You're going with us."

Jimmy said, "Fat chance."

"RC saved us yesterday, and now he's in as much trouble as we are. You'd be shot full of holes if not for RC."

Gratitude was not Jimmy's strength. He glared hard at RC. "Do you want to come?"

"I hadn't thought about it," RC lied. He hadn't thought about much of anything else. He'd decided to write the story but put off publishing it until after the geeks at the White House committed themselves to a historical cover-up. Think of the impact: sex, lies, corruption, homosexuality. He could work the Mafia angle. It had everything, if he waited. Alberta would give him his job back.

Kirsteen would shyly murmur at cocktail parties, "I used to *kneppe* RC Nash, before he became famous."

There was the danger that if he waited too long no one except Internet conspiracy nuts would believe him. Journalism school professors would dismiss him as paranoid or, worse, ignore him. But RC had that contingency covered. He had proof. Honey had shown him her Baggie full of curly hair.

Honey said, "Of course RC wants to come. How about you, Farlow? We'll need you to carry the heavy stuff."

Farlow opened his eyes. "I'll have to talk to my placekicker."

"He can come too," Honey said.

"Jesus," Jimmy said. "Let's buy a bus."

Farlow unwound his legs. They wouldn't unwind themselves without being shoved and pulled by both hands. His knees had been operated on so often they looked crosshatched, like waffles.

He said, "I think I'll stay."

Honey forgot the girl-with-the-cornbread crisis. This was serious. "But I need you close by. What if Jimmy does me dirty again?" She hesitated. "Or someone else breaks my heart?"

As Jimmy went into *Dirty again?* and *Someone else?* and the general blah-blah of ruffled feathers, Farlow and Honey stared into each other's eyes. Unspoken Tender Shit flew back and forth between them. RC felt like an intruder.

Finally Farlow said, "It's time."

Honey said, "I'm not ready." She looked about to cry, and this one wasn't manipulation. This one was real. "I thought you were dependable. I'm supposed to be able to count on you."

Farlow's voice was sad. "I can't spend my whole life as your safety net."

"I don't see why not."

"I need to explore a healthy relationship."

Jimmy snorted.

Farlow ignored him. "I need to stay here and play football. That's what I do." Farlow blinked, remembering the situation. He broke the eye lock with Honey and turned to RC. "Unless you think they'll throw me in jail or shoot me or something."

Honey sniffed back tears. "RC can keep your name out of it." She also looked at RC. "Can't you?"

They were all looking at him now. Even Jimmy had worked his way from the "someone else" back to RC. RC didn't know what to say. He was a journalist. Journalists report; they don't advise.

He said, "All those dead people in your house make it awkward."

Honey stood up. Her voice quavered. "But you can do it. You're competent. I never met a person so competent as you."

Jimmy said, "I'm competent."

Now it was everyone's turn to stare at Jimmy. His ears reddened, and he seemed almost embarrassed—for Jimmy, anyway.

He said, "I am."

Sleet was waiting in the library when the Olivetti clan got back from mass. It was a library only in the loosest sense. The second Mrs. Olivetti collected Silhouette romances and shelved them by the color of the spine. She bought two of every title Silhouette published, read one before donating it to Washington Literacy, and saved the pristine copy for posterity. She said they were the one truly American literature.

Gino had turned on *Meet the Press,* and Eldon was wishing his grandfather hadn't shot the computer monitor, when Ace came out of the library and said, "Sleet is here."

Louise said, "Does he want an espresso?"

Gino said, "No, Sleet doesn't want an espresso." Eldon trailed along, through the double doors into the library, where Ace stopped him.

"What do you want?"

Eldon said, "A book. I have a book report due at school." Patrick Diprisco would have chased him out, but Ace was new to the job and didn't realize the harm in witnesses.

Sleet stood along the red-spine wall with his hands at his sides. He was the thinnest and scariest-looking person Eldon had ever seen. He looked like a killer. Sleet dressed all in black, with slicked-back hair and skin the color of pissed-on snow. As Eldon understood organized crime, from movies, television, and slips by protégés, a hit man should not look like a hit man. He should blend in, be instantly forgettable. Sleet looked like John Cusack in a coma.

And he was watching Eldon. Eldon knew because of the skin prickle. Sleet's head didn't move, but his eyes followed Eldon to the bookcase, where Eldon proceeded to hyperventilate. Think fish under the gaze of an osprey.

While Sleet was scaring the wadding out of Eldon, Ace brought Gino up to snuff. "You remember Nick Floreano's little brother. I don't know his name, but he's on probation for boosting a dialysis machine from Sibley Memorial."

"Tell me this has something to do with me," Gino said.

"He called while you were gone—Nick Floreano's brother. He works at a Zippy Mart out by Lanham. He said Jimmy was in about dawn, buying cigarettes."

Gino hated breaking in a new lieutenant. "Why didn't you say this right off instead of a bunch of foolishness about dialysis machines?"

Ace shrugged. "Jimmy was with the football player whose house it was where Patrick . . ." He drifted off, unsure whether to say "bought it" or "got whacked." "Nick's brother spotted him from a picture in the paper."

Eldon made it to the blue wall without passing out. As he pretended to search for a book, he could feel Sleet's eyes on the back of his neck like a hot cigarette lighter, the electric kind in cars. Eldon took *A Passionate Illusion* by Tory Cates off the shelf. On the cover a woman with cleavage gave comfort to a rugged-looking man who might have been a protégé at a company retreat. There was a mountain in the background.

"When they left, Nick's brother followed them," Ace said.

Gino said, "Why?"

"We offered a thousand for whoever snitches Jimmy."

"I didn't offer a thousand."

"You said to do whatever it takes." Ace flashed on a good line, one he would use regularly for the next few days. "Patrick okayed it."

Eldon smelled Freon and realized Sleet was standing behind him, too close, reading the book over his shoulder.

"That is an interesting story," Sleet said. The voice was Mister Rogers meets Elmer Fudd.

The woman on the cover had Mormon hair and painted fingernails. "You've read it?" Eldon asked.

"Of course."

Behind them, Ace was saying, "They drove across the Beltway to the new football field and went in."

Gino said, "That greasy snake is holed up in the stadium. If you can't find Jimmy, find the football player and follow him to the girl and the girl to Jimmy, then get my money and kill everybody."

Sleet's eyes stayed on Eldon a moment before he turned to Gino and said, "I'll take fifty percent for returning your investment."

Gino said, "That's three hundred thousand."

Sleet stared at Gino with black-hole eyes, from which no light escaped. He didn't argue. He didn't threaten. He waited.

Gino tugged on his spatulate earlobe. Ace kept his eyes on the floor. Outside, a jet from Andrews broke the sound barrier, and everyone but Sleet simulated a heart attack.

Gino said, "Your price includes whacking Jimmy and the girl?"

"Of course. I'll kill them for the entertainment value."

Eldon quietly slipped the book back into its slot, between other blue-spined books with *Passion* in the title. He wasn't sure anymore that he wanted to take over if running crime machines meant having people like Sleet in your house. Maybe he would hire Sleet to cap Papaw, then be done with the whole nasty business.

Gino said, "You got the picture?"

Ace handed the photo to Gino, who handed it to Sleet.

Ace said, "Patrick had it filed under 'Shit Heels.'"

Gino said, "He thought if he was the only one knows where things are, I couldn't replace him. Let that be a lesson."

Sleet stared at the photo.

Ace said, "It was taken at Hooters. The Labor Day Blow-Out."

Sleet passed the photo to Eldon. His fingers were translucent against the white border. Eldon thought if Sleet touched him, he would die.

"What do you think, boy?" Sleet said. "Should I kill these two?"

Jimmy sat in profile, his mouth in a Sean Penn sneer, a brown cigarette in one hand, a Coors Light in the other. Honey sat on his lap, looking directly into the camera, as if she knew a juicy secret about the photographer. She was wearing a white top thing and shorts. She was barefoot.

"He deserves to get shot," Eldon said.

"What about the girl?" Sleet's eyes were Confederate gray with huge pupils. When they focused on Eldon, it was like facing eternity alone from a rain-filled grave. It took all the courage of his twelve years for Eldon to speak.

"No, sir."

"I shouldn't kill the girl?"

"No, sir."

"Why not?"

Eldon stared into Honey's eyes, which were the exact opposite of Sleet's. Honey's eyes promised life.

"She has a nice smile."

Ace sniggered, but Sleet gave him a look that would have shut up Jesus. He looked back down at Eldon and said, "Those are the ones you have to kill first."

Lonicera stood in the second-floor East Wing hallway, looking out one of the big windows with multiple panes at the White House lawn, where in a couple months she would be lighting a Christmas tree chopped down in Maine or Vermont or someplace. If she was still First Lady in two months. That was beginning to look doubtful.

Washington had the feel of a change of seasons about it. The trees along Pennsylvania were at the color peak—cherry and maple reds, birch yellows. Civil servants had gone to the beige trench coats they wore like a uniform. The gnomelike woman who stood out on the sidewalk all summer holding a sign condemning the use of genetically altered corn in taco shells was gone. Lonicera kind of missed her, standing out there in her faded blue dress, setting down the sign only long enough to eat a pimiento-cheese sandwich packed in waxed paper. The woman had been so certain that her opinion was right. Lonicera had never been certain enough about anything to carry a sign in public. Few people are.

She heard footsteps and turned to see Chip Allworth coming down the hallway, dressed for the ten-o'clock meeting. Chip smiled his world-famous smile and hugged her. Lonicera felt her eyes go slick from gratitude. No one had hugged her in a long time, not since the wife of the president of Latvia, and she was a fat stranger who smelled like potato pancakes, so the hug hardly counted.

Chip said, "I'm sorry."

Lonicera pressed her face to his shoulder. "Thanks for coming so quickly."

"I would have been here sooner, but the red phone didn't work."

She held on tightly. "You and I are the only ones who really like Charles."

Chip said, "Millions of people love him."

"I suppose so." Lonicera broke the hug. "But we're the ones who like him."

They moved down the hallway and sat on a concrete bench that should have been outside and was until Eleanor Roosevelt had it moved.

"Tell me what I can do to help," Chip said.

Lonicera held both Chip's hands in hers and studied his face. The Vice-President was so young and earnest. The earnestness tended to make people underestimate him. Chip believed in his ideals and listened to others, two traits often misinterpreted as stupidity in Washington. At the moment, he also had a white flake lodged in the upper edge of his right nostril.

"You remember when we took over?" Lonicera asked.

Chip nodded. "Those clowns on the way out turned all the paintings in my office to face the wall."

"The country was a pitiful mess."

Chip said, "Pitiful."

"And now things are better. People have jobs. Crime is down. The poor don't have to humiliate themselves to see a doctor. Charles gave the nation hope."

Chip's eyes misted over. He loved this kind of shit. "If President Franklin is dead, God forbid, I promise to carry on the battle."

Lonicera patted his hand. "I know you will." She thought, The press is going to gag at Chip's eagerness. The one thing they respect less than a politician who lies to them is a president who wants to please.

"Charles was—is—a great president, Chip, but men like Claude Hammer only care about power, right now. Not yesterday. It's up to you and me to protect Charles."

"From Claude?"

"From anyone who would spoil Charles's memory. Charles Franklin deserves to go down in history for what he did for the country."

Chip said, "I couldn't agree more."

"If word gets out that he died while committing adultery, the press and those self-righteous historians will make him into a laughingstock."

"You think so?" Chip sniffed and swallowed. His coke throat had left him with a dry mouth. "I would like to believe that balancing the budget and cutting gun violence in half is more important than the way a man dies."

"You're sweet," Lonicera said. "But naive as a baby. When it comes to sex scandals, nothing else matters."

"I'll remember that."

"Keep your penis out of politics, Chip. If you get into trouble, make sure it's for stealing money, like a Republican."

Chip narrowed his eyes, as if he were searing Lonicera's words into his frontal lobe. "What about drugs?"

"Not as forgivable as influence peddling, but still safer than sex."

That's how Chip had figured the deal, but it was good to hear the truth from an expert.

"Before we go into the meeting, I want you to blow your nose," Lonicera said. "You've got a visible rock the size of the Hope diamond."

Chip felt around until he found the flake, which he inspected closely, then rubbed into his gums.

Lonicera watched, fascinated. She thought, *Only in America.*

"There's one more favor I'd like."

Chip said, "Shoot."

"If Charles is dead, I don't want to spend the winter in Wisconsin. I want you to appoint me ambassador to Tahiti."

Chip nodded. "You betcha."

"Don't hang up."

"Who is this?"

"I was driving home yesterday, after we talked, and I fell into the scoop of the century, maybe even the biggest news story in the history of journalism."

"Is this RC Nash?"

"You're not going to believe this one, Alberta."

"I fired you, Nash."

"We can print it now, but I think if we hold on a few days, until the White House covers itself with lies, we can blow the lid off America. I'll give the *News* an exclusive, but I keep book and movie rights myself."

"I don't believe a word out of your mouth, but what's the story?"

"Not till you promise I can have my job back."

"You must be drunk out of your mind to call me at home with this trash."

"I'll give you a hint. Do you know where the President is today?"

"I don't care where the President is—if you call me again I'll get a restraining order."

"You're going to look back on this conversation and slit your wrists, Alberta."

Alberta Chamberlain slammed the phone down and rolled over between her black silk sheets to face Tubby Fitzhugh, senior senator from Georgia and the only Republican to announce two years before the election that he was running for president.

"Where were we?" Alberta cooed.

Tubby asked, "What was that?"

Alberta put her hand on Tubby's chest and snuggled closer. "Just some idiot I fired yesterday, trying to weasel his way back into a job."

"I heard something about the President."

Alberta nibbled on Tubby's earlobe. "RC Nash claims he has the scoop of the century."

Tubby moved his head away from Alberta's tongue. "What if he does?"

"Nash is a fluff writer. He wouldn't know a real story if it bit him on the butt. Which is what I'm going to do to you in about one minute."

Tubby pushed Alberta's hand away from his crotch. "Did he say what he had on the President?"

Alberta lay on her side, perplexed, "He asked if I knew where the President is today."

"Do you?"

"He had the flu yesterday. I suppose he's still at the White House."

Tubby sat up, letting the sheet slide to his lap. "Call him."

"I can't call the President."

"Call that reporter. I have to know what he's got."

"He's got nothing."

"Call him anyway."

Tubby swung his legs off the side of the bed and stood, leaving Alberta to marvel at the senator's hairy ass.

Alberta said, "He wasn't home. I heard street sounds behind him."

Tubby bent to retrieve his jockey shorts. "Call his cell phone."

"We canceled it yesterday. Tubby, come to bed. Nash will say anything to get his job back. He's a worthless hack."

Tubby sat on the bed to pull his pants on over both feet. He always did it that way so no one could say Tubby Fitzhugh put his pants on one leg at a time.

Alberta's voice trembled. "Tubby, what did I do wrong?"

"You had information I need and you let it go."

"But RC was lying."

"You don't know that." Tubby's face was a mask of anger as he pulled his undershirt on over his head. "Get up, we're going to find Nash, and if we can't find him, we'll find Franklin."

"But Tubby—"

"Listen, Alberta. I don't fuck you because I like baggy old women. I fuck you so you'll dig up dirt I can use to crush that shit-for-brains in the White House."

Tears sprang to Alberta's eyes. "I thought you loved me."

"Jesus," Tubby said. "You're pathetic."

A glass filled with two-percent milk and Hershey's dark chocolate syrup sailed through the air into the rock fireplace mantel, where it exploded into a chocolate mess, much of which splattered onto a framed six-by-eight of Rat's Ass's father shaking hands with Bugsy Siegel while Dwight Eisenhower beamed nervously at Bugsy's side.

Eldon gave it everything he had. "Take me to the football game!"

Gino hurried to the mantel, his handkerchief already out and ready to blot, when he remembered who he was.

"Clean that," he said to Ace.

"You got paper towels?"

"Use your shirt."

Eldon howled again. "I have to see the football game!"

"You never said anything about football before," Gino said.

"All the other kids' grandfathers take them to games. But not you. You're too busy *killing people*."

"That's not fair," Louise said. "Your papaw doesn't kill people." An odd thing to say, since Papaw had killed her grandfather. Or had him killed, Louise was never certain which it had been.

"I'll bet you can't even get tickets."

"Of course I can get tickets."

"Good ones?"

"Best in the damn stadium."

When Eldon was seven, going on eight, he had whined for a puppy and his father said no. That afternoon Eldon's mother sat him down at the dining room table, and over her Merlot and his cherry Sprite, she taught him the routine of getting around Daddy.

"You've got to break glass," she said. "Most men won't listen until glass gets broke. Aim for a brick or a rock or something hard, because if the glass bounces and doesn't break he'll never take you seriously."

"What if there's no glass around?" Eldon asked.

"There's always glass around. If you have to, find a heavy object worth a lot of money and heave it through a window."

Eldon nodded, already working out how he would present this conversation to his therapist.

"When you've got his attention, scream out what you want real loud. Let's hear you scream."

Eldon screamed.

His mother had a thoughtful look on her face, like a chef tasting soup. "You'll have to do better than that."

He screamed again.

His mother patted him on the knee. "We'll work on it. Next, what you do is accuse him of not being able to deliver even if he wants to." She made her voice husky. "You won't buy me the necklace because you can't afford it. You're poor. I knew all along you were lying to me."

Her voice went back to its own sweet self. "He'll deny that he can't give you what you want, and you say 'Prove it,' and *ta-da*, you've won."

Eldon said, "*Ta-da.*"

His mother smiled and sipped Merlot. "You've forced him to put up or shut up."

"You think I can do it too?"

"When you start off, throw your fit in front of a neutral third party, somebody Daddy doesn't want to look bad in front of."

"Like you?"

"I'm perfect."

Eldon tried his mother's method the next day and, to his amazement, it worked. He got the puppy. It didn't matter so much that a UPS truck squished the puppy dead a week later, the lesson had been learned.

"We're supposed to be bonding," Eldon said, "but all we ever do is eat and watch TV. If you really want to bond—and make Mom happy—you'll take me to the football game."

"What would it hurt?" Louise said.

Gino said, "Jesus."

Louise said, "All you had planned for the afternoon was a nap."

Gino snatched the photo from Ace, who was only smearing it anyway. Gino said, "Get three tickets to the fucking game."

Ace said, "Yes, sir."

Eldon turned to Louise. "Can I have more chocolate in the next one, Grandma?"

They met in Jonathan Weathers's conference room in the Treasury building. Chip Allworth sat at the head of the table, playing with a toy whose challenge was to get little steel balls to settle in the eyeholes and navel of a belly dancer under glass. Lonicera Franklin sat at his right, wearing a tasteful black sheath with a matching Barneys of New York sweater. She was settling into her mourning wardrobe. Claude Hammer sat at Chip's left, and twice he dropped his Waterman pen on the floor so he could bend down to retrieve it and take a look up Lonicera's dress at her purple underwear. Lonicera figured it out the second time and stood up and paced. She was more comfortable moving, anyway. Jonathan Weathers sat opposite Chip. Since he had called the meeting and it was his office, he felt free to lead the discussion.

"We have to go public soon," Weathers said.

Lonicera turned at the east end of her pacing path. *"No."*

Claude Hammer said, "Face it, Mrs. Franklin. We have no ransom note, no body, no nothing. We can't keep the lid on much longer." Claude felt that Lonicera was overdoing the loving-wife act a bit. She should be bereft as hell in front of the cameras, but this was behind the scenes, where everyone knew what a sham their marriage had been. She didn't have to dance and sing the grief deal here. Everyone in the room knew she loved him more than she loved Charles, except maybe Chip.

Chip rubbed his nose and said, "Why not?"

Claude said, "Because, you idiot, they will crucify us."

Chip glanced up at the "you idiot" crack. That was no way to treat the leader of the Free World. Still, he had both eyeball balls in and all he needed was the navel without losing an eyeball, so he let the crack pass. Instead, he said, "Who exactly will crucify us?"

Jonathan Weathers said, "The press." Jonathan knew Chip's brain was pinging through the coke ozone and Claude was trying to see up Lonicera's skirt, and he was, frankly, disgusted. Jonathan had joined the Service under Ike and Mamie Eisenhower, back when presidents had dignity. In his opinion, there hadn't been a dignified president or First Lady since, except maybe Rosalynn Carter, but she came and went so quickly he never was certain if she had dignity or a tight ass.

Claude Hammer said, "This nation would be a nice place if we shot all the reporters and chopped them up for emergency food for the Congo."

Chip said, "Can I quote you on that?"

As always, Claude ignored him. "No doubt that Nash character is on the phone to his agent this minute. They're working out back-end points on a movie deal."

"If I ever catch up with RC Nash, I'm going to personally cut off his balls," Jonathan said. He blamed RC for the loss of Greg Gamble. He'd forgotten he was probably going to eliminate Greg himself.

Lonicera stopped pacing. "What about Charles's legacy?"

Claude and Jonathan exchanged an embarrassed look.

Claude said, "Legacy?"

Chip's little steel ball lodged in the belly dancer's navel. *"Score!"* He held up his arms and made cheering-crowd noises.

The others were staring at him. Time to say something pertinent. "The press will crucify us either way. I'm for putting it off as long as possible."

Claude did what he always did at crisis meetings: he ran scenarios. "Under one scenario, we're fools. The other scenario, we're fools in prison."

Chip set the toy on the table. He was finished with it and ready to move on. "Since when is lying to the public illegal? If we get caught, we'll say we spread disinformation to protect national security. Charles spread disinformation every day."

Lonicera blurted, "Got that right," then wished she hadn't.

The intercom buzzed. Jonathan punched a button and barked. *"What?"*

"There's a man throwing a fit out here. I told him you were not to be accessed, but he says it's a national emergency. I called security."

Weathers said, "What's his name?"

The sound of a scuffle came over the intercom, and what must have been a falling chair, then RC Nash's voice. "Get away from me. Weathers, tell this crazy woman how much you're spending looking for me."

Jonathan sprinted to the lobby reception area, where he found RC flattened against a wall by two security guards and an off-duty agent. His receptionist, Ida, held a stapler to RC's throat.

RC croaked. "Call off the goons."

Jonathan said, "Let him go."

The guards and the agent released RC, but Ida was teed off. The jerk had gone around her desk and tried to enter the inner sanctum without her permission. She wasn't going to stand for it.

She said, "Let me staple his mouth shut."

Jonathan said, "He's the one we're looking for."

RC arranged his clothes and winked at Ida and said, "I like your hair that way."

Ida snarled, like a bobcat.

"Follow me," Jonathan said.

RC followed down a hallway to the conference room, where Jonathan didn't bother with introductions. "Is the President alive?"

RC said, "No."

Lonicera slumped forward with her weight on both hands on the table. Somehow, she had never really believed Charles was dead. In her heart or subconscious or wherever denial breeds, she had been certain he was off somewhere, nose deep in pubic hair, and he would call in with a bizarre story that would make her furious. He had survived so many scandals and near scandals she had come to have faith—like Charles himself—that he would always land on his feet.

Chip stood up. "How did he die?"

"Near as I can tell, he was running and he tripped over his undershorts and hit his head. Can I have some water? Your goons hurt my throat."

As RC crossed to the pitcher on the table and filled a glass, he tried to put a finger on the room vibe. Claude Hammer looked triumphant, as if only good manners kept him from breaking into "I told you so." The Vice-President's face showed sadness, then a flash of hot-damn-I'm-president, then back to sadness. Actually, he looked royally buzzed. Jonathan was a robot. Only Lonicera didn't seem to be acting the way her position dictated that she act. She'd lost her husband.

"Why was he running?" Lonicera asked.

RC drank from his glass. "Jealous boyfriend."

Lonicera nodded. That's how she had it figured. "Is the girl a prostitute?"

RC took offense. "Honey DuPont is the victim here. He used the presidency to take advantage of her."

"But Charles is the one who's dead," Lonicera said.

Chip had dry mouth and could have used water himself, but now he was president he felt someone else should offer to pour it. Charles had never poured his own water. Chip said, "I don't get where the football player fits in."

RC said, "Farlow doesn't know about the President. He thinks they are on the run from Rat's Ass Olivetti."

Claude said, "You expect us to believe that?"

RC sat in Lonicera's chair. It was the only one not being used. "You don't have much choice."

Ripping out balls did not appear to be an option, at least not at the moment, and Jonathan couldn't simply shoot RC in front of the Vice-President and First Lady, or President and former First Lady. He was at a loss as to the appropriate action.

He asked, "When did you join the assassination team?"

"Let's get this straight," RC said. "There is no assassination. You can't even pin manslaughter on these kids."

Claude made a face where his upper lip curled and exposed his eyeteeth. He said, "They killed the President, and you're in it up to your neck. Can you even dream of the trouble you are in?"

RC leaned across the table toward Claude. "Cut the crap, Claude. You folks don't threaten me and I won't threaten you."

"Threaten us?" Chip asked.

"The American people are not going to be happy to find out their president has been dead two days and you kept it a secret. Can you picture how self-righteous that pig on Fox is going to be? He'll call for a lynch mob. Jay Leno will win an Emmy."

The gang of four looked at their hands or the floor or the walls, anywhere but RC, who decided to go for the kill. "And what if it gets out that he died while porking a twenty-year-old girl. From Texas." He focused on Chip. "There won't be another Democrat elected for fifty years."

Chip gave up and poured his own water, then, for lack of anything better to do, sat back down. Lonicera glided up behind him and rested her hand on his shoulder. Or it looked as if her hand was resting; she was actually digging her fingernails into his flesh.

Jonathan said, "And you came to us with a proposal."

"Pardons for any crimes we may have committed, a guarantee against reprisals, and passports and tickets to somewhere safe. Honey likes New Zealand."

Claude said, "Out of the question."

Jonathan said, "No."

Lonicera dug in her talons and Chip kind of yelped. "We accept."

"You can't accept this," Claude said.

Chip said, "Watch me."

Claude said, "But—"

"I will not turn this nation over to the Republicans simply because Charles Franklin couldn't keep his tallywhacker dry." He leaned forward, toward RC. "Tell us what you want done."

RC was amazed at how easy it had been. He'd brought along a presidential hairball he got from Honey, in case they put up a struggle, but now he could save that surprise for the guarantee-against-reprisals negotiation.

"You'll need a double, or whatever it is you do in these situations."

Jonathan said, "We have a mask."

"No kidding? A mask might come in handy later."

Lonicera's eyes turned suspicious. "Why?"

It was Jimmy's idea to ride up the elevator and break into a skybox, but Honey gave only token resistance. After reading the *Daily News* and filing her toenails, it hadn't taken long to get bored, and while she considered herself as emotionally flexible as the next girl, boredom was a condition Honey did not tolerate.

"RC said to stay put," she said.

"Is RC your father, 'cause he's not mine."

So they sneaked out of the L-shaped cubbyhole and rode to the top of the stadium, where Honey tried the first door they came to and found it locked. "Think you can get us in?" she asked.

Jimmy looked at her like she'd insulted him. "Of course I can get us in." He knelt on one knee and shut his left eye so he could peer into the keyhole with his right. Ten seconds later the door swung open. "Let's see Mr. Competent do that."

"If you don't back off about RC, I'm going home—to Texas. You're the one in trouble, Jimmy. Not me. I'm only here out of loyalty, you know."

Jimmy had always wanted to see the inside of a luxury skybox. He was a little disappointed that it had the ambience of a lounge at the Comfort Suites. There was a carpet that smelled of carpet glue, and a refrigerator, wet bar, ice maker, and a buffet counter.

The furniture was new and high-end generic. The bathroom was luxurious only compared with a slop bucket. TVs had been placed strategically in case you needed food or a knob job and didn't want to miss a play. Whoever decorated the room liked plastic plants and oil paintings of football stars in action poses.

Honey headed for the open end, where captain's chairs set up on two levels like a jury box faced a sliding glass panel overlooking the field.

"It's pretty up here," she said.

Jimmy said, "Let's check out the liquor cabinet."

The seats Honey looked down on were color-coded according to class structure—yellow for the gentry, red for the commoners. The field itself was a pleasant green. The place looked more like a Lego stadium than reality. Little toy men crossed back and forth over the grass. Someone with a machine was freshening the white stripes, which from up here looked plenty fresh already.

From across the suite, Jimmy said, "There's a closet full of girls' clothes over here. You should take a look."

"What size are they?"

"How would I know?" Jimmy came up behind her, smoking a Cuban cigar and holding a weak-tea-colored drink.

"What's that over there?" Honey asked

"Where?"

"The end zone. Looks like a drive-in movie screen."

"That's the JumboTron."

"Is this where you got the idea for naming your tool?"

Jimmy slumped into an end seat and puffed up a cigar cloud. He couldn't honestly tell Cuban from regular. He only smoked them because they were illegal. "You should see the food over there. Oysters and sushi and mushrooms stuffed with slimy stuff. Why are we hiding in that basement closet when we could be up here?"

"For one thing, there's a game this afternoon."

"I'd be willing to clear out for home games."

"We have to be ready to do RC's plan."

Jimmy twisted his head back and blew smoke at her. "That's another thing. Who died and made RC Nash boss? What's he doing with us, anyway? I didn't invite him along."

"He's helping us."

"He's waiting to screw you, is what he's doing. And you're encouraging the old fart."

Honey sighed and waved her hand to clear the smoke. Time for lap girl. Some days she felt as if she'd spent her life on men's laps, coaxing, teasing, faking baby talk. Her father was the first, and both grandpas, then various other male relations and their golf buddies. Then her junior high geography teacher. They all wanted baby-girls who called them Daddy and did lap dances.

Honey slid into Jimmy's lap with her left arm around his shoulders. She giggled and said, "Let's get rid of the phallic symbol," then she took the Cuban cigar and snuffed it out in the built-in ashtray on the next chair over.

He said, "That means fake prick, doesn't it?"

She giggled again, as if he'd made a joke. Then she bumped her nose against his. She said, "You have to understand, pumpkin, Mr. Nash is a reporter, and to him Charles being dead down there is a big deal. He thinks he can get a bunch of money off it. That's why he's following us around."

Jimmy sulked. Men with women in their laps tend to start out sulking. It's the ritual. "I don't like it when you flash your tits in his face, and you give him that lick-me look of yours. It's embarrassing."

"Don't be a silly old bear," Honey cooed, not quite baby talk but close enough to turn her stomach. "I have to flirt with Mr. Nash. You know I don't want to, but I'm doing it for you. We need him."

"I don't need him."

"He's making a deal for us, to get away. You and me wouldn't know who to talk to about a deal." She hated saying "You and me" instead of "You and I," but it was men who set the rules. All she did was play by them.

"He can make our deal without you being a cocktease."

Honey almost gave up and decked him, but she didn't. She pulled herself together. "Listen close, Jimmy-poo. RC can print his story before we're safe in New Zealand or after. If I have some harmless fun with him, he'll protect me and not sell his story till after."

"Just so harmless fun doesn't mean screwing him."

Honey sat up straight and laughed, apparently amused no end by the absurdity of her screwing RC. "Mr. Nash is an old man. He probably can't even get a stiffy."

"The dead guy was old, and he got one."

"Yes, but Charles had power, and power begets hard dicks."

"Begets?"

Honey leaned toward Jimmy and nipped lightly at his earlobe. She said, "Jimmy, the only reason old men get laid is if they're famous or rich. Mr. Nash isn't either one. Why on earth would I sleep with him?"

In a rare leap of insight, Jimmy said, "Because he's there."

Kid squatted on a Raleigh trainer stool and taped Farlow's ankle, his stringy hands flying fast as a con artist on a shell game.

"Giants coaches teach the crack-back," Kid said. He tore tape with his teeth, clamped down the right ankle, and without a pause went on to the left. "They give prizes for whatever lineman breaks the most legs."

Farlow was mesmerized by Kid's hands—bony knobs, scars, and strings, visible tendons, a thumb that had been broken over and over. Watching his hands move was like reading Kid's biography. Farlow said, "If they do, they'll get caught. There's too much profit in telling secrets these days. Some tackle goes on TV, says, 'The Giants teach crack-backs,' then he turns free agent and makes a bundle 'cause he's got good character plus he knows how to crack-back."

"All I know's Otis Wilson's the best ever at breaking legs, and he's their line coach. Man with a skill like that would tend to pass it on. You want a shot in your knee there?"

"I'm okay. I appreciate you asking."

Farlow turned down the cortisone because he was planning to make this a one-play day. RC had called Farlow's cell phone a half-hour earlier and told him to fake a twisted ankle on the opening kickoff.

"Why should I do that?" Farlow said. "I'm in my zone. After two days with Jimmy, I need to hit somebody."

RC was calling from a pay phone at Burger King, so he had to talk over a busload of high school civics students from Parkersburg, West Virginia, who were on a field trip to see historical roots and lose their virginities. A million schoolkids a year visit our nation's capital, making it a great spot to own a Burger King or a condom machine.

"We need you to get hurt and go down to the training room, where you'll tell whoever's there you're going to walk it off, then go get Jimmy and the body and take them to the tunnel." A teenage hardbody with her shirt cut off mid-ribs and her pants hanging five inches below her navel was staring at RC with all the intensity of a lip reader.

He cupped his hand over his mouth and went on. "Leave Jimmy and clear out quick. I told these people you don't know about the dead guy."

"They'll never believe he could have carried that much weight upstairs."

"Nobody will ask. Make certain Jimmy brings all the parts. I wouldn't put it past the bastard to try something cute."

"I'd rather leave Jimmy down in the hole."

"He started this mess, and we've been cleaning up after him ever since. It's his turn. You think you can convince Honey to stay down there till it's over?"

"How well do you know Honey?" Farlow asked.

"I guess that's a no." The girl with visible flesh was whispering to her friend, the spiked body princess. Now they were both eyeing RC. He said, "Just tell her to hang back and try not to say anything. We need to lay the responsibility on Jimmy in case there's repercussions."

"In case, my ass."

The two high school girls came over by the phone and the spiked one drank from the water fountain while the skin exposer stared at RC from all of two feet away.

"You waiting on the phone?" RC asked. He could have been speaking Chinese for all the response she gave him. "'Cause if you aren't, leave me alone. I'm a grown-up." Into the phone, he said, "I've got to get over to the White House. You take care of yourself, and if I don't see you again, I hope everything works out with the placekicker."

The girl said, "We know who you are."

RC hung up the phone and said, "Pretend you don't. I'm underground." Then he walked out, wondering who the girls thought he was.

Back at the stadium, Farlow sat in front of his locker, looking at the cell phone in the palm of his hand. A couple of rookies were having a wet-towel fight near the showers, and a fifteen-year veteran had his upper body encased in ice at one of the trainer's tables. Otherwise, Farlow was alone. He'd come in early to see if the Secret Service was waiting to nab him, and when they weren't he knew RC would soon be calling.

A wistfulness settled over Farlow, not unlike the last game of your senior season, or the last time you sleep with someone before a breakup. You know it has to end, you even want it to end, but at the same time you remember back when there was optimism. In all likelihood, this was the last time he would ever save Honey. That had been the driving force of his life for so long it would be sad to see it go.

Farlow punched numbers on the phone and called his placekicker, whose name was Martin and who was in Phoenix for a game with the Cardinals. Farlow checked his watch to see what time it was there, but he couldn't remember if this was the half of the year Arizona was in Mountain Time or Pacific. The state jumped back and forth, or to be precise, Arizona stayed put and the states around it jumped back and forth an hour. He was fairly certain Martin wouldn't be at the stadium yet.

Martin answered. "Hey."

Farlow said, "It's me."

"Well, hi there. I was just thinking about you. Shouldn't you be in your yoga psych-up trance about now?"

"I already did that."

"What's the matter, Farlow?"

"Nothing's the matter."

"You never call while you're in the zone. How you going to kill a linebacker if you're hot from talking to me?"

"I miss you, that's all. What are you wearing?"

"Silk kimono and a jock strap. Don't give me that 'Nothing's the matter' jive. I know you."

"I'm fine, Martin. Can't I call you without there being a problem?"

Five seconds of dead air later: "Whatever."

"I wanted to hear your voice before kickoff."

"Now you've got me rattled, I'll probably shank an extra point. If you aren't going to be open with me I wish you wouldn't call."

Four seconds of dead air later, Farlow said, "I love you."

"Me too."


Kid was three minutes into a story about Otis Wilson breaking a tight end's pelvis in the rain in 1962, and Farlow wasn't listening, when Coach Czeneck came out of the bathroom, zipping himself up. He stood beside the trainer's table with his arms crossed over his belly, breathing like the asthmatic drunk he was.

Kid said, "How's the restraining order, Mal?"

Mal said, "Fuck you."

Kid had been around forty years, and Czeneck was a special-teams coach. No respect was due.

"Lots of people looking for you, Stubbs," Mal said.

"I'm right here."

"Place was crawling with Feds on your trail two hours ago. I don't know where they went."

"Why don't you give them a call?"

Czeneck tapped Kid on the shoulder. "Don't waste time on Stubbs. We're starting Blackthorne on kickoffs."

Farlow's stomach turned over. "You're benching me?"

Czeneck shook his thick head in mock sympathy. "You're distracted 'cause of having your house shot up. I can't risk you missing an assignment. Is Blackthorne here yet?"

Kid said, "I haven't seen him."

"You do, have him come talk to me."

Czeneck hummed as he wandered back to the coaches' office.

"That song he's stuck on sounds familiar," Farlow said.

Kid stood up and admired the wrap on Farlow's left ankle. He'd done good work. "It's 'Ballad of the Green Beret.' He always hums it when he screws over a player. Stand up."

Farlow stood and shifted his weight from ankle to ankle.

"You wouldn't have missed an assignment," Kid said.

Farlow said, "You better look for Blackthorne."

"It was an accident, but an embarrassing accident, one we can't talk about, and we lost the body."

Turk Johansen said, "I understand."

"You do?"

"No."

Stonewall and Turk were in what Stonewall considered the most interesting room in the White House, the room the million teenagers who visit Washington each year never see. Turk sat in front of a makeup mirror while Stonewall stood behind him, admiring his professionalism. On all four walls of the room, museum cases displayed the executive branch masks.

Early in American history the government had used doubles, but good doubles are hard to find and even harder to train—Warren Harding's double once got drunk and peed in the sink at the German embassy—so the moment Hollywood developed high-quality latex facial impressions, the doubles were dumped. Now it takes a body double, and these aren't hard to find, except in the case of Nixon.

All the presidents from Herbert Hoover on were lined up around Stonewall and Turk. And the vice-presidents, most of the First Ladies, and a few others, such as Kissinger and James Watt. Hubert

Humphrey had two, so he could be in three places at once. Because of its weight, the Lyndon Johnson mask came with detachable ears.

The original purpose had been for safety issues such as personal appearances in the wake of a death threat, or a national emergency conflicting with a social obligation, but the presidents also used their substitutes for more private reasons—avoiding another March of Dimes reception or the Easter Egg Roll, where ankle-biters drooled and parents videotaped. Very few people know that the real Richard Nixon didn't go to China. He stayed home and worked acrostics while his double did the work. The last year he was in office, what we thought was Ronald Reagan was in fact an Italian immigrant known in the Service as Frodo. The Kennedys used to swap masks with one another, in case Bobby wanted to be president for a day or Teddy wanted to get blown by Marilyn Monroe.

From the neck down, Turk was a perfect match for Charles Franklin, and as Stonewall watched the transformation, it was as if Franklin entered Turk's body. His posture changed. He had control over each eyebrow so he could do Franklin's infamous you-and-me look. Even the Adam's apple was Charles's.

"So do I fall and hit my head or have a heart attack or what?" Turk asked.

"Probably hit your head, but we'll have to wait and see the body before we decide. Our source was vague about what condition he's in." Stonewall's hand drifted to the incisor in his front pants pocket. He was more than a little concerned about Charles's condition. "All we know is that he's naked."

"The neck seam will show if I die nude."

"You won't die at all." Stonewall knocked wood on a pencil. "When we make the exchange, we'll put your clothes on Charles while you slip downstairs."

Turk bent to tap in the blue contact lenses that gave him Franklin's eyes. "I don't like the sound of this."

"You'll be okay. What you'll do is go down the same staircase as the guy who gives us the body. I want you to follow him."

"Is he armed?"

"We have to assume so."

"I'm in my underwear, following an armed man who just gave up the dead President, and you can't tell me who he is or why he has the body?"

"Right."

Turk raised his head and looked at Stonewall in the mirror. He had become Charles Franklin. Even Lonicera couldn't have told them apart.

"Are you sure you know what I'm doing?" Turk asked.

"Of course I'm sure," Stonewall said, although of course he wasn't. "You have to tell us where the guy hides. He thinks he can cause the President's death and walk away a free man, but we can't allow that. If this one gets away with accidentally killing the President, everyone will think it's okay for them too."

Turk said, "That makes sense."

Large parking lots made Eldon nervous, with cars every which direction and any one of them liable to whip around a corner going for an empty space and instead running down an innocent child. And large crowds made him anxious, especially large crowds of aggressive fat men painted red, many of them wearing pig snouts. Nervousness and anxiety triggered Eldon's asthma. As Ace drove up and down the parking lot rows, Eldon could feel his lungs shrinking like a stepped-on toothpaste tube.

"What do Redskins have to do with pigs?" Ace asked. "I don't get it."

"Fuck this shit," Papaw said. "Drive up front, an operation this big must have valet parking."

They did, so at least Eldon was spared the misery of walking a mile across pavement. He'd left his inhaler back at the house, which was shaping up as a mistake. Eldon began to doubt the wisdom of coming to the game at all. The stadium was loud, with people running right and left, shoving and yelling and selling cheap junk for high prices. He'd never find Sleet in this mess, and if he couldn't find Sleet he probably wouldn't find Honey and he'd have an asthma attack and have to be rushed to the emergency room. Maybe he'd die, which wouldn't be so bad if Honey knew he died for her, but there would be no one to tell her. His mother would be mad at Papaw for taking him to a football game if he stopped breathing and keeled over while walking up a thousand flights of stairs, which, once they got inside and circled for about an hour looking for the right ramp, is what they had to do, although at the top Eldon discovered there were escalators they could have taken.

Ace yammered on about how good the seats were and how he'd called in favors and made irrefutable offers, but Eldon didn't think the seats were special—nothing to phone home about. At least they were yellow. Papaw Rat's Ass would have had a cow if he'd ended up sitting with the rabble. No one in the yellow Club seats wore a pig snout.

"There's a kid selling food," Rat's Ass said. "You want something?"

"I'd like a popcorn bag," Eldon said, and Gino misunderstood and bought him a bag of popcorn. Eldon figured it didn't matter; you probably couldn't buy popcorn bags without popcorn anyway.

He dumped the popcorn out on the concrete at their feet.

Ace said, "What'd he do that for?"

Eldon cupped the open end of the bag around his mouth and breathed in and out, concentrating on the shrink wrap around his lungs.

"What's he doing?" Ace asked.

Gino made a gesture like shushing mosquitoes. "Whenever Eldie wants attention he has a breathing attack. I told his mother if she ignores him he'll be fine, but like always, she didn't listen. What's he gonna do, hold his breath till he dies?"

As Eldon inhaled, slowly and evenly as possible, he swore to God on high that he would live to kill the fucker.

Meanwhile, the Giants came sprinting out of their tunnel and the crowd booed and hissed and generally made sounds you'd expect from drunks painted red. Then the Redskins ran onto the field, and guys were standing and screaming while music came over the speakers so loud you couldn't tell what the song was. A man on the P.A. was talking that roller-coaster way P.A. announcers and no one else on earth talks.

Eldon breathed in, breathed out.

Stuck in the midst of eighty thousand people, Gino was feeling insignificant, as if the masses around them didn't know how important he was, even though he was the only one in their section wearing an Armani suit, silk tie, and diamond pinkie ring. Instinctively, Gino compensated by being especially arrogant to Ace.

*Get me a beer. Buy Eldon a program. This isn't beer, it's cow piss. Go find me a real beer.* All spoken loudly so everyone nearby knew he had a lackey.

Eldon stood up to look for Sleet, but Gino told him if he was going to stand he had to take the silly bag off his mouth.

"You look like you got polio or something. Need an iron lung."

Eldon had no idea what an iron lung was, but two rows back he heard a father tell his son the funny-dressed men were in organized crime and if the kid didn't behave himself the men would put a horse's head in his bunk bed. Ace turned to stare at the guy, who stared right back, but somehow, being recognized as dangerous put Gino in a better mood. To Eldon's mortal embarrassment, his papaw pulled out the rat's ass on a string and announced this was the rat's ass he didn't give for which team won the game.

There were mutterings and stares, and by kickoff an ugly scene was in germination.

Eldon said, "I gotta go the bathroom."

Rat's Ass said, "You want Ace to go with you?"

"I can potty by myself."

And the father who'd warned his son about the dangers of fooling with organized crime said, "That's the spirit."

It takes more manpower to move a president across town than it does a vice-president or First Lady. Eight motorcycles—four ahead, four in the rear—three Crown Victorias, three black SUVs, and a Lincoln limo paraded out of the White House drive. Each intersection was blocked by Washington's finest. An F-16 patrolled the skies.

They stuck RC in the back-facing seat between Stonewall Jackson and Claude Hammer, as if they expected him to bolt from the car and flee to Wyoming. RC had no intention of bolting. He was having fun riding around with the President and First Lady, even if the President was fake. He was doing something that mattered for the first time in a long while. Being a person who didn't matter was hard on RC. He'd rather be in a life-threatening situation than feel superfluous, which was how he felt sleeping with a Danish swizzle stick and writing celebrity puffs.

Nobody bothered introducing the artificial President to him, either as Franklin or whoever was in there. The resemblance, however, was remarkable. RC caught himself staring at the false Franklin the way a child would, as if the person being stared at couldn't see back.

"That's the most amazing mask I ever saw," RC said.

"You can buy yourself one for thirty dollars on Hollywood Boulevard," Claude Hammer said. "That's where we found ours."

Lonicera said, "Isn't there some way to get Charles and still strangle the girl?"

An embarrassed silence fell over the three men facing her and the false Franklin, although his silence wasn't so much embarrassment as cluelessness. RC wondered if she meant "strangle" in the literal sense, or the way most people mean it when they say, I could just kill such-and-so. Usually you know what people mean, but at the highest level of government and commerce, hyperbole loses its symbolism.

"Claude," she said. "We can't simply stand by and let her fly away. She seduced Charles and now he's dead."

"She's got hair," RC said.

Lonicera said, "I beg your pardon."

"Honey cut hair off the President. She's hidden it in a safe place with a to-be-opened-if-I-die-strangely note."

"Hair doesn't prove anything. Lots of people had access to Charles's hair." Lonicera tried to come up with an example. "Barbers, cleaning ladies."

"Not hair from this part of his body."

Lonicera said, "Oh."

Stonewall Jackson was interested in the body-parts-as-insurance concept. He said, "How'd she set up the note? I mean, what if the person she left it with gets curious?"

"She sent it to a lawyer in one of those living-will packets that tell people what to do in case you turn vegetable and there's no one to pull the plug. He won't open it unless he needs to."

"I hadn't thought of that," Stonewall said.

"We all did," RC said. He was flying by the seat of his pants here. The pube Baggie was still in Honey's purse, except for one curly lock behind the photo window of the billfold in RC's back pocket. "We divided the hair four ways."

"Why would Farlow need blackmail evidence?" Stonewall asked.

Claude's cell phone buzzed. He listened a moment with his eyes on Lonicera. He was hoping she would look his way so he could wink. Maybe she would wink back. He needed a sign that this jealousy over the girl who had freed them was an act, but Lonicera put on her sunglasses and stared out the window at a chain office-supply store.

Claude said to the others. "The game started. We're set for the exchange."

RC tried to figure out a subtle way to ask his question, but it couldn't be done, so he dived right in. "Was Farlow hurt on the kickoff?"

Claude repeated the question into the phone. They waited until he said, "Mr. Stubbs was on the bench for kickoff."

RC said, "Oh, shit."

Lonicera said, "Why?"

"Farlow has to fake an injury so he can go to the locker room, then slip off to the hiding place and let Jimmy out."

Lonicera studied RC's face to the point where he felt discomfort. She said, "You're lying."

He said, "How can you tell?"

"I lived with Charles for twenty years."

RC went to his fall-back position. "Okay, try this one. The President weighs two hundred pounds, more or less."

It was Claude who said, "One-eighty."

"I don't know what you found out about Jimmy, but he's a skinny runt. He couldn't carry a hundred pounds up stairs. We need Farlow."

Quick as a prosecuting attorney, Claude snapped, "But you claim Farlow doesn't know about the body."

"He knows there's a body in the bag, but he doesn't know who."

Nobody believed that one.

Claude said, "Bag?"

Stonewall said, "He's in a beanbag chair," and immediately wished he hadn't.

Lonicera took off her sunglasses and leaned forward. "Jonathan hasn't said anything about a beanbag chair. How is it you know and he doesn't?"

"I guessed," Stonewall said. "Just now, this second. There were styrofoam pellets on the floor at Jimmy's apartment, then yesterday a woman in Landover found a dead man in a beanbag chair, in her living room. By the time the police arrived, the body was gone."

"Jimmy lost him for a while," RC said. "But I got him back. You mind stopping at a 7-Eleven? I need to pee."

The false Franklin finally opened his mouth. He said, "You are part of a presidential convoy. We do not stop at 7-Elevens."

Claude punched buttons.

RC said, "Who's he calling?"

Stonewall said, "Gail Van Vleck, I imagine."

Gail Van Vleck inherited the Washington Redskins when a chain-mail-covered horse jumped a retaining wall at the Medieval Times theme restaurant and landed on her parents. Before she took over the football team, Gail had been a big-game hunting guide, specializing in Dall mountain sheep, and it was rumored that she slept with either the head cheerleader or the tailback, depending on which supermarket tabloid you swore by.

"Gail, Claude Hammer here. The President and Lonicera are on the way to your game."

He listened for an inordinate amount of time, then said, "That's not within the FBI's jurisdiction."

Claude listened some more. Lonicera crossed her legs, and Claude felt his heart leap into his throat. He had never beheld a woman of such grace.

"The President wishes to see one of your players in action. Farlow Stubbs." Long pause while RC shook his foot to relieve the bladder tingle. "It seems Charles dated Farlow's mother back in college and he didn't realize Farlow was here in Washington until the excitement yesterday."

Lonicera was glaring at him, so Claude winked. She didn't wink back.

"I know, it's always a shame to lose a member of the Secret Service. But the important thing is, the President has his heart set on seeing his old girlfriend's son play."

RC said, "I didn't know the President had this much power."

Stonewall said, "He can name the score if he wants to."

Claude held his hand over the mouthpiece. "Only the once, against Green Bay. It was politics."

Back on the phone, he said, "It's a deal, Gail. I'll have the FBI look into the break-in at your skybox, and you make certain Stubbs is in the game."

Claude hung up and turned his gaze on RC. "Tell me the body isn't in the owner's skybox."

RC said, "The body isn't in the owner's skybox."

Amid the chaos and roar of the sidelines, Coach Bobby Dean pressed his hand against the earpiece of his headphones and strained to hear Jimbo McMichaels, the defensive coordinator, who was high above the field in the coaches' box.

"They're kicking our butts on the right side," Jimbo shouted. "You've got to pull Cross into the line of scrimmage. Go red eagle zone six—"

Suddenly McMichaels's voice fuzzed out in a series of static pops and Gail Van Vleck came on. "Bobby."

Bobby Dean said, "Who the hell is this?"

The Giants ran a counterplay for another in a series of first downs. Bobby groaned.

Gail said, "Your boss."

"I'm fighting for my life out here, Gail. You can't call on this line."

"President Franklin is on his way. He wants Farlow Stubbs in the game when he gets here."

"Who?" Farlow was so far down the defensive depth chart it took Billy a moment to remember him.

"Stubbs. Franklin nailed his mother back in college and now he wants to see the boy play."

"I can't change the defense for a politician."

"Bobby, do you know how much tax the Redskin organization paid last year? None. Do you know why? Because we respect our president."

Bobby Dean said, "Fuck."

Farlow sat on the bench with his feet propped on his helmet, not watching the game, deep in a fantasy about an end-zone wedding in the spring during cherry blossom season. He and Martin were surrounded by family and friends. They wore mauve tuxedoes, the flowers were red star orchids set off in baby's breath. Music from the *Titanic* sound track played over the loudspeakers, or maybe *The Bodyguard*. Martin was barefoot, like Julia Roberts when she married Lyle Lovett, before she went off the deep end. Honey gave Farlow away, and as Martin slipped the ring onto Farlow's finger and they kissed, fifty thousand fans erupted in cheers. The JumboTron flashed fireworks.

It was during the kiss that Coach Czeneck kicked Farlow's helmet out from under his feet.

Czeneck barked. "You're in the game, Stubbs."

Farlow leaned to the side to look past Czeneck at the Giants, who were lined up for second down on the Redskins' thirty.

"Nobody's punting," Farlow said. "I'm here for punts and kickoffs."

"Your daddy wants to see you play."

"My daddy's dead, Coach."

"President Charles Franklin isn't your daddy?"

"Not that I know of."

"He says he popped your mama's cherry back in college and now he wants to see his kiddie kick some ass."

Farlow worked out the math. "My mother was working at a Dairy Queen in Levelland, Texas, the year before I was born."

"She must have turned tricks behind the barn. You're going into the game."

The Giants saw that the new defensive end wasn't somebody who should be there, and ran the next play right at him. All-pro Willie Grimes was the ball carrier who ran at Farlow, while offensive tackle Joe Don Patton was the one assigned to knock him out of the way.

Instead of cooperating, Farlow slipped Joe Don's block and stuck his helmet into the ball and his shoulder into Willie's sternum, blowing the air out of Willie's lungs and causing the football to fly upfield and bounce twice before the Redskins pounced on it. Joe Don was so humiliated at missing the block that he pretended to fall forward and rolled up the back of Farlow's legs, which made Farlow's ACL snap like a worn-out fan belt.

The pain was similar to a lightning bolt in the knee. Farlow landed on Willie, who was already doing a fish-on-the-shore gasp from having had his breath knocked out. Trainers came running from both sidelines while the network went to a commercial.

Farlow rolled off Willie and lay on his back staring at the sky, which was a nice whitish blue, not true blue like in Texas, but more your East Coast high-humidity blue. As an alternative to screaming he resumed the spring wedding fantasy, in which he stood under the goalposts with his back to the boys and threw his orchid bouquet over his shoulder, and it was caught by RC Nash, wearing a beige evening dress with pearls. Farlow and Honey found each other in the happy throng. He smiled; she gave a thumbs-up. Although the pain was there in the unendurable range, it was also familiar to Farlow. He'd been here before. The only question was whether this would be the one that ended his career.

Kid knelt over Farlow and lifted his calf to bend the knee slightly. He said, "The cap's still out of socket. Relax so I can pop her back in."

Farlow said, "I am relaxed, goddamnit."

Next to him on the turf, all-pro Willie Grimes was revived enough to sit up and call Farlow a fucking fag. From the flat-on-his-back position, Farlow threw a punch that caught Willie in the voice box. The referee threw a flag. Willie stood and kicked Farlow in the knee. The line judge threw another flag, but Farlow didn't see it because silver lights exploded in his eyes and even though he didn't lose consciousness he did lose awareness of the situation until he came to on the Redskins training table with Kid pumping up the ice pack on his leg.

Kid was talking away, as if Farlow had been coherent all along. "I warned you they'd crack-back. Didn't I say it? The Giants teach that shit. Joe Don was getting high fives in the huddle after you went down. He's the one you should of popped. Not Willie Grimes."

Farlow tried to sit up. Kid pressed a palm against his chest and firmly put him back down. "This is the NFL. We can't have third-stringers punching out all-pros. Hell, all he called you was fag. Willie calls ever'one who tackles him fags."

"Did we recover the fumble?" Farlow asked.

"You bet. You're on the highlight reel."

Farlow sat up again. "I can walk it off."

"Like hell you can."

"No, Kid, all I need is a minute and I'll walk it off. I'll be back by halftime."

"You'll be in ice till halftime, then I'll X-ray. I don't think the ACL is snapped. You probably just tore some old scar tissue, and if we clamp a DonJoy 4Titude on her you'll be back in a month or so."

"I don't have a month. I have to go somewhere now."

"Listen, Farlow, I've been around since the Dark Ages. When the human knee says *stop,* you stop. It don't take *go* for an answer."

The Redskins marched down the field and scored in five plays. Eighty thousand fans screamed and stomped, and to Jimmy and Honey three stories underground, it sounded as though the building was falling down.

Jimmy smoked long brown cigarettes, one after another. He said, "They're fucking us over. I can feel it."

Honey was nervous too. There was nothing to do but wait, and waiting had never been her strength. "Nobody's fucking us over, Jimmy. You always think other people will do what you would do in the situation, but they don't." He gave her an odd look, as if he was having trouble following the train of thought, so she added, "At least not all the time."

"If they're not fucking us over, why isn't Farlow here?"

"Farlow is coming."

"He should have been here a half-hour ago. Our plane tickets will be in the tunnel in five minutes."

Honey was concerned about Farlow. He'd never been late to pick her up, not in all their years of knowing each other. She was late as a matter of policy, but Farlow took promptness with her as a religious duty. "Maybe he got held up."

"Maybe we're being double-crossed. Maybe your boyfriend sold us out and we'll haul the body up there and he'll be waiting with a million cameras and cops. We walk through the door and I'm shot all to hell like Sonny Corleone at the toll booth. You'd like that, wouldn't you? It would make your day."

"Jimmy, get hold of yourself."

"He wants you for himself, and he'll do anything to get me out of the way." Jimmy puffed smoke like a tire afire. His face kind of twitched and he slung his wrist this way and that, flicking ash across the room. He said, "RC Nash hates me."

Honey couldn't very well deny it, so she changed the subject. "Jimmy, sweetie, we have to go upstairs now and get the tickets. I'm not spending another night in this hellhole with a dead man and no TV."

Jimmy threw his cigarette butt to the floor and stomped on it. "You go up."

"Farlow's not here. I need you to carry Charles."

They both looked at the green trunk with the workout bag sitting on top. "I can't carry that upstairs," Jimmy said. "People weigh more dead than they did alive. It's a scientific fact."

"We could put him back in the bag, and I'll carry one end while you take the other, the way you and RC did on the golf course."

Jimmy tapped his foot against the trunk. "Far as I know, you're in on the double-cross. You and Noah, scheming to get me killed so you two can set up house in New Zealand and feed each other kiwis while you dog-style on the beach. That's what you want, you might as well admit it."

Honey thought, *Where is Farlow,* but she said, "Jimmy, don't be a dick."

"Tubby, sweetheart, what are we doing here?"

"We're watching," Tubby Fitzhugh said.

"For what?"

"For whatever that bastard is up to." Tubby raised his binoculars to check out a flurry of Secret Service activity up by the VIP entrance to FedEx Field. "I know this man better than my grandma back in Georgia knows the Book of Job, and he's up to something. There's more evidence than that phone call you screwed up."

"I said I was sorry."

"Sorry don't pick cotton."

Alberta Chamberlain and Tubby Fitzhugh sat behind the tinted windows of a *Daily News* delivery van, not thirty yards from where remnants of the White House press corps had set up their cameras. Alberta's attention was divided between the tunnel and her *Daily News* reporter, who was sharing a joint with the guy from the *Post*. The impulse was to storm out of the van and give her man a colon cleansing, but then she'd have to explain why she was there.

"He supposedly had the flu yesterday but not the day before," Tubby said. "I never heard of a one-day flu bug."

"Maybe he got well," Alberta said.

"Well enough to suddenly decide that it's time to hit a football game? Hell, half the press corps took the day off. Franklin hasn't gone to a game yet without it being a national event, announced weeks ahead of time."

Alberta said, "They must be close. Jonathan's clearing the tunnel."

"And that's another thing. Jonathan Weathers doesn't work in the field, especially on Sunday. Jonathan's strictly a modem jockey."

Jonathan wasn't a modem jockey today. As soon as the presidential convoy rolled to a stop, Jonathan rushed to open the limo door. Tubby focused on the President as he stepped out of the limo, spoke a few words to Jonathan, then turned and waved an arm to the press corps and the smattering of loiterers attracted by all the fuss. Tubby tracked Franklin walking toward the tunnel. He hated that cleft chin, and the swollen nose. He hated the character crags on Franklin's face. He hated the way the man led with his crotch, as if he had a silver dollar stuffed up his butt. Now Franklin stopped and smiled at someone behind him. Tubby hated Franklin so much that the sight of him left a tinfoil taste in his mouth.

Lonicera came into view, wearing white slacks and a Redskins-red pullover sweater that would have been Claude Hammer's idea. In Tubby's opinion, she wasn't smart enough to think of wearing the hometown colors herself.

"Come the campaign, we're going to crucify that little Jazzercise princess," Tubby said.

Beside him, Alberta gasped.

Tubby said, "What?"

"RC Nash is with them. In the limo."

Tubby swung the binoculars to the open limousine door. "That's the man you said couldn't find a story if it bit him in the ass?"

Alberta didn't answer. Seeing RC Nash with the President and First Lady was a nightmare come true. A true newsman would have heard an alarm in the way RC had said, You'll slit your wrists, with such confidence, and Alberta would have heard it if Tubby hadn't been so seductive. A professional would have lied, promised RC his job back, then denied saying it later. That's what Woodward and Bernstein would have done.

"Why is he dressed like a condo-share salesman?"

"That's what he was wearing when I fired him yesterday."

RC joined Charles and Lonicera, who were talking to Claude Hammer. The four walked to the VIP entrance, and together with Jonathan Weathers and another Secret Serviceman, they went in. Two more Servicemen moved to block the doorway.

Tubby lowered his binoculars, thinking. He said, "I don't know what the hell is going on, but I do know somebody tried to tell you and you hung up the phone."

"I said I was sorry, what else do you want?"

Tubby said, "As God is my witness, Alberta, you'll never suck a Republican dick again."

Stonewall and RC dropped behind the others as they walked through the tunnel. RC was trying to determine where the nearest bathroom was. Normally, he could locate a bathroom even in a place he'd never been. It was an innate gift of his, like being able to find a gourmet coffee shop in a strange town. For years RC's life had rotated between coffee shops and bathrooms, and now he didn't know whether they drank good coffee in New Zealand or not. Be his luck to find sanctuary in a tea country. They had to have public restrooms, although he'd been in countries that didn't. The thing he liked best about France was that the men peed wherever they were when they got the urge. He took public urination as the sign of an ancient civilization.

"Your file says you're from Wyoming," Stonewall said.

RC nodded. "Cody, but it's been a long time."

"I've got five acres outside Spearfish, South Dakota. It's on a stream, real pretty place."

"I went through Spearfish once, on my way to Deadwood fishing."

"Deadwood's a den of gambling now. It's worse than Sturgis."

RC wondered why they were having this conversation. If the world were coming to an end in twenty minutes, would men still shoot the shit?

"You planning to retire in South Dakota?" RC asked.

"I was, before Honey screwed the President. Now I don't know."

RC said, "Honey didn't screw the President. They gave each other head."

Stonewall glanced at him. "All this trouble is over a blow job?"

"She's really a sweet girl."

"I don't doubt it."

The sweet girl and Jimmy stood in the alcove beside the elevator and staircase, behind the beanbag chair, which surprised RC some. The last he'd seen of Franklin, he was in a trunk. Honey was wearing a short black skirt and an old "Free Winona" tank top. She was carrying the silver lamé clutch. RC couldn't see her feet because they were behind the beanbag chair.

Honey smiled at RC. She was a sweet girl.

Jimmy said, "You bring the passports and tickets?"

Claude held up a manila envelope.

Jimmy said, "How do we know you won't kill us?"

Claude said, "How do we know you won't go on *Letterman*?"

"I said I wouldn't. Jimmy Sebastiano is a man of his word."

This caused Lonicera and Honey to titter, then they each realized the other was tittering and stopped.

Honey said, "I like your name."

Lonicera said, "I don't understand why Charles chose you."

"He would have gone home with anybody. He was terribly lonely."

"He didn't have to be."

Honey shrugged. To RC, it was a gesture of innocence.

"So why did you choose him?" Lonicera asked.

Honey thought. "He needed me so much. It made me feel okay, to be needed."

Lonicera knew what Honey meant. "He made everyone feel needed."

Honey said, "Most men who would rather lick clit than fuck are like that."

Stonewall nodded toward the beanbag chair. "Is the body in there?"

Jimmy unzipped the bag and pulled out the Frostbite Falls beer sign.

Claude said, "What is this?"

RC said, "Bullwinkle."

The elevator went *bing,* the door opened, and Sleet stepped out with a pistol in his right hand.

Sleet said, "Hi, Jimmy."

Turk, in the Franklin mask, said, "Jesus Christ, who's this?"

Sleet was staring at Jimmy, who had gone newsprint white, a shade whiter than Sleet's normal pissed-in–snow skin.

Sleet's voice was nearly a whisper. "Rat's Ass wants his money."

RC felt Stonewall kind of easing behind him, which meant a gun other than Sleet's was about to come into play, and what RC wanted least was to find himself between two people pointing weapons at each other again.

RC said, "We're in the middle of something right now. I don't know who you are, but how about waiting your turn?"

Sleet gave RC the dead-eye stare until RC was properly intimidated, then one by one he turned his power on the others. Turk-as-Franklin came last.

"You look familiar," Sleet said. "Are you on TV?"

Turk said, "I am your president."

Sleet almost blinked on that one. "Do you have Rat's Ass's money?"

"I know nothing about any Rat's Ass, but as your president I order you to wait and shoot Jimmy after we have finished our business."

Sleet slid into that little milk-curdling smile of his. "You may be president, but I'm the man with the gun." He turned his attention back to Jimmy. They'd never met, but Jimmy knew Sleet by reputation and he was close to wetting his pants. "Besides, I'm not going to shoot Jimmy."

"That's good," Jimmy said.

"Not yet, anyway. First I'm going to shoot everyone else, one at a time, until he tells me where the money is, starting with her." He pointed the pistol at Honey.

Jimmy said, "I don't have the money."

Which pissed Honey off. "Jimmy, he's going to shoot me."

Jimmy pointed to Claude and Lonicera. "They took it."

Lonicera had had enough. "You two gangsters kill each other later. I want my husband, now."

Sleet fired a shot at Lonicera's earlobe, but missed. "You're next, lady. I always kill the women first. It cuts down on whining."

Sleet turned the gun back to Honey. "Okay, Jimmy. You know the drill. Count to three. One—"

Honey pushed a switch on Bullwinkle's back that made his arm come up while his tinny voice said, *"Watch me pull a rabbit out of my hat,"* only instead of a squirrel wearing an aviator hat and diapers, Bullwinkle pulled the President's head—which had deteriorated considerably in the last thirty-six hours—out of the hat. Charles Franklin's head said, *"Oops. Wrong hat."*

Sleet finally blinked. He said, "What the fuck?" and Claude Hammer said, "Jesus, what happened to Charles's face?" Lonicera gave a gasp, then Eldon leaped onto Sleet's back and dug his fingertips into Sleet's eyes.

Sleet screamed and spun in a circle, with Eldon kicking and

yelling and biting him on the back of the neck. Stonewall and Turk went for their guns, but Sleet managed to yank Eldon's hand off his right eye in time to put a shot through Turk's mask.

Sleet yelled, *"Drop it!"* with his gun aimed at Stonewall's chest. Stonewall hesitated a moment, then dropped his gun.

Honey nailed a bullet into Sleet's heart.

Then there was silence. It had happened so quickly RC's eyes were still on Franklin's pasty head in Bullwinkle's white-gloved hand. It took a few seconds before it registered that Sleet and the fake Franklin were dead and Honey had a gun. Eldon was lying on his back on the floor, staring big-eyed at Honey.

Lonicera said, "Holy shit."

Stonewall picked his pistol up and said, "Get them out of here."

RC helped Eldon up, then gave Jimmy a little push. He said, "Grab Bullwinkle. We've got to clear out anything we don't want reporters finding."

Claude said, "This is yours," and thrust the manila envelope into RC's hands.

RC stood between Honey and the dead men. As he carefully took the pistol from her hands, he said, "Honey, are you okay?"

Honey said, "What happened?"

RC turned to point Honey's gun at Sleet. "Whoever that is just killed the President."

RC beelined for the slop bucket, and after sweet release he returned to find Jimmy throwing a tantrum.

"I said *no guns.* They everyone of them had guns. You even had a gun," he said to Honey. "I can't trust anybody now."

"When were you planning to pull yours?" Honey asked. "After he shot me?"

"He said I had till three. I was waiting for him to say two."

RC fingered Honey's little pistol in his front pocket. "What I want to know is where you came by a gun."

Honey smiled sweetly at him. "You gave it to me."

RC's face showed the look of a clueless male.

Honey said, "At Farlow's house, before you threw Vinnie out the window you tossed his gun to me under the couch thing."

"I didn't even know you were under the couch thing."

"Well, you threw me the gun. I put it in my clutch with the pube Baggie and my Carmex."

"What the hell are you looking at?" Jimmy asked. Eldon was standing beside the weight bench, gazing up at Honey with love in his eyes. His breathing was fine.

Eldon said, "You did a perfect shot. If the bullet had gone clear through Sleet it would have got me, but you made sure it didn't."

"You knew that man?" Honey asked.

"My papaw hired him to kill you and this guy"—indicating Jimmy—"but I saved you."

"You sure did." Honey kissed Eldon on the mouth. RC thought a quick peck was appropriate—the kid had saved their lives—but after two seconds of contact, he cleared his throat. Her lips had been up against his this morning and he had at least thirty years on the boy. The age spread was disturbing. And the kiss-as-reward thing bothered RC. He wasn't certain the motivation for kissing him differed appreciably from the one for kissing Eldon.

Eldon's own mouth was clamped shut, and his eyes appeared near popping out. His body went stiff as late-stage rigor mortis.

Jimmy said, "Enough already."

Honey pulled back and stared into Eldon's unblinking eyes. She said, "My hero."

Jimmy said, "Ask him who Papaw is."

RC said, "My bet goes to Gino Olivetti."

Jimmy's gag reflex kicked in. "Rat's Ass is your papaw?"

Eldon nodded, but the kiss had left him speechless. His fantasy had come true, and even young as Eldon was, he knew that was a dangerous thing.

Jimmy turned to RC. "What's a papaw?"

"Grandfather, I think."

Honey rested her fingertips on Eldon's shoulders. "Did your grandfather bring you to the game?"

Another nod.

"You better find him before he starts to worry."

Another nod.

"I won't forget what you did," Honey said.

Eldon left without a word.

Later that afternoon Eldon sat on the love seat in the living room with Gino, Louise, and Ace Columbus, watching a black-robed Supreme Court justice swear in Chip Allworth as president of the United States. Chip wore a dark brown suit with a yellow tie. His hair was freshly cut and he blinked more often than people who aren't either under stress or on drugs.

Gino Olivetti said, "Maybe I'm old-fashioned, but you won't catch me showing respect for a president named *Chip*."

"I heard he went to that California college on a beach volleyball scholarship," Ace said.

Louise said, "His eyebrows are twitching."

Eldon didn't say anything. He was trying to determine how many years he had to wait before proposing to Honey so that she would take him seriously and not simply smile and say, "You're sweet." If he revealed the depth of his feelings now, she would think of him as just another sixth-grader with a crush on an older woman—who could blame her?—but that was the furthest thing possible from the truth. Eldon's love was unique. It was adult.

He figured he should wait at least until he was sixteen, but four years without Honey's constant companionship loomed like a lifetime without air. A lot depended on how old she was. He thought she was probably a senior in high school, or maybe even a college girl, although in Eldon's experience most college girls had studs in their belly buttons. He'd seen Honey's belly button when she raised her arm to gun down Sleet, and he couldn't recall seeing a stud. Her nose was clear, he knew that much, and there was only one ring in each ear, which meant she was probably in high school, say seventeen or eighteen.

Eldon wondered if Honey and Jimmy had gone all the way. Papaw had called her a slash, but he called all girls slashes or cunts, and it didn't necessarily mean she wasn't a virgin. Eldon didn't care either way, so long as she kissed him again.

A mug shot of Sleet came on the TV, and the announcer speaking in a somber voice said, "The lone assassin has been identified as twenty-eight-year-old Ivan Greene from Paterson, New Jersey."

Louise bolted upright on the couch. "Gino, that's your friend Sleet."

The announcer went on. "Greene was identified from fingerprints obtained during two prior arrests for cruelty to animals. In an exclusive interview with CNN, Greene's mother, Sylvia, maintained his innocence."

Louise said, "Why would Sleet kill President Franklin?"

Ace said, "Gino, I don't get it."

Gino used his penknife to clip the end off a cigar, then he lit a kitchen match with his thumb and held the cigar to the flame, rotating the cigar slowly for an even burn. He said, "I want men in every airport from Newark to Baltimore. You cover Dulles personally."

"Jimmy generally boosts a car when he needs transportation."

"I don't know what kind of shit went down out there, but I do know it's get-out-of-the-country shit, and Jimmy'll need more than a hot car. Check the international flights. He'll be on one."

"Maybe Patrick was right," Ace said. "Maybe we should forget the money for a few days, till we know what the deal is."

Rat's Ass took out his rat's ass. "I don't give a fuck about the money. I want Jimmy Sebastiano."

"Why?" Louise asked.

"That turd-for-brains has cost me four employees. He's doing this to make a fool out of me, and I won't stand for it."

Louise said, "You're saying Jimmy had Sleet kill President Franklin just to make you look bad?"

The TV cut to Lonicera Franklin in black mourning clothes from Ralph Lauren, stepping into a limousine. The announcer said, "In a historic break from tradition, Lonicera Franklin announced that her husband will be cremated. In a statement released by her press secretary, the First Lady said, 'It was Charles's wish that his ashes should be spread across the front lawn of the Sigma Upsilon Kappa house in Madison, where he spent his happiest years.'"

Louise said, "You could tell by looking at Sleet he was the sort to kill somebody."

After the swearing-in, Chip held a press conference in the Rose Garden, because he'd always wanted to hold a press conference in the Rose Garden and now he could. The reporters sat on folding chairs numbered in red ink on the back, with cameras spread in a semicircle behind them, while Chip stood at a lectern with about twenty microphones stuck in his face. Jonathan Weathers and Claude Hammer flanked Chip, a little off his back pockets. Jonathan's face showed nothing; Claude ground his molars behind a grimace the reporters misinterpreted as grief.

Throughout the inauguration ceremony Chip's brain had had a neon sign in his frontal lobe: BE PRESIDENTIAL. It was his new personal mantra. Be Presidential meant behave with decorum and dignity, as if the weight of the world rested on your shoulders. Be Presidential meant lose the slang.

Now Chip repeated to himself, *Be Presidential.* To this end, he held the lectern with both hands and spoke distinctly, as called for by the occasion.

"At this point in time we have no reason to believe Ivan Greene was acting in conjunction with other parties."

A bunch of reporters tried to interrupt, because with this bunch the question mattered more than its answer. Being Presidential, Chip ignored the rabble.

"I am, however, appointing a blue-ribbon commission to investigate this heinous crime. The commission will be a bipartisan committee made up of a consortium of the most unimpeachable men and women in government service and the private sector. It will be headed by the chief of the American Secret Service, Jonathan Weathers."

Jonathan didn't react. He was quietly harking back to Mamie.

Chip said, "Mr. Weathers has my personal directive to leave no stones uncovered in his relentless search for the truth. Let me make myself perfectly clear"—he paused for emphasis—"when Mr. Weathers and the blue-ribbon commission have completed their inquiry, we will know the truth, there will be no questions without answers."

The few reporters who actually took notes all had shorthand scribbles for phrases along the lines of "At this point in time" and "Let me make myself perfectly clear," so Chip's speech took up only a couple of lines in their notebooks.

Chip breathed out, breathed in, whispered "Presidential" to himself, then said aloud, "We will now entertain questions."

The reporters started screaming, "Mr. President! Mr. President!" which gave Chip a buzz. He basked in the warmth of power for a few seconds before he chose a woman from *Newsweek* because Charles Franklin had told him you always choose her first or she'll trash you in her column.

Chip said, "Joan?"

Joan said, "Joan Prince, *Newsweek* magazine. Mr. President, what is your opinion of Lonicera Franklin's decision to have her husband cremated?"

Chip nodded and began his answer with, "That's a good question,

Joan." Charles had taught him to say that. He said people need to have their questions complimented. "At this point in time, my opinion is that Lonicera Franklin is the bravest woman on the planet."

Joan said, "But won't cremation raise doubts in the conspiracy community?"

"I am certain my blue-ribbon committee of unimpeachable members will thoroughly examine President Franklin's body before it is cremated. I understand a high-level autopsy will be conducted this evening."

Much to Chip's irritation, Joan wouldn't let it go. "But the American public has a right to disinter their fallen heroes."

"Lonicera can and will do whatever she knows is best for America." Chip stared into the camera from NBC, because it was the network with the prized demographics.

"After all"—Chip's voice practically dripped it was so earnest—"Lonicera is an Aries."

Behind Chip, Claude Hammer smote himself on the forehead.

Farlow Stubbs was a large man and the hideout door was wide but less than three feet high, so Farlow had to turn around and drag himself in backward, more or less pulling his right leg along like a duffel bag. No one jumped up from what they were doing to help. Besides the fact that Farlow weighed so much that grabbing him by the armpits and pulling would have been more symbolic than helpful, a kind of general lethargy had settled on the room. The heightened awareness of the moment of being present when people are shooting at one another is almost always followed by loginess. Imagine the post-sugar-buzz crash times ten.

Honey and RC were playing poker, with each of them trying to lose so as to bolster the other's self-image. Honey won most of the hands even though she seldom held so much as a jack's high pair. Jimmy was cleaning the gun he hadn't used in either of the shoot-outs they'd been involved in the last two days. It depressed him no end to know he could have killed in self-defense but instead shot a golf ball and a man in the foot.

Farlow pulled himself to his feet. He looked at Franklin's head, which still hung from Bullwinkle's white-gloved hand.

He said, "You were supposed to get rid of Franklin."

Jimmy said, "You were supposed to carry him upstairs."

Farlow nodded toward his DonJoy 4Titude brace, which gave him the look of a human with a robot leg. "I got hung up. Why is the head hanging from a beer sign?"

Honey looked up from her diamond flush. "Jimmy played a joke."

"I thought it was funny," Jimmy said.

Honey said, "No one else did."

Jimmy snapped in the clip and set the gun on the end table next to the manila envelope holding their tickets and passports. He said, "A girlfriend should be supportive. You never support anything I do."

"Maybe I shouldn't be your girlfriend."

"Yeah, right," Jimmy said as he slid his thumbnail along the envelope flap. He dumped the contents out on the table.

RC stared at his two aces and trash, and wondered what "Yeah, right" meant. It had been spoken sardonically, like when you say "That'll be the day," knowing full well that day will never come. There were two possibilities: Either it was beyond Jimmy's comprehension that Honey would leave him, or he had no intention of letting her go. RC hoped it was the first possibility and Jimmy was wrong, since the second came with implied violence. RC'd had enough violence.

Jimmy spit the words. "There's three tickets."

Honey said, "We wanted three."

"I didn't." Jimmy squinted at the top ticket. "And who the hell is Mohammed Das?"

"You are," RC said. "From now on."

"You named me Mohammed?"

"They didn't have time to print a new fake passport, so they glued an old mug shot of you on one they already had."

Honey said, "I fold," which left RC with the winning hand. She got up, walked over to Jimmy, and took the passports from him.

She glanced at them, then raised an eyebrow at RC. "Connie Chung?"

"Do you like it?"

"Why not Parthenia?"

"I didn't know you'd rather be Parthenia."

"I'd rather be anything else, so long as it has four syllables and doesn't end in *ie* or *y*."

Jimmy said, "I'm not spending the rest of my life answering to Mohammed."

Honey said, "This picture isn't me."

"I cut her out of a *Sports Illustrated* Swimsuit Issue."

"How sweet."

Jimmy studied his passport photo, which had been taken after a reckless-endangerment charge brought on by a senior citizen in a Hyundai Accent who cut him off on the interstate. "Why aren't you Mohammed Das? I don't see why I have to take the crappy passport."

"I already had a passport."

"But it's your real name."

"Rat's Ass isn't after me. I don't need a new name."

Farlow's knee hurt like fire, and the only place to sit was on the trunk, but before he sat down he opened it and looked in, confirming his fears. "So what are we going to do with him?"

"They're sending a limo to pick us up at nine. Once we're in the air, we'll tell them where the body is."

"So where will Charles be?" Honey asked.

Farlow said, "Not here."

Jimmy was still seething over his passport. "What's the matter, Farlow? Afraid of losing your love nest?"

"We went to a lot of trouble to decorate."

RC was surreptitiously checking to see what Honey had been

holding when she folded, and just as he suspected, she'd let him win the hand when she knew she had him beat. "I did a story on Dulles's lost-luggage room once. We might hide it there."

Honey put her fingertips on his wrist. Her voice was serious. "I need you to go back and get some things."

RC's wrist tingled where she touched him. He realized this was love, and he'd never felt it before, and it scared him so bad he needed to pee again.

Honey said, "I can't escape to New Zealand without clean panties. And my hair extensions I ordered from Raquel Welch on TV, and my Pooh bear, and my diary, only you have to promise not to read it."

"You expect me to break into the apartment and pack your stuff?" RC asked.

"I left a half-pack of cigarettes by the bed. Don't forget them," Jimmy said.

Honey borrowed RC's checkbook to write the list on a blank deposit slip. She said, "The tampons are in the bathroom medicine cabinet, beside my birth control pills."

Farlow lowered himself heavily on the trunk and tugged his right leg up on the lid so it stuck out straight. He said, "Bonnie and Clyde didn't go back for tampons."

Honey said, "Bonnie didn't have a killer period."

RC let himself in with Honey's key and cut across the living room, which the technicians had left in mid-deconstruction. Fingerprint dust lay in a film on the regular dust, and they'd accidentally left an ultraviolet light used to see sperm that was invisible to the naked eye. RC knew the ultraviolet light couldn't tell sperm from Woolite. He'd written a story about an egotistical rapist who splashed Woolite over the floor of a woman's kitchen so the police would think he put out fourteen ounces of jizz.

The first thing RC did before going to work was make coffee. In the excitement of the day, he hadn't had a caffeine opportunity. His only chance was Burger King, and there the lip-reading hardbody got him so flustered he forgot to buy a cup. For RC, an experience didn't count until he'd had time to think about it over coffee. Sometimes he wondered if maybe there wasn't a connection between this and frequent urination.

While the Mr. Coffee dribbled, RC explored. In the bedroom, he felt under the mattress for the diary that he fully intended to read, but it wasn't there. He hadn't thought it would be. People searching with tools that can ID dandruff weren't likely to miss a diary between the mattress and box springs. On the chest of drawers he found what appeared to be sections of a horse's tail, sewn together and glued to a clip. As he ran his fingers through the curtain of hair, he heard water running in the bathroom.

The water shut off and Lonicera Franklin came out, drying her hands on a Motel 6 towel. There was a chance she'd been crying in the bathroom, but RC couldn't tell for certain. She might have simply worn her contacts too long.

He said, "Would you call this a hair extension?"

Lonicera said, "An incredibly cheap one."

RC said, "She bought it from Raquel Welch, on TV."

"Figures."

RC felt under the bed and found the carry-on suitcase Honey had told him would be there. He opened it and dropped in the hair. He didn't ask Lonicera why she was in Honey's bathroom, and she didn't ask RC why he was in the bedroom. It was as if they'd been expecting each other.

"What's that smell?" Lonicera asked.

"I'm making coffee." RC lifted a pizza box off a pair of panties—pink and cut high at the sides. The box contained a full pizza's worth of crusts.

Lonicera said, "Eighty-five percent of all presidents since Washington had mistresses."

RC sniffed the panties, decided they weren't clean, and dropped them back where he'd found them. "What's your source?"

"Charles told me. I don't know where he got it. Presidents have access to so much secret information they're hell to disagree with."

"Any idea where Honey keeps her clean clothes?"

"Try the closet floor."

When RC opened the closet, the Abs Roller fell out.

"I had to come here one more time," Lonicera said. "After all Charles and I have been through, I just can't grasp that it ended in this dump."

The pile of clothes on the floor of the closet depressed RC. He'd never know clean from dirty or the stuff Honey wore from the stuff she didn't. He looked at Lonicera standing against the wall with her arms wrapped around each other, as if she had a chill.

"You want a cup of coffee?" he asked.

She nodded.

"I hope you can drink it black. The only milk I found has lumps."

They sat across from each other at the kitchen nook with two month's worth of junk mail and a raspberry jelly stain on the Formica top. The Pooh bear RC had been sent to find lay facedown between salt and pepper shakers that proclaimed they came from Stuckey's. Lonicera held the mug someone had gotten as a premium for donating to National Public Radio with both hands.

She said, "I don't know how many there were. The last one I found out about had a ring in her nose." She blew across the coffee surface and sipped. RC had enough experience with women to keep his mouth shut.

"My husband betrayed me for a girl with a ring in her nose. Imagine how that makes me feel."

"I don't think Charles had mistresses," RC said.

Lonicera's voice was bitter. "What would you call them?"

RC drank and wished he had cream. Cream-in-coffee dependence is almost as bad as coffee dependence. "One-night stands. Compulsive emissions. I don't think who he was with mattered."

"Are you trying to make me feel better?"

"When I was married I used to masturbate by fantasizing about being with different women, but that doesn't mean I cheated on my wife."

"What Charles did wasn't masturbation."

"I think it was." RC drank more coffee. All Honey stocked was this hazelnut-flavored preground mix from Starbucks. Normally, he wouldn't touch flavored coffee, but today wasn't normally. "Remember that joke we all heard in junior high that asks why a dog licks his balls?"

"Because he can."

"Right." RC waited for Lonicera to make the connections. She was a smart woman and he hoped he wouldn't be lowered to spelling it out.

"First you say Charles was masturbating, then you say he was licking his balls."

"Either way, it wasn't cheating on you."

Lonicera and RC both stared at her thumbs against the NPR mug. It was hard for RC to tell if he had been a comfort to her. He knew there was a difference between giving comfort to a woman you were sleeping with or would be soon and giving it to a woman you weren't. He didn't have much experience with the weren't group.

Her eyes came up to meet his. "How are you planning to word this scene in your book?"

"I beg your pardon?"

"The wife of the dead president and the"—she tried to come up with the word, but failed—"whatever you are for the assassins, sitting around the kitchen table, chatting over coffee."

"There's not going to be a book."

Lonicera stared at him.

RC said, "I promise, I won't write the story," which amazed the hell out of him, because he hadn't known until that moment that he wasn't going to make journalism history. Now he was certain.

Lonicera's eyes showed equal amounts of hope and skepticism. "Has the girl put her hooks into you too?"

"No. Well, yes she has, but that's not why I'm killing the story."

"Why, then?"

RC tried to figure out why he was pissing away his life's dream, not to mention walking away from fame, money, and sex with women who are turned on by winners.

He said, "There's people who would use the way your husband died to undo the good he did for the country."

Lonicera said, "I can give you a list of names."

RC tried to think of a way to word "doing the right thing" without sounding dorky. "A man deserves to be remembered for how he lived, not how he died." He paused to look into Lonicera's eyes to see if she bought it. "That's a dorky way to say it," he said.

She blinked away tears and said, "Truth is always dorky."

"You think so?"

Lonicera nodded. "Thank you."

He said, "Can you let yourself out? I'm going to be a while, sorting underwear."

As RC pushed Honey's carry-on bag through the half-door into the hiding place, he heard snuffled crying sounds coming from the back of the L.

Jimmy's voice was fairly whiny. "I said I was sorry. What more do you want?"

RC crawled on into the room while Honey said, "I want you to have some idea what you're sorry for."

"I'm apologizing. Isn't that enough?"

"It doesn't count if you don't know what you did."

"Hell, Honey, I never know what I'm apologizing for with you."

RC came around the corner to find Honey sitting on the unmade bed, twisting the double-wedding-band quilt on her lap, tears leaking down her cheeks. One particularly endearing tear perched along the top edge of her upper lip. Jimmy stood beside her, blinking in frustration.

"Hi, kids."

Jimmy saw RC and reverted to tough. "What do you want?"

RC ignored him and asked Honey, "Are you all right?"

Honey sniffed. "I'm dandy."

RC said, "You don't look dandy."

"I have a boyfriend with the sensitivity of a salad fork."

RC thought, *Salad fork?* He wasn't certain how to respond.

Jimmy did the lip-curl thing that he meant to come off as a snarl. "Did you get my cigarettes?"

"I forgot."

"You forgot? I don't believe this shit."

Although they all knew he wasn't sorry, RC said, "Sorry."

"I'll bet you remembered every little item on Honey's list, but *forgot* the one thing I asked for."

RC nodded, admitting the truth of Jimmy's bet. "Cigarettes are bad for you, Jimmy. And secondhand smoke is bad for me."

"Fuck secondhand smoke. It won't kill you half as fast as I will."

Honey's tears shut down like a turned-off hydrant. To RC, even her cheeks looked suddenly dry and flushed. She said, "Ever since he killed the President, Jimmy thinks he's Billy the Kid. Do this or I'll kill you, do that or I'll kill you. It's time to grow up, Jimmy. Recess is over."

For an instant, RC thought Jimmy was going to hit her, and he considered the appropriateness of leaping to her defense. She might be impressed, but then again, she might see it as belittling her ability to take care of herself. You never could tell with modern women. Besides which, Jimmy's gun had to be factored into the equation.

RC's train of thought came to nothing, however, when Jimmy said, "I'll get my own damn cigarettes."

Jimmy stomped across the room, expressing his rage by making as much noise as possible, and flung open the door. Then he stopped. A look of consummate slyness stole across his face, the obvious kind of consummate slyness, like when a dullard fancies himself as wily. Without leaving, he slammed the door shut.

Jimmy froze, waiting.

Before long, Honey's voice came from the back of the L. *"Hmm, that feels good."*

Jimmy's mouth twitched and his hand drifted to his revolver.

"I thought he'd never leave," Honey said.

"What'd he do to make you cry?" RC asked.

"I don't know. If he pushes me on it, I'll think of something."

Jimmy's eyes narrowed.

Honey said, "Did you bring my birth control pills?"

Jimmy heard the zip of the carry-on bag being opened.

"The moment we're together, I'm throwing these away," Honey said.

"It can't happen till you've gotten rid of the bagman," RC said. "I don't believe in overlap."

"Oh, RC, I love it when you're noble."

Jimmy quietly unzipped the workout bag, then, holding his hands to muffle the clicks, he spun the combination lock on the attaché case and opened it. Quickly and silently, he transferred the $656,000 and change from the case to the bag.

"You think he'll shoot us when he finds out?" RC asked.

Honey's voice was silky. "Don't you worry about Jimmy-poo. He's all bark until I tell him to bite."

Jimmy closed the attaché case and spun the lock. He zipped the workout bag shut with the money it. Bag in hand, he knelt before the outer door and opened it without a sound, then slipped through and out.

Stonewall Jackson and Parker Swindell parked at the head of the concessionaires' tunnel and spread blueprints of FedEx Field across the hood of their Crown Victoria, holding down the corners with bottles of Gatorade.

"So who hid the body?" Parker asked.

"We think it was Jimmy Sebastiano. He and Ivan Greene both work for Rat's Ass Olivetti."

"But I thought Ivan acted alone."

"We're not certain of anything."

The task of finding the body was made even more difficult than it should have been because Parker thought they were looking for Turk Johansen, who had supposedly been guarding the door the assassin came through and had since disappeared, and Stonewall couldn't tell him any different. As a rule, the two were at the same point on the need-to-know scale, so Stonewall was embarrassed that he couldn't answer Parker's questions.

"Sebastiano could have a tank hidden down on that third level, and it would take a week to find it," Parker said. "We need at least a hundred agents for a proper search."

Stonewall said, "All we have is two. We're it."

"You guys looking for me?" Jimmy Sebastiano emerged from the tunnel, a sneer on his face and a workout bag in his right hand.

"You're under arrest," Parker said.

Jimmy said, "Fat chance."

Parker looked to Stonewall for guidance. Stonewall said, "Off the top of my head, I can think of seven felony charges we can hold you on."

"You still want Hot Dick's body, right?"

Neither agent said anything.

Jimmy went on. "You bust me and you'll never see it again."

"Last time you promised to deliver, we ended up with Bullwinkle," Stonewall said.

"I'll give up the real thing this time, but I want a new deal."

Stonewall turned to Parker. "I need to talk to Jimmy, alone."

Parker said, "Turk was one of us. We can't let this prick talk about one of us like that."

"There's complications," Stonewall said. "Let's take a walk, Jimmy."

Before he and Stonewall left, Jimmy gave Parker his best smirk. "If they told you the truth, they'd have to kill you. But they can't kill me. How does that make you feel?"

Stonewall said, "Jimmy."

Parker stayed by the car, guarding the blueprints and trying to figure how Bullwinkle fit into the puzzle, while Jimmy and Stonewall walked around the outer wall of the stadium. There was a lot of trash lying around because everyone had been so shocked by the assassination and the cancellation of the second half that no one bothered to clean up. They'd all gone home to watch TV.

Stonewall stepped over a package of cold weenies and said, "What's in the bag?"

Jimmy hefted the workout bag. "Nothing to do with you."

"I have to look."

Jimmy considered putting up a fuss, but it seemed a battle he wouldn't win. Besides, the agent should be aware of the kind of man he was dealing with.

"There's no head in the bag," Jimmy said.

"Smells like there has been, recently."

Jimmy shrugged and gave the bag to Stonewall, who opened it and looked inside. He ran his hand through the piles of money, making certain nothing was hidden on the bottom, then zipped the bag shut and handed it back.

Stonewall said, "This is why Rat's Ass sent Ivan Greene after you."

"That's none of your beeswax."

Stonewall nodded and looked back at Parker, who was waiting by the car. It would be so simple to put a bullet through Jimmy's skull. God knows, the little fucker deserved it. But Weathers said they couldn't kill him until they had recovered at least part of Charles Franklin, for the DNA if nothing else. Chip's blue-ribbon commission of unimpeachable men and women needed evidence. Not everything could be faked.

"So what's wrong with RC's deal?" Stonewall asked.

"It stinks. RC stinks. You tell that boss of yours that Jimmy Sebastiano is calling the shots now. Tell him, to start with, I demand another passport. None of this Mohammed Das shit."

"Would you rather be Sherwin Das? He's Mohammed's brother and we have the passport."

Jimmy thought. "Jimmy Mussolini has a nice sound to it. Tell your boss to make me Jimmy Mussolini. And tell him Honey will need a ride at eight, not nine. RC and I will come along later."

"You have alternate transportation?"

"Don't be snotty with me. I'll be arranging for the delivery of your precious dead guy." Jimmy turned to storm away in a righteous fit and stepped on a Redskins doll, the kind with a big helmet and eyes that joggle when you put it on the rear deck of your car. He stopped and turned back to Stonewall. "And New Zealand is for fags. I want a country that's warm, where the slashes run around naked, and they don't sell three-point beer."

"You're asking a lot of your government, Jimmy."

"What'd I tell you about being snotty? I know your dirty secrets, so you'd best show me respect."

Once again Stonewall considered the bullet-in-the-skull option and once again he had to pass it up. "Name a country, Jimmy. I'll see what I can do."

Jimmy had recently seen a show on the Travel Channel called *The Top Ten Beaches of the World,* and the narrator said number one featured hot girls and cold beer.

Jimmy said, "Hawaii."

Stonewall was stunned. Two of his colleagues were dead, the American government had been turned upside down, millions of people were in grief—basically nothing was as it had been before yesterday—and the bozo who caused it all thought Hawaii was a foreign country.

Stonewall said, "Jimmy—"

Jimmy said, "Don't fuck with me."

Stonewall decided not to press the point. It couldn't hurt to have Jimmy thinking escape was impossible without a passport.

"How many tickets do you want?" Stonewall asked. "Two or three?"

Jimmy did the sly look again. He was getting so tricky he was starting to impress himself. He said, "One."

Chip found Lonicera in the gifts-and-photographs room, smashing Nancy Reagan's tea set. Her weapon of choice was a Ping sand wedge given to Charles by the president of Mexico. The Mexican president had given Charles only the sand wedge, not an entire set, which meant the Ping didn't match the rest of Charles's clubs, so he threw it in here alongside the hundreds of other gifts given to the First Couple.

"There are some nervous people out in the hallway," Chip said.

"They should be nervous," Lonicera said. "I am a dangerous woman with nothing to lose."

The sand wedge worked well for Lonicera's needs. Her technique was to line six or seven cups on the reclining totem pole Charles got from the Inuits and quickly chop them overhand, like splitting kindling.

*Whack, whack, whack.*

Chip sat on a twenty-pound cheese wheel from God-knows-where and shielded his eyes from flying china shards as Lonicera chopped her way up the totem pole.

"Who are those people?" Chip asked. "They wouldn't let me come in until I reminded them I'm the President and can go where

I want." Chip looked sad. "You'd think I wouldn't have to tell them who I am."

Lonicera's anger ran out all at once. She dropped the sand wedge on a Popsicle-stick replica of the Jefferson Memorial made by physically challenged middle school students in Baltimore, and sat down hard on a case of self-published patriotic poetry donated by Faith Baptist Church in Clovis, New Mexico.

She said, "My social secretary is out there, and a publicist, and the Secret Service. There's a woman from the protocol office whose job it is to keep me from moving furniture or cracking one of Jackie Kennedy's precious snow globes. She's the one having the anxiety attack over Nancy's teacups."

"I didn't know Jackie collected snow globes."

"East Wing basement. There's a closet full of Jackie's things I'm not allowed to touch." She picked up the surviving teacup and gently knocked the handle off on an elkhorn love seat from Utah.

Lonicera stared at the broken cup in her hand while Chip stared at the love seat, trying to figure out how you were supposed to sit in it. Lonicera considered the political consequences of taking her sand wedge to Jackie's closet; Chip wondered where he was supposed to sleep tonight.

"I heard you're moving to the Four Seasons," he said.

"Only through the funeral, then I'm out of here."

"You don't have to leave so soon."

"I can't wait to get out of this ant farm."

Chip said, "There must be something fun about it. You and Charles worked awfully hard to get here."

Lonicera tried to think of a way to explain to Chip what he was in for. It seemed amazing to her, the lengths to which men would go to find themselves in hell.

"You want an example of what it's like?" she said. "As far as the country knows, Charles has only been dead four hours, and *USA Today* already has an opinion poll on their website where you can vote for what shoes I should wear to the funeral." Her voice caught. "It's nobody's business what shoes I wear to my husband's funeral."

Chip said, "This cremation thing may cause riots. Twenty years from now Oliver Stone will claim it proves Charles didn't die."

Lonicera laughed, bitterly. She said, "Fuck him if he can't take a joke."

Chip laughed also, only his was an actual laugh based on a sense of humor. "Hell, go barefoot to the funeral if you want to. I'll back you up."

Lonicera giggled. She knew her mood swings were out of control, but it had been a bad day. "Claude Hammer would have an aneurysm."

"You say that like it's a bad thing."

"Speaking of Claude Hammer." Lonicera tried to get up, but instead lurched into a moth-eaten stuffed flamingo. Even though she hadn't had a drink all day, she felt drunk. Her coordination was shot and she felt capable of saying absolutely anything.

What she said was, "Charles left you a present."

Chip watched as Lonicera rummaged through a crate jammed full of photographs of Charles Franklin standing beside movie stars. When she couldn't find what she was looking for, she began yanking out photos with both hands and sailing them across the room.

"That Hollywood bunch and Charles had their tongues up each other's butts so high it's a miracle they didn't choke," Lonicera said.

"That's because he's a Democrat," Chip said. "Actors and actresses are hot for Democrats."

"Yeah, well, I don't see you dating teenage starlets," which embarrassed Chip because now that he was president, starlets, teenage and otherwise, were high on his to-do list. It'd been a long time since there'd been a bachelor president. No one could convene a grand jury over his getting laid.

Lonicera pulled out a manila envelope and tossed it over to Chip. She said, "Merry Christmas."

He picked it up off the floor. It was heavy enough to contain a couple hundred pages. The flap was held down by a string looped around a button. "What is it?"

"Charles called it his insurance file. It's a list of every felony Claude Hammer's committed in forty-five years of government sleaze."

Chip unwound the string, opened the envelope, and leafed through the top twenty pages. He felt a glow in his chest, like back in college on the Malibu beach when a volleyball floated up there above the net like a big old moon, just waiting for him to slam it down an opponent's throat.

He breathed the most eloquent words he could come up with. "Oh, boy."

Lonicera smiled. "That's right."

Chip stood up and crossed over bits of broken china to hug Lonicera. "You ever want to be First Lady again, give me a call."

Lonicera said, "I'd rather be burned at the stake."

The hug lasted several seconds, until they were both dewy-eyed from emotion. Lonicera said, "Don't forget Tahiti."

"The present ambassador doesn't know it, but he's on his way to Chad."

"Thank you."

They broke the hug. Chip said, "See you around."

Lonicera said, "I hope not."

Claude Hammer typed an e-mail to his wife:

Crystal,

A powerful attraction sprang to life many, many years ago between myself and Lonicera Jane Franklin, but circumstances and honor have forced us to place the well-being of the nation over our own desires. As of today, circumstances have changed to the point where we can no longer deny the flames that rage between us. My silence has ended. Lonicera Franklin and I are in love!!!

I am certain you will understand, Crystal. You and I married for convenience to save hotel expenses in New Hampshire during the '84 primaries (I trust you knew that was our motive even though it has remained unspoken) and we have had many acceptable years during which we raised two girls to womanhood and you were a helpmate in my career. No one could fault you as a hostess.

Since the girls are out on their own now, the time has come for us to seek our own bliss. We must admit that although we tried, our life together is a cruel joke. We must free ourselves from this awful burden. I know you will want Lonicera and I to be unfettered as the two of us guide our grateful nation through the troubling days upon which we are about to embark. With your prayers, I feel Lonicera and I can lead America.

You may have the house of course. All I want is to keep the Lexus and my collection of classic jazz recordings.

Farewell, Crystal. I wish you good fortune wherever the future may take you and I know in my heart that you wish Lonicera and myself the same.

Sincerely,
Claude

Claude reread the message and added a comma before "of course" and one more exclamation point after "love!!!" He changed "Sincerely" to "With warm regards." Then he clicked Send.

A few seconds later a sign came on the monitor announcing: *Message sent.* Claude leaned back in his chair and closed his eyes. After all the years of hesitancy, he had taken action. There was no going back.

Claude's intercom buzzed and his secretary's voice came from the oval black box on his desk. "The President's press secretary just called."

"Dead president or live?"

"Live. The President says you should meet him in the Capitol Rotunda."

"Tell the President's press secretary to tell the President I'm busy."

"Too late. He already hung up."

The kid working the checkout line at Target had a shaved head and a spiderweb tattoo peeking out from under the short sleeve of his red Target smock. He had a Mepps spinner dangling from the top flap of his right ear, and he mumbled when he told the customer in front of Jimmy to run his debit card through the machine. Jimmy considered the kid a total punk, and himself old and sophisticated by comparison. Jimmy thanked his mother's God he had come through the teen experience five years ago, when Italian boys still took pride in their appearance, even if the black-leather thing looked like a uniform to outsiders. It didn't occur to him that the bald kid with a lure on his ear might take pride in his appearance also.

The kid said, "Thank you for shopping at Target," to the customer who had paid by debit card, then he turned to Jimmy's basket. "Find everything okay?"

Jimmy said, "I can't believe you said thank you to that yuppie slimeball. You've got nothing to thank him for."

The yuppie slimeball gave Jimmy a hard look and left.

The checkout kid talked as he rang up Jimmy's two rolls of duct tape, package containing three pairs of pastel briefs, bottle of Vitalis hair tonic, toothbrush, Lionel Richie CD, and footlong flashlight. "I have to say 'Thank you for shopping at Target' or they'll fire me. You want batteries for this flashlight?"

"No, I don't want batteries."

The kid hit Subtotal. "Anything else?"

"A box of Swisher Sweet Cigarillos."

"Do we sell those?"

"There at the bottom of your cigarette rack, below the GPCs."

The kid studied a rack that stood below a sign reading, "No sales to anyone under eighteen." He said, "I never sold a pack of these before."

He slid the box across the counter to Jimmy, then hit the Total button. "That'll be twenty-eight sixty-four."

Jimmy drew his revolver from his jacket pocket and set it on the counter beside the cigarillos with the barrel pointed at the checker. He said, "No it won't."

The checker said, "You're joking, right?"

Jimmy said, "I'm serious as castration."

The checker said, "Look at the surveillance camera."

Jimmy looked at the surveillance camera. There was a little red light under and to the right of the lens, indicating that it was on.

The checker said, "Look at all these people around here."

Jimmy looked up and down the checkout counters, where people were moving in and out, bagging merchandise, waiting for price checks, trying to keep rugrats from standing in the cart. No one had noticed the robbery taking place at register 6.

Jimmy's checker said, "You don't know the first thing about robbing stores."

Jimmy said, "Don't tell me how to rob a store. I was robbing stores when you were shooting water wads in your mama's bathroom."

"Yeah, well, you're terrible at it. If I was an employee who gives a shit I'd just yell out and you'd be screwed."

"You'd be shot."

"Like what kind of dumbass risks a murder charge for twenty-eight dollars in duct tape and cigarillos?"

The kid had a point. "Okay," Jimmy said. "You're right. Empty the register."

Jimmy unzipped the workout bag and stuffed in his would-be purchases as the checker sullenly shoved cash across the counter.

Jimmy said, "Punk."

The kid said, "Amateur."

Jimmy zipped the bag shut. "Now thank me for shopping at Target."

The kid said, "Stick it up your ass."

"That ceiling is a trip," President Allworth said, leaning way back with his arms crossed over the briefcase clasped against his chest to stare up at the inner dome and canopy over the Capitol Rotunda. He felt like the guy in *High Anxiety* falling forever backward into a pinwheel. "I'll bet high school kids travel from all over the United States just to take LSD in this room."

Jonathan Weathers didn't bother to look at the ceiling. He'd seen the Rotunda thousands of times, and to him, it was nothing but a security situation.

"We'll bring the public in the west doors, two lines, four abreast in each line," he said. "They'll file by on either side of the casket, then exit by those doors over there. The Marine Guard is there, networks there, cable news there. My men will be posted every ten feet in case one of the mourners does something to slow down the line."

The ceiling seemed to be breathing. Chip said, "Far out."

Jonathan said, "Sir?"

"And who's in the casket?"

Jonathan shifted, uncomfortably. A real president wouldn't ask questions with answers he might have to lie about later. He said, "You don't want to know."

"I don't?"

"No, sir."

"Well, how many people did you have to threaten and bribe to get whatever's in the casket in there?"

"As I said before—"

Chip nodded. "I don't want to know."

Actually, Turk Johansen was in the casket, still wearing his mask, and an embalmer and coroner were now nervous millionaires, nervous because they'd been told if the secret ever got out, their wives and children would be chopped up and used as food in the condor release program at Vermilion Cliffs, Arizona.

"We'll let the press access the building at twenty-three hundred hours," Jonathan said.

"That's eleven?"

"And we'll start moving the public at midnight. They're already lined up a half-mile out there."

Chip saw Claude Hammer entering from the Senate wing. Claude was walking fast, not even looking at the preparations for the lying-in-state. His mouth was prissy-pursed, like a man on a mission.

"You mind if I talk to Claude alone?" Chip asked. "We've got some business to attend to."

Jonathan said, "Yes, Mr. President," and before Chip could decide whether he was being sarcastic or not, he'd moved away to consult with the electricians. As Jonathan and Claude passed each other, they both gave a quarter-inch nod, like gunslingers acknowledging each other without actually admitting a kinship.

Claude didn't stand on ceremony. He said, "You better have one hell of a good reason for bothering me."

Chip said, "You think I should take up golf, Claude? I mean, fishing is vice-presidential, but as I read history, presidents play golf."

Claude fought his basic, violent impulses. "Get this straight," he said. "You do not call my office and demand an appearance. I do not serve at your pleasure."

"Let's go for a walk. You need to see America."

Without waiting for Claude to say anything nasty, Chip strode toward the west doors. Claude followed, fuming. Various Secret Servicemen chattered into their sleeves and spread out before and after them.

The outside air refreshed Chip like a cool, damp cloth laid on a feverish forehead. The sun was setting over in Virginia; the birds were flitting; the leaves were turning. Most of the year, Chip longed for Malibu, but he had to admit, fall in Washington was okay.

The crowd stretched off toward the Botanic Garden, as Jonathan had said. District police officers had them eight to a row, waiting to split into two lines as they moved through the doors. To Chip, they generally appeared stunned, their faces showing that slack blankness you see on people in coach class on a long flight. Some wept, although not loudly. No one was showing off. A black woman met his eyes, angrily. A guy in a New York Giants sweatshirt nudged his friend and nodded over at Chip, but for the most part, this crowd was here for a dead president, not a live one.

Claude said, "Don't these people have lives?"

Chip made up his mind. Until now, he hadn't decided what to do about Claude Hammer. Charles had told him that he kept Claude around because a pit bull is a good dog if he's on your side. You just have to be careful not to move quickly when he's hungry. But this pit bull was not on Chip's side. And God knows, Claude was hungry.

Like all politicians, Chip communicated his deepest feelings through the sports metaphor. He said, "Today is the start of a new

season here, Claude, and it's not good to have negative energy gum-
ming up the team. I want to be surrounded by positive players who
believe in America and the nobility of her people."

"Did you bring me out here to rehearse tomorrow's speech?"

They passed a young Hispanic woman with a baby in her arms.
Her dark hair was parted in the middle, and she had excellent posture for a person standing in a line that wasn't going to move for
hours. Chip loved her on sight, and the warmth of his love spread
to everyone waiting to pay respects to Charles. He thought, The
leaders may be fucked, but the people are still cool.

Chip said, "I brought you here to fire you."

Claude said, "Get real, Chip."

"I am real. You're out of here."

Claude said, "You can't fire me, you drug-addled surfer boy."

"Volleyball."

"What?"

"I was never much of a surfer. I'm a drug-addled volleyball player,
and I can fire you. It's in the Constitution. I can fire anyone except
for those old geezers on the Supreme Court." Chip grinned at
Claude. "You thought I didn't know about the Constitution. I know
a lot more about running the government than most people think."

Claude's jaws popped in and out. He appeared to be grind-
ing his teeth, setting himself up for a painful case of TMJ. "Okay,
smartass, the prime goes down, unemployment goes up, and con-
sumable goods stay soft. What do you do?"

Chip said, "Search me."

"Who do you lean on if an American tourist is kidnapped in
Kota Bhuru?"

"That's in Tibet, right?"

"Wrong. What button do you push to force the junior senator
from Oregon to vote for a bill he hates?"

"I wouldn't want to force a senator to vote for a bill he doesn't want to vote for."

Claude said, "I run the country. You charm foreign diplomats and host gala affairs at the Kennedy Center. You light the goddamn Christmas tree, but I run the country."

As Claude wound himself up, his fleshy face seemed to puff up and pass through various shades of purple. Chip found the effect interesting. Claude didn't speak again until he reached the color of a salad-bar beet.

He said, "And if you fight me, I will personally ship you to drug rehab on national TV. Do you understand the implications?"

"Why, Claude, you're blackmailing the President."

Claude said, "It's called leverage. This nation runs on leverage, and I've got it. You don't."

They were almost to the Grant Memorial, which is a huge statue of a famous substance-abuser on a horse. The irony was not lost on Chip. "You think so? I value your opinion, Claude, but this once, I think you're wrong." He opened his briefcase and pulled out the manila envelope with the string holding down the flap. "My leverage beats your leverage."

Without a word, Claude tore open the envelope and started riffling pages. Chip was fascinated by Claude's face, not just the color, which drained from hard-on violet to anemic-nun white, but Claude's cheeks and mouth seemed to shape-shift before Chip's eyes, like a plastic toy in a campfire.

Chip said, "You lose."

"Where did you get this?"

"Lonicera Franklin gave it to me." Chip gently pried the envelope from Claude's fingers. "Boy, does that woman hate you. What did you ever do to piss her off so much?"

Claude said, "But Lonicera loves me. We're going to be married."

"I don't think so." Chip stuffed the envelope back into his brief-case and snapped the clasps shut. "You have ten minutes to vacate federal property. I won't insult you with threats as to what will hap-pen if you open your fat mouth about Charles's death or anything else you've learned on the job. I'm not the kind of guy who insults others. That would be negative."

Claude's cell phone buzzed. As if in a trance, he took it from his belt holster, checked caller ID, and pushed the on button.

He said, "Hello, Crystal."

Chip wandered on to the Reflecting Pool, which reflected a nice, bruise-colored sunset. At the end of the movie *Being There,* Peter Sellers walks across the surface of this pool, like Jesus with the fishing guys, or it might have been the other Reflecting Pool, down by the Lincoln Memorial. Chip wasn't sure which, because he'd seen the movie a long time ago, but that scene had made an impression on him. It came right after the powerful movers and shakers decided to make Peter Sellers president. He played a learning-disabled gardener who was so honest and simple it didn't matter that he was stupid. That was the movie that inspired Chip to go into politics.

"Excuse me, Mr. President."

Chip looked up from his reflected-sunset musings to see he was being addressed by a man with a yellow wire coiling out of his ear.

"You're Secret Service," Chip said. "I don't think I've seen you before."

"Stonewall Jackson. I generally serve the president."

"Which is me now. Do you think I should take up golf?"

With no hesitation, Stonewall said, "No, sir."

"Why not?"

"It's not your style. You're more the pickup-basketball-games-with-the-press-corps type."

Stonewall was right, of course. Chip wasn't golf material. He'd only considered it because he liked the image of himself in Ban-Lon. "Is Stonewall a nickname?"

"I'm afraid not, but it beats the alternative. Mom wanted to name me Buffalo Bill."

"Chip is a nickname. I'm really Graham."

"May I show you something?" Stonewall reached into his pants pocket and pulled out the incisor. "I was one of the two covering Charles Franklin Friday night."

He dropped the incisor into Chip's palm. Chip leaned over to study it in the failing light, then glanced up at Stonewall.

"This came from Charles?"

Stonewall nodded.

Chip bounced the tooth up and over onto its side. "How do you think he got the root white?"

"I don't know that one."

Chip made an O out of his thumb and index finger, with the tooth filling the gap between his fingertips. By closing one eye and peering through the center of the O, he could see the Washington Monument.

"And why do you have Charles's tooth in your pocket?"

Stonewall ran his hand across his forehead and tugged at his right ear. To Chip, he seemed uncomfortable about broaching a sensitive subject. Stonewall said, "I'm not sure if you know how American government works, sir—"

"Why does everyone think that?"

"But when a person knows a secret that could bring catastrophe to whichever party is in power, that person is traditionally either

killed or advanced to a position where it is in his best interests to
stay quiet."

Chip lowered his fingers. "I have no intention of killing you,
Stonewall."

"That is a comfort to hear, but there are others, like Jonathan
Weathers or Claude Hammer, who feel saving themselves from
embarrassment is worth a certain number of casualties. My partner
from that night is already dead."

"Claude Hammer is no longer on the team. He won't hurt you."

This was good news to Stonewall. He'd been more worried
about Claude than Jonathan. Jonathan had lost two agents this
week, and it would look bad to lose yet another one.

Chip rolled the tooth between his fingers, surprised at how
smooth it felt. He didn't think his own teeth were that smooth.

He said, "And Charles's tooth?"

"I have two more in a safe place."

Chip looked back into the Reflecting Pool. The sun had almost
set, and now he could see streetlights shining off the water. Maybe
Lonicera was right. Maybe being president wasn't as much fun as
he'd imagined.

"I've only been president one afternoon, and you're the second
person to blackmail me."

Stonewall's discomfort level shot way up. "I don't mean it as
blackmail, certainly not against you. It's more like insurance to
keep people who work for you from wiping me out."

"Death avoidance?" Chip said.

"Blackmail is when you try to force a person to give you something against his will. I just want to stay alive. I'm sure it's different."

Chip supposed it was different. He supposed he would do the
same thing himself if people were out to kill him. "So what do you
have in mind for advancement?"

"That would be up to you. I would be happy promising to keep my mouth shut and retiring to South Dakota, but I don't think that would satisfy Jonathan. He would see me as a loose end."

"Here's what I don't understand," Chip said. "Was Charles down on the girl, or was the girl down on him, or were they sixty-nining?"

"I believe they took turns, with her doing him first."

Chip nodded, trying to set the picture in his head. "You were right about the golf thing. How'd you like to be my chief of staff?"

"Isn't that Claude's job?"

"Claude's gone. Forget Claude. I have a kick-ass press secretary, and there's a man named Boots I'm thinking to appoint national security advisor, but I need a chief of staff I can trust. Claude was not trustworthy."

Stonewall thought about his Airstream back in Spearfish, and what it would be like to wake up and make coffee knowing he didn't have to speak to a single person all day. He thought about peeing off his porch, about throwing away his TV, cell phones, and razors.

He said, "Shit."

"You'll do it, then?"

"I guess so. How long can you last as president, anyway?"

"Can you start now?"

"I have to work the assassination follow-up tonight. Since I'm the only agent who knows what happened, I have to be the contact with the fugitives."

"Would you do me a favor first? There's a woman back in the viewing line—Spanish girl with a baby—and I'd like to talk to her, only I don't want her thinking I'm taking advantage of me being president and her being a member of a minority and all."

Stonewall couldn't help wondering whether all presidents were pussy hounds before they became president or if something about the job caused satyriasis. At least Chip wasn't as bad as Franklin, and, even if he did get lucky and score, someone else would have to wait outside in the car. Stonewall could live with it.

"Plus I don't want her to lose her place in line, and I can't see wading into that bunch of sad people. They'll think I'm hitting on her, which I'm not."

"I'll see what I can do."

"Thanks, Stonewall. I think this will work. You and I have a positive compatibility quotient."

"I'm certain we do."

From across the south parking lot, Jimmy watched RC and Farlow carry the green trunk toward Farlow's SUV. RC was struggling some because of the way Farlow walked in his knee brace, kind of up and down with a hitch at the top of up. Jimmy saw that they could use an extra hand, but decided he wasn't the one to give it. Instead, he entered FedEx Field and dropped down into the third-level basement, where he found Honey trying to figure out how hair extensions are supposed to attach to hair. The ad on TV said it was simple with the easy-press snap-lock combs—"No heating or messy glues. Do it yourself in minutes." The easy-press snap locks were easy enough, but the combs made her head lumpy.

Jimmy feigned ignorance. "Where's your boyfriend?"

At least gay men have lots of mirrors. Honey had one in front and one behind her head, but she wasn't used to working that way and she didn't feel competent. Her voice was snappish.

"Are you being snide about Farlow or RC?"

"Either one, I guess. You guys should do a three-way. Farlow probably has the hots for RC, same as you."

This startled Honey, because earlier she had been entertaining herself with a delightful fantasy of a three-way with Farlow and RC.

She had been drawing mental pictures of who would be doing what to whom. Her pictures were a bit vague where Farlow and RC were concerned—she wasn't familiar with homosexual positions, other than the basics—but they were quite specific when it came to her own pleasure. Whenever a male suggests a three-way, he invariably means two girls and him, which didn't much interest Honey. The gay male–straight male–girl combination made more sense. Everyone would find something of interest, like a fun version of rock-paper-scissors.

"They took the trunk to Farlow's big Beemer," she said. "He's going to drive it out to Dulles, then wait around awhile and drop it off in the lost-luggage room. Farlow's so sleepy he's talking like a dope. Says he's checking into a hotel and not coming out till I'm on a new continent."

"So is RC coming back?"

"After he finds an ATM. He's worried about getting to New Zealand with no money." She glanced at the attaché case on the floor and crinkled her nose. "And he was going to buy your basic toiletries for the road."

"That's what I did," Jimmy said, opening his workout bag to show her the three pairs of briefs and the toothbrush. He pulled the toothbrush out. "The Target store got robbed while I was there."

Jimmy knew from experience lying to Honey was easier if she couldn't see him, so he moved to the back of the L, where she had set up a primping area. The sink station was a gallon jug of water, a wineglass, and a Betty Manygoats Navajo bowl for spitting.

He tore the plastic off his new toothbrush. "I ran into that Secret Service agent outside. The one who was there when I killed Sleet."

Honey's voice came from the other room. "You didn't kill Sleet, Jimmy. I did."

"Whatever. They're sending a limo for you at eight, then they want me and RC to come at nine. Seems some TV reporters have the airport staked out and they have our descriptions. The Secret Service guy doesn't want us to get there together."

He put Rembrandt on his toothbrush and waited for Honey's reaction. This was when she either called bullshit or bought the gig.

She said, "That doesn't make sense."

"Does to me. They're worried about you bragging about the President tonguing you."

"I never brag about that stuff. That's why men trust me."

Loaded toothbrush in hand, Jimmy returned to the front room. He said, "Tell that to the Secret Service."

Honey just about had the snap locks figured out. Without looking up from her mirror, she said, "I think you're trying to ditch me. I'll go out to the airport and you'll never show up."

Jimmy did his hurt-child impersonation. "You're my girl. I wouldn't ditch you."

Now she did look at him. "Jimmy, I know you. Don't treat me like I'm stupid."

Jimmy pointed the toothbrush at Honey. "Nothing short of death will ever keep us apart." It came across as more threat than commitment. "Tell you what," Jimmy said. With his foot, he pushed the attaché case in her direction. "You take the money. If I don't show up, you and RC split the six hundred fifty thousand."

Honey eyed the case. "It's locked."

"Of course it's locked. But I'll just bet you two can find a way to open it, once you're in New Zealand."

Honey looked dubious.

Jimmy said, "You're right, Honey. You know me better than anyone else does. Am I the kind of guy who walks away from money?"

She considered the question. Jimmy would abandon her in a heartbeat, but he wasn't likely to abandon this much cash.

"I guess not."

"Okay, then. Finish making yourself pretty. You've got a limo to catch."

Honey had never ridden in a limousine before. Although one of her daddy's golf buddies who was always trying to get her on his lap had a Lincoln Continental, which was big inside, the car Stonewall drove her to the airport in was much bigger. There were two seats facing each other in back, with enough leg room between them for a twin bed, should anyone want to put a twin bed in a car.

At first Honey played with the console buttons that controlled the TV and the DVD player and made a bar pop in and out of the wall. There was a sound system that made Jimmy's at the apartment look chintzy. But soon she felt Stonewall's eyes on her in the rearview mirror and she moved up to the front backseat so she could talk to him if she could think of something interesting to say.

Stonewall said, "Your hair looks different, since the tunnel."

Honey said, "I brushed it out. What do you think?"

"It seems longer."

They were driving along a boulevard in Cheverly that could have been lifted up and plunked down in any city in America—franchise restaurants, barbershops and office supply stores, clusters of doctors' offices, a beauty college: businesses of absolutely no interest to Honey. She had a fantasy where someone from Odessa Permian saw her in the limo and went back home and told everyone, but that wasn't likely, because she was probably the first person from Odessa to ever ride down this street, and besides, the side window was so dark she'd have to find an excuse to roll it down before anyone could recognize her.

"Will you pull into that Popeye's up there?" she asked Stonewall. "I haven't eaten since I killed that Mafia guy."

A policeman was directing traffic in the center of the intersection where they turned into a mall with a Popeye's Chicken in the parking lot, and when they went past, Honey saw tears running down the policeman's face.

She said, "The policeman is crying."

Stonewall met her eyes in the mirror. She was twisted around so she could see out the front. "I imagine he's unhappy about the President being dead," Stonewall said.

He stopped at the drive-up order speaker, and Honey rolled down her window to order two pieces of dark meat and a large onion rings. She hadn't thought about how the President's being dead would affect strangers who didn't know her or him personally. It dawned on her that people all over the country were probably upset. As they pulled around to the window where you pick up the food, she said, "It wasn't my fault."

Stonewall was digging for his billfold to pay cash for the order. "What's not your fault?"

"That Charles is dead. If he hadn't of run, Jimmy wouldn't have hurt him, at least not much. He should have stayed and fought for me." She tried to remember exactly what had happened. It was only the night before last, but a lot had gone on since then. "Charles didn't have pants on," she said. "I've been in similar places before, and the guy with his penis out is generally intimidated by the guy with pants on."

Stonewall paid and got the food. He turned to pass it back through the open privacy panel. "I read your diary."

When Honey bit into her first onion ring, two inches of onion strand pulled free of the breading and drooped down her chin. "You did?"

"It was between the mattress and box springs."

"What kind of person reads another person's private diary?"

Stonewall's feelings were hurt. "It's my job. The President was missing and I had to explore every clue. If the President hadn't disappeared, I wouldn't have read it."

Honey sucked in the onion like a kid slurping spaghetti. "I guess it's okay, then, if you had to."

Stonewall watched her take a huge bite of chicken. She seemed to enjoy it thoroughly. "Did you really do those things that were in the diary?" he asked.

"Which things?"

"You know, like the time in the Smithsonian basement, in the room where they keep the Indian bones?"

"Oh, that." Honey's face did a cute remembrance thing. "The janitor told me he was seventy-three and a virgin. He was so sad. He said he didn't want to die a virgin. He even made a funny joke about being laid in his grave."

"He might have been lying."

Honey stopped, her lips poised over another onion ring. "I don't think so. After I blew him, he thought he'd lost his virginity, and I didn't have the heart to tell him different."

She studied the onion ring carefully. "Here's the part that amazes me. If a married man gets blown by a virgin, he's committed adultery but the girl who blew him hasn't lost her virginity. He's had sex but she hasn't. Doesn't that sound like a double standard?"

Stonewall said, "I've never been married."

Honey said, "Can I ride up front? Talking through a window feels weird."

Later, as they were driving on the Beltway, Honey said, "I think Jimmy's planning to ditch me."

Stonewall said, "You'll be better off without him."

She hooked her hair behind her ear. "Why is that?"

"Besides the fact that he's a horse's ass?"

"Besides that."

He glanced over at her, then back at the freeway. Traffic was light. People were home, glued to their television sets. "My boss isn't about to let Jimmy live happily ever after. You can't kill a president, even accidentally, and expect no consequences. You'll be better off far away from Mr. Sebastiano."

"But what about RC?"

"What about RC?"

"If Jimmy ditches me, what's he going to do with RC?"

Stonewall considered the question for several miles. Personally, he didn't care what Jimmy did to RC Nash. RC could have brought this farce to an end yesterday, and Greg might still be alive. But Stonewall figured he should say something to reassure Honey, even if it was a lie. Out of everybody involved, she was the innocent party.

"Why don't you give me Farlow Stubbs's cell phone number. I can call and have him check on RC."

"I thought you Feds could get any number you want."

"I'd rather not go through official channels on this one. My boss isn't happy with RC."

Honey reached into her clutch for a scrap of paper on which to write Farlow's number. "You're a very nice man," she said. "I feel like I ought to repay you with a hand job or something."

What Jimmy banked on was RC's urinary tract. He figured RC would crawl through the door and head straight for the slop bucket before he even noticed Honey was missing, much less her carry-on bag and clutch. If RC realized Honey had cleared out, he might become wary, but the man didn't have the bladder to notice anything until it had been drained.

Which is exactly what happened. RC came in, said, "Hey, Jimmy," and practically ran for the back of the L. He pried the lid off the slop jar, unzipped, pulled himself out, started his flow, and only then said, "Where's Honey?"

Jimmy swung the footlong flashlight and clipped RC solidly at the base of his skull. Still clutching his penis and peeing, RC went down cold as a poleaxed pig.


He awoke sometime later wrapped in two rolls of duct tape. His legs were girdled from ankle to thigh, his arms from wrist to elbow. His mouth was sealed to the point where a stuffy nose would mean death. Every movable inch of RC—except his eyes and the thing hanging out, which Jimmy wouldn't touch—was cinched tight.

RC did the grunt-and-jerk maneuver that tightly bound people always seem to do in spite of the fact that it never helps. He rolled onto his back with his legs and arms stuck up in the air and saw Jimmy, standing by the bed, counting the five hundred dollars he'd taken from RC's pocket.

Jimmy said, "The Redskins are out of town the next few weeks, but Dallas comes in next month. I imagine Farlow and his lover boy will find you nice and ripe."

RC didn't attempt yelling through his taped-shut mouth. He knew that was useless. Instead, he expressed radical contempt—along the lines of "Fuck you, creep"—through his eyes.

Jimmy chuckled. He said, "That'll teach you to mess with my woman."

Then he left.

Jimmy took a taxi from the stadium to the airport, and he considered it an act of civic-mindedness on his part that he paid the seventy-five-dollar fare with money he'd taken off RC, instead of rolling the cab driver. The driver grumbled about the lack of a tip, which Jimmy saw as a sign of ingratitude.

Jimmy said, "Be happy you're still alive," but the driver didn't thank him for the favor.

He found Honey sitting in the passenger lounge area between the ticket counters and security, painting her toenails a new shade she'd found in one of the shops there. It was an oily kind of yellow, like the spots you see when you're fixing to pass out. She bought the color because it reminded her of her parents' bedspread from back when she was growing up. Painted on top of black, her toes came out somewhat like van Gogh's sunflowers. Van Gogh was Honey's favorite painter.

Jimmy sank into the seat next to hers and said, "This assassination shit is exhausting."

Honey looked across the lobby. "Where's RC?"

"He went home to pick up some papers. He'll join us on the plane."

Honey said, "I don't believe you."

"What? You think you're the only one with a life? He went home to pack. He's coming later."

Honey had just started on her left big toe when a pair of government-issue Florsheims appeared beside her foot.

Stonewall said, "They didn't have Mello Yello. Will Diet Pepsi be all right?"

Honey smiled as she accepted the can of soda pop. "Thank you, Mr. Jackson. You're sweet."

Jimmy said, "Jesus Christ, Honey. What is it with you and old farts?"

Stonewall said, "Come on, Jimmy. We need to have a conversation."

"So converse."

"It's not a subject you want discussed here."

Jimmy stood and reached for the workout bag, but Stonewall said, "Leave it. This'll only take a second."

Jimmy looked down at Honey, who was being careful with her brushstrokes. He knew that when Honey was working on her toes, nothing could break her concentration.

Jimmy said, "I'll be back. Don't leave without me."

She said, "Uh."

Stonewall walked off toward the foreign currency exchange booth, and Jimmy followed. The moment they rounded the corner next to a bank of pay phones, Jimmy said, "You got my ticket to Hawaii?"

Stonewall patted his breast pocket.

Jimmy said, "What about the passport?"

"My boss is bringing it. Where's the head?"

Jimmy shook a cigarillo from the box. "It's where you can't find it. Why isn't my passport here yet?"

"Because they don't grow on trees. And don't even think about lighting that."

Jimmy considered the value of pulling a power move to show who was in charge, but Stonewall had the dangerous aspect of a man looking for an excuse to pistol-whip.

Stonewall said, "We had a deal with RC. You give us the head before takeoff and call in the body location once you're in the air."

"RC didn't tell me about that part of the deal."

"Maybe he thought he was going to be here. Now, where's my head, Jimmy?"

Jimmy said, "Fuck you. RC's deal is gone. I'm the main charge now."

Stonewall grabbed Jimmy by the throat and threw him against a pay phone, one of those high-tech phones that take only credit cards and won't even fool with money. Stonewall said, "Listen, you punk. You screwed me before, and you're not leaving till I get my head. There's a bipartisan committee that needs DNA, and you're going to give it to them."

Jimmy choked through his compressed larynx. "Chill out, for Chrissake."

Stonewall relaxed his grip the least amount possible, just enough for Jimmy to gasp. He said, "Okay, if it's that important to you."

"It's that important to me, Jimmy."

"Wait here and I'll go get your precious head."

Stonewall released his hold on Jimmy's throat.

Jimmy straightened his cuffs and tucked in his shirttails, trying unsuccessfully to reclaim his dignity. He said, "But there better be a passport here when I get back."

What neither of them saw, down the line at a phone that did accept real coins, was Ace Columbus, digging through his pants pockets for a quarter.

Gino Olivetti hung up the phone, then immediately lifted the receiver and punched numbers. He said, "Bring the car."

As he hung up a second time, Louise said, "You're not going out, are you? It's our last night with Eldon."

"Ace spotted Jimmy out at Dulles."

Eldon had been lying on his back on the couch with his head in Louise's lap while she fed him popcorn like a mama bird feeding babies. He was wearing paisley jammies. Because of the assassination, he'd been allowed to break his mother's one-hour-a-day-of-TV rule.

He said, "I'm going with you."

Gino bent down to slip on his shoes. "Don't be a schmuck. You're going to bed."

Eldon sat up. "No, I'm not, Papaw. I'm going to the airport with you."

Gino ignored his grandson. He said to Louise, "Put the kid to bed. I'll be back in a couple hours."

Eldon made fists out of his hands, only they were little-boy fists, with the thumbs inside the fingers. "If you don't take me with you, I'll tell. I'll say Sleet was at the football game killing someone for you but he got mixed up and killed the President instead."

"That's not true," Louise said. She turned to Gino. "Is it?"

Gino spoke softly, which was a thing he did when he wanted to be menacing. "Who are you going to tell, Eldon?"

Eldon pointed to Tom Brokaw on the television screen. "Him." When his grandfather's expression didn't change, Eldon said, "And everybody else. I'll tell a policeman. I'll tell Mom."

Gino snarled, "You're not telling anyone anything."

"I will if you don't take me with you to the airport."

Taking the kid tonight wasn't so bad, but Gino saw this as the first in a series of demands. *Buy me a computer game or I'll tell. Buy me a motorcycle or I'll tell. Buy me a casino.* Once you give in to a blackmailer, the demands never cease.

Gino said, "You better watch yourself, sonny. I'm not too old to whack my own grandson."

Louise said, "Don't be ridiculous, Gino. You can't kill Eldie."

"Used to happen all the time when I was his age."

"Well, it doesn't happen now."

"If you whack me, Mom will know," Eldon said.

Gino said, "Hellfire." Here he was, the most powerful crime boss in the District, and he was being bluffed by a twelve-year-old. The world had gone to hell. Or maybe he was too old to cut it anymore. His ruthlessness had gone the way of his erection.

"Okay, but this is the only time you use that I'm-gonna-tell shit. I hear it again and you're floating facedown in the bay."

"I promise, Papaw," Eldon said. "It won't happen again."

Then he hopped off the couch and ran to change his jammies.

"You go on through security, I'll wait and see if RC shows up," Honey said when Jimmy came back from his walk with Stonewall Jackson. "Besides, my toes need to dry."

Jimmy checked out the line of dull-eyed travelers waiting to pass through security and into the Dulles concourses. The line wasn't long at this time of night, but it was slow. The guards seemed to be making every other person through take off their shoes.

"These X-ray guys aren't going to understand my piece."

Honey kind of shrieked. "You're still carrying a gun!"

Jimmy said, "*Shhh.*"

"What kind of an idiot brings a *gun* to the airport?"

A couple of businessmen glanced at Honey and Jimmy and moved quickly away. A follower of Reverend Moon who had been about to hit them for a love donation decided against it. He decided to hang out at the cinnamon-roll stall instead.

Jimmy said, "You're right. I'll go get rid of it." He picked up the workout bag. "If I'm not back by the time the plane boards, you go through security without me. I'll catch up."

Honey blew on her toenails. "Is this when you ditch me?"

"Hell, I'm not going to ditch you. You've still got the money, right?"

Jimmy took off past the Saudi Arabian Airlines ticket counter with Parker Swindell hot on his trail. Parker had orders not to lose Jimmy under any circumstances, but Jimmy spotted him right off. It was the Florsheims. In a city reeking with government-regulation shoes, Secret Service footwear sticks out like zits on a swimsuit model. It's easier to spot than the FBI.

Jimmy followed a Japanese tourist wearing a checkered sports jacket like you see in Florida nursing homes and carrying a video-camera into the men's room, where Jimmy karate-chopped the tourist, which knocked him down but not out, so Jimmy kicked at his head until the tourist pretended to be unconscious just to make it stop. Jimmy stripped off the tourist's jacket, took the video-camera, and went back out the door. The process from going in to coming out spanned all of ten seconds.

What Parker Swindell saw was a video lens aimed at his face and a bad jacket while the guy whose face he couldn't see muttered senseless syllables in a Japanese accent, or what passed for a Japanese accent on old racist cartoons. Parker turned away, but the guy with the camera stayed right in his face. Parker held up his hand to shade his eyes, and the mad video taker moved on down the hall, still muttering things like *"Kawasaki"* and *"Mitsubishi."*

Around the ticket-counter corner, Jimmy dumped the jacket and camera in an abandoned Smarte Carte and ducked through a door marked "Authorized Personnel Only."

Ace Columbus, who witnessed the proceedings, thanked God he was in the Mafia instead of the Secret Service. He wandered over and fished the videocamera out of the Smarte Carte but left the checkered jacket for someone else.

Jimmy's "Authorized Personnel Only" door led to a hallway that led to a stairway that went down to a vast luggage-sorting room where bags and boxes zipped along on conveyor belts, being whisked here and there between connecting flights and carousels. The room was laid out like the wiring on a jukebox. Only a professional would have any idea what belt took what bag where.

At first Jimmy thought the room was deserted, but then he saw a couple of employees in coveralls, smoking in a corner where obviously they weren't supposed to smoke. They were so fearful of being reported that when Jimmy made his way across and under belts to their corner, they didn't ask what he was doing there.

Jimmy demanded, "Lost-luggage room."

One of the men made a sign that he didn't speak English.

Jimmy turned and yanked a Kelty Calypso backpack off a conveyor belt and threw it to the floor. "This is lost. Where does it go?"

The other man pointed to a double door at the back of the room, where one of the belts dead-ended into a canvas cart.

Jimmy started that way but then spotted a small animal carrier with a red ribbon through the side airhole and a homemade Magic

Marker sign on the front that read "Annie." He snagged the carrier off a moving belt, opened the front gate, and dumped a dachshund onto the concrete floor, where it yelped once and ran off into the tangled web of luggage control. Jimmy hefted the carrier in his left hand—perfect size for a head.

With the carrier in his left hand and the workout bag in his right, he hip-bumped open the double doors and stepped in to find RC Nash sitting atop the green trunk in a room full of luggage.

RC said, "Are we kidnapping pets now?"

Jimmy recovered quickly. "How'd you get loose?"

"Farlow came back."

"That fag. He said he was checking into a hotel."

"The agent—Jackson—thought you might be up to no good, so he gave Farlow a call. I figured you'd come along sooner or later. Jackson wouldn't let you fly away without giving up part of Franklin."

"I need his head."

"The head's not here, Jimmy. We changed the plan to body first, head later."

"That's stupid."

"It was Honey's idea. She thought you'd be less likely to steal the security deposit if it was too heavy to run with." RC leaned forward on the trunk. "You owe me five hundred dollars."

Jimmy slyly pulled the zipper on his workout bag, talking to cover the *click-click*s. "I didn't kill you before, because I owed you one, but I don't owe you two."

RC nodded toward the bag. "You don't have a gun in there."

"Why not?"

"Even you aren't stupid enough to bring a gun to an airport."

Jimmy laughed. "You know why I always win?"

"I didn't realize you ever win."

"Because smart guys like you underestimate me." With a flourish, Jimmy whipped out his revolver. "You can start begging now, hotshot."

RC braced himself for the bullet, wishing his life had lasted a little longer. Having a baby with Honey would have been a hoot. It seemed like a sick joke that he should figure out what mattered only to die before he could act on it. Just before RC's past flashed before his eyes, he noticed something peculiar.

So did Jimmy. The heart of his revolver, where the cylinder was supposed to be, was nothing but air. You could see through it to the other side.

Jimmy said, "Shit."

RC said, "Don't you need that piece in the middle?"

Jimmy stood frozen, backtracking in his mind. The cylinder had been there when he robbed Target; it had been there when he left RC in a duct tape cocoon.

"Motherfuck." The truth hit him like a brick to the brain pan. *"That bitch!"*

He tore open the workout bag and yanked out its contents, throwing each item to the floor—panties, red halter top, "Free Winona" shirt, a book called *The Vagina Monologues,* a stuffed bear, a birth control wheel.

*"That fucking bitch."*

"What were you expecting in the bag?" RC asked.

*"That double-crossing cunt."*

RC stood up. "You are talking about the woman I love."

"I'll cut her twat out."

"Does this mean we fight fair this time?"

Jimmy said, "Hell, no." He reached into his jacket pocket and brought out his switchblade—*swick*—the very knife he'd thrown at the President and into Kurt Cobain's neck less than forty-eight hours ago.

RC said, "Let's not go there, Jimmy."

Jimmy said, "Every bit of it is Honey's doing."

Then he lunged. RC jumped back and fell ass-over-head over the green trunk. Jimmy scampered around the trunk and just as he stabbed, RC slapped a lost Samsonite twenty-six-inch Oyster bag with cartwheels to his own chest.

His mind snapped back to the last time he'd been in a fight— Cody Middle School. Lunch period. That fight had been over a woman also. Teddy Nubolt beat the crap out of him, and contrary to popular western myth, Katie Willins fell in love with the winner instead of the loser.

Jimmy's knife stuck in the suitcase, which, had the suitcase lived up to advertising, should not have been possible. RC kicked. Jimmy grabbed his groin and fell.

RC leaped to his feet, holding a lost aluminum deep-sea fishing-rod canister made by St. Croix. Jimmy bounced up with the knife extended in his right hand.

Breathing like lung-shot lions, the two men faced each other in a room filled with lost baggage.

As soon as Jimmy went around the Saudi Arabian Airlines corner, Honey packed up her nail polish, put on her jelly sandals, and walked over to stand in line at the security checkpoint. A stout black woman in a uniform with a name tag that said "Gus" asked to see her ticket and a photo ID.

Honey handed Gus her passport and the envelope holding her plane ticket.

Gus said, "Miss Chung, there are two tickets in here."

"The other one belongs to my ex-boyfriend. He decided not to come after all."

"Well, if he changes his mind, he won't be able to get past here without a ticket."

Honey said, "That's the point."

She passed through the metal detector without a beep, but on the other side, a man big enough to be a retired football player so he reminded her of Farlow was frowning at the X-ray screen.

He said, "Rusty, look at this," and another man, in chunky black glasses, bent to look. The big one, who didn't have a name tag, pushed a button that brought the attaché case and Honey's carry-on out of the machine. He picked up the attaché case and asked Honey if she minded them looking in it.

"It's locked," Honey said. "My ex-boyfriend knows the combination, but he doesn't trust me enough to tell me what it is."

"Did you pack the case yourself, and has it been in your possession at all times?"

"Heck, no. Mohammed would never let me see inside his case."

"Mohammed?" Rusty and the big man without a name tag exchanged a look. By then, Gus and another female employee with an electric wand that could detect metal had wandered over to listen in.

Honey said, "Mohammed Das. We broke up, five minutes ago." She pointed. "Over there."

A chill went through the security crew. The big man said, "We have to look in the case, ma'am."

"You can keep it. I'm sure there's nothing of Mohammed's that I would want." Honey lifted her carry-on from the belt. "Do you mind if I go catch the shuttle to my concourse? You're supposed to be there an hour ahead."

The man said, "I'm sorry, but you can't go until we've opened the case."

"But I have a plane to catch."

This time Rusty said she couldn't go, and he didn't preface it with being sorry.

"What did your machine show is in it?" Honey asked.

The big man said, "It X-rays as empty."

"I guess that makes it suspicious."

"Yes, ma'am."

The black woman Gus and the woman with the wand, whose name tag said she was Ellen, stood with Honey while the big man and Rusty used a serrated knife to saw the side off the attaché case. Rusty told the big man they would have to tear off the lining and any layers of lamination.

The big man said, "I know that."

Ellen was talking about her feet and how much they hurt, when Honey interrupted her. Honey said, "See those three men over by the flight insurance machine."

Gus said, "They look like Feds."

Ellen said, "They're awfully upset about something."

"The cute one on the left is President Allworth's chief of staff," Honey said. "He drove me out here tonight."

"He doesn't look like anybody's chief of staff," Gus said.

"I think he starts the job tomorrow. He's a very nice man."

A male voice came over the public address system. It said, *"Will Stonewall Jackson please meet his party at Baggage Claim Ten. Stonewall Jackson, meet your party at Baggage Claim Ten."*

"That's him," Honey said.

Ellen said, "Look at them take off. They must be meeting someone important."

Honey said, "I imagine so."

Jonathan Weathers, Parker Swindell, and Stonewall Jackson fairly flew across the lobby. They sprinted down an escalator, taking two steps at a bound, and Jonathan actually knocked an elderly southern lady to the floor. He and Parker continued running, but Stonewall stopped to help her up.

He said, "Sorry."

She said what southern women will almost always say when you push them down from behind. She said, "Well, I'll be."

The main baggage-claim area was a beehive of people picking up and waiting for bags. Loved ones reunited. Businessmen and bureaucrats walked with cell phones clamped to their ears. Baggage Claim 8 was surrounded by a traveling Riverdance troupe— Stonewall had never seen so many ruddy cheeks—and 9 and 10 were off to the left, down another, shorter escalator.

Stonewall tore around number 9, which was deserted, and found Jonathan and Parker staring at number 10, where a single green trunk slid along the far side of the oval track. As Stonewall watched, the trunk made a slow U-turn and briefly slipped from sight behind the baggage chute before it reappeared, borne back ceaselessly toward the waiting Secret Servicemen.

As the trunk slowly came toward them, Parker said, "I wish you'd tell me what's going on."

Eldon came through the line while Honey was watching Rusty and the big man who reminded her of Farlow tear up Jimmy's attaché case. Gus made Eldon go through the metal detector twice because his inhaler set it off the first time. When he finally cleared the machine, he walked up to Honey and said, "Hi."

Honey said, "You turn up in the strangest places."

"I saw you over here and used my dad's credit card to buy a ticket so they'd let me in. He won't mind."

"Where's the ticket go to?"

Eldon pulled the ticket from his jacket pocket and read it. "Qatar."

When the men finished ripping apart the attaché case, it looked like a road-kill cardboard box. Rusty said, "You want this back?"

Honey said, "If Mohammed tries coming through here, give him the case."

"Thank you for your cooperation."

Honey picked up her carry-on bag and clutch and started into the terminal. She said, "Since you're here, why not walk me to the shuttle station. I'm supposed to be meeting my new boyfriend—we're going to New Zealand to have a baby—but I'm not sure if he'll show up. Some men rush into a commitment like this and then get cold feet. Why did you buy a ticket to Qatar?"

Eldon sucked in a puff of his inhaler and held his breath as long as he could, which was seven seconds. He said, "I wanted to ask you something."

Honey said, "Would you be a gentleman and carry my bag?"

Eldon took the bag from Honey, mentally kicking himself for not volunteering to carry it.

"What did you want to ask me?"

"I want to know if you'll marry me."

Honey looked down at the boy beside her. She didn't stop walking, but she did slow down. "This is so sudden."

"Not right away. I know I'm only twelve, but I love you seriously as a grown-up. I'd be willing to wait till I'm sixteen, if that's okay with you. I mean, I'd be willing to wait any amount of time, but sixteen seems right. Don't you think?"

Honey stopped. "What's your name?"

"Eldon Bergstein. My papaw is Gino Olivetti but everyone calls him Rat's Ass. I'm planning to take over the Mafia, or at least the part of it here in Washington that Papaw bosses. I'll be stinking rich and powerful, and we can live in a big house, after we're married."

"Oh, Eldon, I don't want stinking rich and powerful if you have to be in the Mafia to get it."

"Papaw says slashes are suckers for power."

"Not me. My ex-boyfriend Jimmy lied and cheated and stole from innocent strangers who never did a thing to him. He would have killed too if he wasn't such a fuck-up. I don't want another guy like that."

Eldon said, "I don't understand."

Honey touched his cheek, then dropped her hand to his shoulder. "If you grow up to be a sleazewad who treats women like slashes, you'll never get a girlfriend worth having."

Eldon's bottom lip quivered. "I don't want a girlfriend worth having. I want you."

Honey held Eldon's hand and pulled him over to a chair that was welded to a coin-operated Internet connection. She sat down and turned sideways to hold Eldon with her hands on both his shoulders. She stared him straight in the eyes. "Eldon, listen."

He swallowed.

Honey said, "Here's what I want. I want you to grow up to be straight and true. And kind. I want you to treat women with respect, as if each girl you meet is me. I don't want you breaking any laws at all. Not one. Do you understand me now?"

Eldon nodded. He was afraid to speak for fear he would start crying.

Honey said, "You grow into a good, honest man and in ten years you come find me. We'll talk. No promises, but I may just up and marry you. Wouldn't that surprise your papaw?"

Eldon's lungs filled with air. There was hope! In his wildest imagination they had run hand in hand to the nearest airplane captain and been married on the spot, with second choice being a promise to wait till he was sixteen and a Godfather, but deep down, in Eldon's superrational brain, he'd known he was being a kid.

Turned out his brain wasn't so smart after all. Right then, Eldon swore to himself he would never break any law again, at least for ten years.

"What about the new boyfriend that you're running off to New Zealand to have a baby with? Do you think he'll be a good sport about it, when you marry me?"

Honey laughed that laugh of hers that made men fall in love. She said, "RC Nash is pretty old. I can't picture him lasting ten years with me."

Parker and Stonewall each took an end and pulled the green trunk off the baggage carousel, then they stood there next to Jonathan Weathers, studying it.

Parker said, "Maybe he booby-trapped the lock."

Stonewall said, "This is Jimmy Sebastiano we're talking about."

Suddenly there came a voice from within the trunk. *"Get me the fuck out of here."*

Stonewall said, "That's him."

Jonathan said, "Open it, for Christ's sake."

Stonewall flipped the center clasp, which had a keyhole but wasn't locked, then the two latches, and opened the lid to find Jimmy on his back like an upside-down turtle, lying on a naked, dead, headless body.

Jimmy said, "Jesus fuck shit damn."

Jonathan stepped closer to the trunk to check out the body under Jimmy. It'd been dead almost two days and had turned a bluish yellow, like a slowly rotting banana. The enclosed air in the trunk concentrated the odor. Imagine Greeley, Colorado, on a hot day.

Stonewall said, "Ish."

Jimmy's hands clawed for purchase. "Get me out, Goddamnit. His dick's sticking in my back."

Nobody moved to help Jimmy out of the trunk, but after a few seconds of scrambling he managed to extricate himself. He leaned forward with his hands on his thighs and shook like a wet dog, all the while spewing a continuous string of curses, as if the filth had lodged in his mouth.

Jonathan said, "You'll never get the smell off."

Parker stared at the naked, headless body. "Is that—"

"Yep," Stonewall said.

Parker said, "Then who—"

"Where's the head, Jimmy?" Jonathan said.

Jimmy spit a pizza-cheese-colored glob. "That shitheel RC Nash stole it. You better get Nash. He's dangerous. Him and that bitch are in it together. They're both fucking criminals."

Jonathan said, "You're the only criminal I've got now." He almost but not quite smiled. "At this point in time."

Jimmy spit again, trying to get the dead-body taste off his tongue. "What's the charge? You can't hold me, Mr. High-and-mighty. You've got nothing on me. Nothing."

"I found you lying on the dead president's dick."

"Tell that to Congress, you jerk."

Parker still had not connected the dots. "So this guy actually killed President Franklin?" he asked. "Not the other guy?"

Stonewall said, "Right."

"Then who did the other guy kill?"

"It's a long story," Stonewall said. "We'll talk later."

Parker shifted his stare from the body to Jimmy. "You want me to cuff him?"

Jimmy's voice was particularly snide. "You can't touch me, you loser. Where's my ticket to Hawaii?"

Stonewall turned to Jonathan. "It's your call. Do we cut the punk loose?"

Parker said, "How can we cut him loose?"

Jimmy chanted: *"Losers, losers, you're a bunch of losers."*

They all waited for Jonathan Weathers to make a decision, but he was stuck. He wasn't about to let this creep kill the President and walk, but the alternative was to slit his throat, and there were witnesses—travelers looking for the right baggage claim, people standing outside the glass wall, waiting for cabs, a lost woman in search of the can. He scanned the room, adding up how many people would have to be bribed or threatened. It wasn't like the old days, when you could buy silence. Now everybody has to go on talk shows.

Jonathan stared into space and said, "Give him the ticket."

"And my passport."

"And his passport."

Stonewall said, "We can't let him go."

Jonathan said, "He's free."

Stonewall followed Jonathan's line of sight back past baggage carousel 9, where Gino Olivetti, Ace Columbus, and two other generic hoods wearing black suits and pinkie rings were watching the action.

Stonewall handed Jimmy his ticket and the new passport. "Okay, Jimmy. You're free as a bird."

Jimmy said, "Damn right I am, loser."

He took two steps away and saw Rat's Ass. Jimmy said, "I changed my mind." He turned back to Stonewall. "I confess. I did it."

Stonewall said, "Did what?"

"I killed the President. Franklin. I killed him and there he is." He pointed to the body in the trunk.

Jonathan said, "Too late, Jimmy. We already have our assassin. It would confuse the public if we had two."

"But it was me." Jimmy looked over his shoulder at Rat's Ass, who smiled, like wax.

Jimmy shouted, *"I am the assassin!"* The three or four non-affiliated witnesses within earshot looked embarrassed and hurried away. Jimmy shouted even louder. *"I killed the President. Doesn't anyone care?"*

Olivetti reached into his breast pocket and pulled out a string that was tied to a tail, two legs, and a furry asshole. He dangled it in the air for Jimmy to see, then gently rocked it side to side.

Honey threw herself at RC and smacked him with a major kiss—a movie-moment kiss. He liked it a lot.

She said, "I am so happy you showed up. I was afraid you'd get scared. I mean, you only ended a relationship yesterday. I didn't know if you'd want to start a new one right off."

"Nothing could have kept me away," RC said.

Honey said, "You are so cool," and she kissed him again, this time slower, with more tongue.

When she finally broke lip contact, she kept her right arm around RC and turned to Eldon. "RC, this is Eldon. You remember him from before."

"Is he going with us?" RC asked.

Honey laughed. "Don't be silly. Eldon has school tomorrow."

"It's called off on account of the assassination," Eldon said.

"Aren't you a lucky boy," Honey said.

Eldon didn't like Honey kissing the old man, and he figured he'd better remind all parties of the terms of the deal. "You'll die, and then I get to marry her," Eldon said to RC.

RC said, "That sounds fair," but when he saw how Eldon was looking at Honey, he added, "So long as you don't ask your grandpa to bump up the schedule."

"Eldon is done with having people killed," Honey said. "Aren't you, Eldon?"

"I never really did it, anyway. But I was going to if Papaw didn't start acting nice."

"No killing, no drugs, and no being a crime lord," Honey said.

Eldon nodded, but he wasn't happy. He suspected the old man might try to have sex with Honey. He knew how babies were made, and Honey had said they were going to have a baby, but she was different from other girls. She'd find a way that didn't involve an old man lying on top of her.

"Good-bye," Honey said, without letting go of RC.

"See you later," RC said.

He shook Eldon's hand, and Eldon said, "I hope you die soon."


Honey insisted on sitting at the front of the nearly empty shuttle so they could see where they were going, even though it was pitch black outside and they were only going to another concourse. She held RC's hands and talked about the cottage they would live in by the ocean and how RC would make waffles from scratch while she breastfed their baby, who would wear a linen gown and go right to sleep whenever they wanted to make love.

"We'll build you a studio out past the garden, where you can see me and our baby playing in the front yard while you write your celebrity profiles."

RC told Honey the secret he had never told anyone, not even Kirsteen. "I was thinking I might write a novel."

"*Wow,*" Honey said. "That is so wonderful. I always all my life wanted to fuck a novelist. You can dedicate the book to me and the baby. I thought we'd name it Farlow if it's a boy and Evangelina

Lillian if it's a girl. Nobody would dare treat a girl named Evangelina like an airhead."

"Farlow if it's a boy?"

"Soon as Farlow destroys his knees forever, we'll make him and his lover move to New Zealand. They can babysit while you and I walk the country lane down to the village to buy kiwis from the farmers' market."

RC was a born sucker for enthusiasm, maybe because he never had much himself. Whenever he was around an enthusiastic person— especially an enthusiastic woman—he couldn't help but get a second-hand high.

"I have an idea for a three-generation epic about missed opportunities," he said. "I'll tell you the plot on the airplane."

"Am I in it?"

"You're the star." RC decided he'd better bring up an unpleasant subject before they got on the plane. "The only problem is, I don't know how we'll live. I only have four hundred and twenty-five dollars."

"Don't worry about money. We'll live on love."

"Can people really do that?"

They held hands awhile, each thinking their thoughts of New Zealand and the cottage, the baby, and RC's novel. RC made a quick check under the seat, in hopes that he had missed something.

"What happened to the attaché case Jimmy's been carrying like a third arm for the last two days?" he asked.

Honey hooked her hair behind her ear. "The nice man at security kept Jimmy's case. It was locked and empty, and that made them suspicious."

"I was kind of hoping it had the money Jimmy stole from Olivetti."

"It was empty. Do you think we can have hummingbird feeders at our cottage? When I was a little girl my grandma had humming-bird feeders in her backyard."

"I don't see why not, if they have hummingbirds in New Zealand."

"Everybody has hummingbirds."

RC looked at the approaching lights of the concourse. "I wish we'd get there," he said. "I have to pee."

The Secret Service owns a fleet of dairy-products-delivered-to-your-door vans rigged with high-tech equipment they use to spy on possible troublemakers and agents' wives. In a pinch, which happens more often than you would like to think, the vans double as undercover hearses. Stonewall had parked one of these next to an executive-branch-jet hangar where common airline travelers aren't allowed to park. Even the CIA isn't allowed to park there. Every clandestine affairs agency has its own secret parking at Dulles, and if you park in another agency's spot it causes no end of friction.

"There's still time to stop RC and Honey, if you want to," Stonewall said.

Jonathan popped open the back doors to the van and looked in to see if any listening devices had fallen on the floor. "Chip Allworth gave me orders not to bother with the other two unless it was necessary to get Jimmy. Chip seems to think Honey only did what any American girl would have done when propositioned by her president."

"Did he think that way before he became president?"

Jonathan shrugged. "And he said to hold off on RC. We'll watch him until he makes a deal to tell the story, then we'll initiate termination. Otherwise, Chip doesn't see a need to punish RC."

Stonewall watched as a 747 took off directly over his head. The roar was amazing. He imagined it was the plane taking Honey DuPont away. He wondered what she would have said had he offered to go with her.

When the roar died down and they'd secured the trunk carrying the dead president inside the van and slammed the doors, Stonewall said, "RC is basing his future on Honey. I imagine, in the long run, that's punishment enough."

Parker had been silent ever since Ace Columbus led the blubbering Jimmy away, but now he finally had to speak. He said, "I still don't understand what happened to President Franklin's head."

*tuesday*

Alberta Chamberlain sat at the counter in Damien's Donuts, staring sadly into the worst cup of coffee imaginable. It was so terrible a grounds film had formed on the sides of the cup. When she stirred powdered Coffee White into it with her Poly King stir stick, the coffee turned the color of Tubby Fitzhugh's ass, which depressed her all the more since chances were quite good she would never see the ass that she loved above all others again. She'd be lucky to see any senator's ass again, at least any senator beyond his first term. Word was out among the high and powerful—Alberta Chamberlain was passé.

As if a metaphor for Alberta's mood, the President's funeral was being broadcast on a nine-inch color TV with a coat-hanger antenna Leonard Levinson had set up at the end of the counter, down by the black schizophrenic with the greasy shopping bag and the odor of hockey socks, who was writing in a little red notebook. The TV was set to Fox News because Leonard, being a poet, had a fine sense of irony. For example, Bob Burnett and Trudy Tamburro, the newscasters describing the funeral procession to the millions of mourning viewers, were chosen because of the dynamite job they had done at last winter's Rose Bowl Parade.

Trudy said, "Former First Lady Lonicera Franklin looks regal in her black ankle-length gown by Jean-Paul Gaultier. She is truly American royalty."

"Isn't Gaultier from France?" Bob Burnett said.

"Oh, Bob," Trudy gushed. "This is no time for carping. The nation should draw together today and celebrate Lonicera's style. Just look at those accessories."

There was much conjecture as to the identity of the dignified Latina beauty standing beside President Allworth. Bob and Trudy agreed that she had magnificent posture, even with a baby on her arm. Bob said he'd heard she was a Bolivian diva.

"Looks like my maid," Alberta said.

"Let me pour you more coffee," Leonard said. "It'll go well with your bear claw."

Cranford Nix, the black schizophrenic, said, "A fed bear is a dead bear," and over by the window, Mr. Gelfino and Mr. Sawtelle nodded as if Cranford had said something that made sense. The only other customers were a table of GS-11s in beige trench coats who, if possible, were even more morose than Alberta.

"So tell me exactly what RC said when he was here Saturday morning," Alberta asked Leonard, for the third time. Even though it was too late to save her Tubby relationship, Alberta had become obsessed with what RC knew and when he knew it. She was fairly sure he had had prior knowledge of the assassination attempt, but she had no clue what RC had been doing at FedEx Field. The White House denied he had even been in the tunnel with Charles Franklin. They claimed Alberta had mistaken RC for an agent named Turk Johansen, who had also been killed. No one, not even Tubby, believed Alberta when she said RC went in and never came out.

"He told me the history of Foggy Bottom," Leonard said. "I think he was afraid to go home on account of his girlfriend was pissed off. She thought he was sleeping with Heather Graham."

Just then the dishwater blonde, whose name was Sparkle, walked up from the back room, tying an apron around her exhausted hips. She'd been up all night with colicky twins, and it showed in every part of her body as she paused to watch the funeral on Leonard's little TV. A riderless Appaloosa stallion with back-facing boots in its stirrups was prancing down Pennsylvania Avenue, and instead of explaining the ritualistic symbolism, Bob Burnett described which fashion icon had designed the boots and how many ounces of silver were in the stirrups.

Trudy Tamburro said, "That's a lot of silver, Bob."

Sparkle turned to the conversation around the cash register. "Are y'all talking about that reporter, writes about movie stars and uses the toilet ever'time he comes in?"

"That's the one," Leonard said. "Did you see him this weekend?"

"He was by Saturday noon and tried to borrow the company phone. When I explained how it's against policy, he threw a fit."

Alberta perked up. This was her first lead. "What kind of fit?"

"The kind men throw when you don't do what they want. He said it was a national emergency."

"Did he say what kind of emergency?"

"Just national. He ended up using Cranford's cell phone."

Alberta followed the lead to Cranford, who answered her questions by saying, "My vegetable love should grow vaster than empires."

Alberta said, "Jesus Christ."

In Cranford, she saw herself in ten years' time, if she didn't solve the mystery—stumbling across the national mall, muttering vile curses at tourists, hoarding Kleenex, eating her own hair, searching each face for RC Nash.

She said, "Shithead."

Leonard thought she was talking about Cranford. He said, "Ma'am, we're all the same in this doughnut shop."

Alberta looked at Cranford, Sparkle, Mr. Gelfino, and Mr. Sawtelle, and the table full of depressed GS-11s, and she said, "I may kill myself."

Cranford said, "The stream interrupted by rocks is the one that sings most nobly," then he gathered his Bic pens, his little red notebook, and scraps of a chocolate éclair, and dropped them into his shopping bag. Rising with a groan, Cranford crossed to the door.

Leonard followed him outside and spoke quietly so the others couldn't hear. Leonard said, "I'm sorry, Cranford, but you've got to take a shower before I can let you back in."

Cranford said, "I stink, therefore I am."

Leonard touched Cranford's arm. "You know what you said about rocks and the stream that sings? Do you mind if I use it in a poem?"

Cranford jaywalked E Street and was almost run down by a limo containing the Greek ambassador in a rush to the funeral, late because his electrolysis session had run over schedule. Cranford had learned long ago that the only way a street person can deal with Washington traffic is to ignore it. If he looked at oncoming cars, the drivers knew he saw them and ignored him, instead of the other way around, which left Cranford shuffling on the curb like a little boy who has to use the restroom, but if he simply stepped on out into the street without looking, the cars swerved and slammed on the brakes.

The driver of the Greek limo both swerved and stomped his brakes, dumping the ambassador in a heap between the seats. Cranford heard a shouted curse in a language foreign to his ears, although he did catch the gist.

Once in Rawlins Park, Cranford launched into a free-ranging monologue on the subject of hygiene in plantation slave quarters during the early 1800s. He'd found self-ranting kept the Jesus freaks and spare-changers at bay, although as cell phones shrank and became more hands-off, half the people in the park seemed to be talking to themselves. Lately, Cranford had had trouble telling the schizophrenics from the tech weenies.

Talking all the way, he cut diagonally across the sidewalk grid, forcing joggers and nannies to deal with it. Near the center of the park, Cranford passed a barricade of yellow crime-scene tape strung around the chalk outline of a dead nun. Police technicians were photographing and measuring the general area. Stonewall Jackson stood on the nun's outlined neck and sighted a metal rod at Sleet's sixth-floor window in the Downtowner Hotel, a block and a half away. As Cranford shuffled by, Parker Swindell was saying, "I don't understand."

At the east end of the park, Cranford dropped to his knees beside a juniper hedge and, pushing his shopping bag before him, entered a dry culvert. He felt blindly in the dark until he located the disposable flashlight he'd left there the evening before. He flipped the flashlight on, held it between his teeth, and started crawling forward.

Because of his bag and an intense fear of spiders, Cranford's progress was slow. He kept forgetting where the flashlight was, so when he resumed talking to himself it fell into the grimy residue at the bottom of the culvert, but finally he passed under the street to a place where his culvert emptied into a tunnel large enough for him to stand up and walk.

The tunnel had electric cables and sewer lines strung along the roof. It ran deep under the Department of Interior building, and had Cranford wanted to, he could have walked all the way to the Tidal Basin. Instead, he left the tunnel by way of a wrought-iron ladder that led to a trapdoor that should have been padlocked but wasn't and on through a rotted vent into a hallway in the subbasement of the Department of Interior.

From there, Cranford proceeded to the long-forgotten storeroom where he'd stashed a pile of blankets, several candles, and a couple thousand three-inch-by-five-inch notebooks containing his collected poetry and observations. The notebooks were lined up, neatly, on shelves that covered the south wall from waist-high to ceiling. Each notebook was dated on the inside front cover— although sometimes with the wrong date—and signed on the inside back cover—*Cranford Nix, live person.*

Below the shelves and in front of his blanket pile, Cranford had built an altar from cinder blocks, on which he kept his treasures, such as feathers from a seagull killed by a foul ball at the 1989 World Series, a tattered copy of Andrew Marvell's *Complete Poems,* two bites of a bratwurst sandwich he'd seen Serena Williams drop into a trashcan at the zoo, an empty Coke bottle given him by the love of his life back at Howard University the night she left him, a photograph of his mama from the time when pictures came back from the drugstore printed on ragged-edge paper, a sketch by Jackson Pollock he'd stolen from the Hirshhorn Museum, and a bottle of pills the doctor at the Farragut Square free clinic had said would make him better.

Dead center on the altar, Cranford kept a copy of the single book of poems he had published before he lost himself. The cover was blue. On the back there was a picture of Cranford, looking young and full of potential, a blurb from Jimmy Baca saying it was a fine book, and a quote from *Publishers Weekly* calling Cranford "the brightest star in a constellation of young contemporary poets." Next to the book lay a yellowed newspaper clipping of the review by Jonathan Yardley in *The Washington Post* that had ended his career as a published poet and a rational man, the review Cranford read every evening when he awoke.

Cranford struck a match and lit two candles but not three, because three on a match is bad luck. He turned off the flashlight, and humming the bass line from "All Blues" by Miles Davis, he placed last night's notebook on the right end of the line on the top shelf, bookended by a brick from the Capitol construction.

He sat cross-legged before the altar and reached into his shopping bag for the remnants of the éclair. Chewing thoughtfully, he pulled out two pens, a can of Vienna sausages, a half-roll of toilet paper, the cell phone he'd found on the side of a fountain over by the Boy Scout Memorial, and Charles Franklin's head.

Cranford spoke to the head. He said, "That'll teach you what happens when you ruin a good poet with a bad review." He placed the head on the altar, between the seagull feathers and Andrew Marvell, then, quietly contemplating Charles Franklin's eyes, Cranford opened his tin of Vienna sausages.